Please return or renew by
latest date below

I, Weapon

I, Weapon

CHARLES W. RUNYON

DOUBLEDAY & COMPANY, INC.

GARDEN CITY, NEW YORK

1974

All of the characters in this book
are fictitious, and any resemblance
to actual persons, living or dead,
is purely coincidental.

Library of Congress Cataloging in Publication Data

Runyon, Charles W   1928–
  I, weapon.

  I. Title.
PZ4.R943Iap [PS3568.U53]   813'.5'4
ISBN 0-385-06491-8
Library of Congress Catalog Card Number 73–22537

First Edition

I, Weapon

Background

Human history since the sidereal year one of space, the year 1970 of the Gregorian calendar, the year 1390 of the Muslim calendar, saw the outpouring of the human race into the surrounding spiral arm of the galaxy. Planets hung like ripe fruit free for the picking, and the Directing Council, set up to judge conflicting boundary claims, made the genocidal wars over colonies no longer valid. In a flush of anthropocentric benevolence the D.C. telemapped the entire visible universe and reserved for each race and political group a conical section of Creation extending into infinity, with each point anchored upon the planet earth.

Five hundred years passed with only minor skirmishes where borders overlapped or survey lines were hazy, and mankind again fell prey to the arrogant fallacy that he was heir to the universe, ordained by God. That naïveté crumbled when a colonizing ship belonging to the Sha'al, an Arabic-speaking people pursuing their manifest destiny in the Fomalhaut region, encountered the leading edge of the Vim empire.

The Vim were a plated erect bipedal marsupial race with a mace-like bone at the end of a prehensile tail. They lived entirely on the blooms of a flowering vine, similar to the Kudzu of ancient earth, so rapacious that it smothered all other forms of vegetation. The Vim method of colonizations was to land a few agricultural workers in a sheltered valley, plant it in kusa vines, then move on to the next planet. A following wave of settlers would find the plants ready to harvest; they would then begin the orgy of eating and breeding which would overpopulate the planet within a century.

It was ironic that Vim should clash with man when both races were young, brash, and aggressive. With half the galaxy unexplored, their chance encounter might not have been repeated for a thousand years, at which time both might have developed traditions of interstellar diplomacy. Ironic, too, that each race had a deep-seated, unconscious prejudice against the other. The Vim regarded erect bipedal humanoids as domestic animals, to be ridden, worked, and eaten. Humans looked upon all scaly, tailed marsupials as creatures to be avoided, eaten, or stomped underfoot. Irony coupled with destiny to arrange that the Sha'al spaceship should land in the only valley then inhabited by the Vim crop tenders. The Arabs were an elite para-military group, composed of officers, soldiers, and their wives and concubines. For such men, to encounter resistance is to draw one's dagger—and there was no doubt that the Vim were hostile from the moment the Arabs began setting up their defense perimeter. The Vim saw their crops being trampled and ground to pulp by the vehicles of the colonists; they attacked with bare hands and macelike tails—and were burned. Those who ran were hunted down and eaten, since the Arabs were starved for meat after a three-year diet of ship concentrates.

The Vim proved to be indigestible. Half the company died in foaming convulsions, the rest became helplessly ill. The last communication from the ship commander stated that a few seemed to be recovering; true, their minds were totally blank, but the only physical aftereffect was a slight yellowish tinge around the eyeballs.

It is not known how the Vim took control of the humans who had eaten them. That they did is an established fact. The planet Hwu Hsi reported that a ship landed there and left behind three humans for medical treatment. That was the last word from Hwu Hsi. The planet Yakovitch reported a similar visit, before they too were swallowed up in silence. Many more must have been infiltrated and been unable to report it. At last a customs agent on the Spanish-speaking planet Rinconcito put the ship in a quarantine orbit and would allow nobody to disembark until it was determined what had caused their eyeballs to turn yellow. The Vim apparently realized that their chance to assimilate mankind was shattered; the only option left was annihilation.

So it was that the human race, knowing only that an Arab ship had been detained somewhere on the periphery because of the jaundiced appearance of its passengers, was hit by the greatest fleet ever assembled anywhere. More than a billion spaceships converged on the bubble of man's infant empire. There was no waste, no duplication of effort. One ship would destroy a planet's governmental center. The others would circle the planet like angry hornets, laying waste all centers of population. Then came the landing, the embarkation of mace-tailed soldiers armed with weapons which fired small coated projectiles. These would, upon striking any part of a metal object, dissolve the entire structure within minutes—whereupon the defenseless humans were either burned or shot with a serum which dissolved cytoplasm and turned them into puddles of slime. After all resistance had ceased, the survivors were somehow converted into Vim puppets and sent out to fight their own kind.

Within ten years the civilization of man was smothered under an avalanche of mace-tailed marsupials and yellow-eyed humans. But once they arrived at the planet earth, the Vim found themselves exhausted. Conquest is not like colonization, which feeds itself as it grows. Conquest is a cancer, feeding on the health of the organism, drawing from a limited source, taking out and putting nothing back. Vim were starving on the inner worlds. There were not enough Yam-ships, even if battle losses could be made up—for the number of Vim had doubled during the conquest and the food supply had been halved as Vim were thrown into combat.

So the Vim pulled back . . . back beyond their original perimeter, leaving behind a hundred billion mindless humans whose thinking powers had been irrevocably shattered by the brief control of the alien Vim.

The worlds of man lay in waste. Imbecile survivors wandered among machines they could not repair, feeding themselves on stored foods and starving when they ran out. Some followed their brute instinct to breed, and their offspring had normal intelligence—but they knew nothing of earth or of humanity, only that they were alive and that the purpose of life was to live.

Many were eaten by predators. A few grew to adulthood, and produced children of their own. Some worlds were cold, and only the hairiest or the fattest survived. Some worlds were hot, and only the laziest, or the smallest, or the tallest, lived to reproduce themselves. Many of these died out before the third generation, struck down in the ecological backlash of a world reverting to its natural flora and fauna. On one world out of a thousand, survivors managed to dig in and begin the building of a culture, but these were adaptations to local conditions, and owed nothing to human history.

The sole exception was the Jovian moon-people. At the time of the Vim disaster they numbered only about thirty thousand scientists and their retainers scattered over the moons of Ganymede, Callisto, Io, and Europa. They grew their own food in hydroponic tanks, mined the minerals needed to synthesize their own air and water—in short, were self-sufficient, intelligent, and highly adaptive. Some were involved in advanced research in space flight, others used the planet Jupiter as a high-pressure testing laboratory, and others worked in vacuum chemistry. The Vim came so swiftly that there was only time for everyone to take cover in the great pressurized cavern on Ganymede—and then the Vim were gone, leaving the earth a smoking, radioactive ruin. Attempts to contact other scientific colonies on the moons of Saturn, Neptune, and Uranus were met with a harsh cackle of static, and the scientists did not dare embark rescue ships without being sure they would find food for the return journey. (There was an element of prudence involved, since they could not be sure the departing Vim had not left behind drone ships to annihilate anything that moved.)

Of course, everybody agreed they should do something in the face of this unparalleled disaster. Since the Jovian moons were dominated by English-speaking scientists, their response was to call a general election of all mankind and elect a new Directing Council. The Deek's first act was to establish what became known as the Three Priorities:

To preserve the culture of earth;
To regain the Empire of Man;
To destroy the Vim.

Once again, the human race was reduced to a nucleus which regarded itself as the Chosen. (In all the ancient mythologies the same event keeps recurring, from Gilgamesh to Cadmus to Noah.) As centuries passed in the caverns of Ganymede, the descendants of the original scientists came to confuse the coming of the Vim with the Great Flood, and to equate the lost Empire of Man with the Garden of Eden. Only the Librarians who kept the ancient tapes and microfilms knew the line between history and mythology—and since the Jelk* culture had become rigidly stratified, they did not communicate with those outside their group.

For hundreds of years the population of the Jelks held at 28,243— the number present at the first roll-call election. One person's death was followed immediately by the issuance of a birth permit, so that mourning was overlapped by rejoicing, just as it had been in the ancient days on earth. Every ten years a survey ship went out and circled the planet earth, and each time returned to report that no landing was possible. At last, in the year 520 P.V. (Post-Vim), the ship returned with good news. The earth was still a tectonic hell, with volcanoes spewing and lowlands deadly with radiation, all the continents covered by swamps and giant fungi . . . but—the air was clearing. Though temperatures were fifty degrees higher than they used to be, it was probably that the islands near the North Pole— Ellsmere and northern Greenland, Spitzbergen and Franz Josef Land, plus the entire south polar continent, would be ready for human habitation within a hundred years.

Typically, the Jelks planned the move right down to the last bolt and paper clip. Old maps were studied, property was assigned, exchanged, and reassigned, cities were planned, and the largest estates were reserved for those heroic men and women who undertook the reexploration of man's lost interstellar empire. These early explorers carried out their missions on tiptoe, so to speak, with eyes peeled sharply

---

* The Jovian Lunar Confederacy, called J.L.C., and finally Jelk.

for signs of the Vim. Still, nobody can deny their courage. Only one out of three ever returned; the others fell prey to hostile natives or meteorites or else were stranded by mechanical failure on unknown planets and forced to survive on the means available. It was a slow process, not only because the ships were a drain on the carefully balanced resources of the Jelks, but also because the human breeding instinct was hesitant to shift into high gear after half a millennium of forced control. Another contributing factor was the widespread use of Sen-sex,* an electronic sensory hookup which made flesh contact a rather dull, irritating alternative, to be carried out for the sole purpose of begetting children.

The exploration might have crept on for centuries, hamstrung by personnel shortages, had not the starship *Medusa* landed on a planet in the Hyades cluster. It happened to be a frontier world of the Hossip archate, one of those feudal states which always crop up in the ruins of a collapsed empire.

It must be noted here that man in his outward push had encountered many nonhuman races, and had followed his usual practice of sub-jugating all who were inferior in brains, weaponry, or ferocity. Among these were the Hossip—a large, six-legged oviparous noctural creature which became a popular pet. They were docile and friendly as long as you gave them an adequate supply of meat, for they were carnivo-rous. During centuries of domestication, they learned to talk and smile and even to wear clothing . . . and after the Vim left, they turned on their now imbecilic human masters and indulged in an orgy of eating. The Hossip realized that they would soon use up the supply of meat, so the largest and fattest humans were culled out for breeding. Within a hundred years, by elimination of rebellious traits (i.e., the killing of intelligent individuals) the Hossip created vast herds of human animals whose mental powers were limited to growing their own food supply. The Hossip called them Unguls, in an attempt to imitate the guttural sound the beasts made during rut. In the course of time the Hossip selected certain individuals on the basis of cleverness and do-cility, and created a special breed of herders and domestic servants. These "Grithies" (word origin unknown) came to regard the life-style of their Hossip overlords as the ideal, and aped them in everything possible, including their appetite for the meat of the Unguls.

So it was that when the *Medusa* landed on one of the outlying ranch planets of the Hossip, four billion Ungulate humans grazed under the watchful eye of fifty thousand Grithy overseers. (The seven hundred Hossip rulers were all asleep, hanging upside down from their perches, since it was daytime.) The arrival created panic among the herds, and the seven Jelk crew members stared dumbly from the

* See Appendix I.

ports as a vast wave of naked shaggy humans raced bawling and slobbering across the rolling landscape. Shock became horror as big-eared Grithy herdsmen, riding on the backs of enormously shouldered, long-legged Unguls, turned the stampede by blasting the heads off those in the front rank. Horror turned to nausea as the Grithies began to butcher their kill, and to load the quartered carcasses on carts pulled by trunk-legged draft Unguls. At this point distraction appeared in the form of an armored vehicle. It stopped in front of the ship and discharged a single, uniformed human, who marched up to the entry port and hammered with his baton. (This was HaM'ho, head of the Grithy militia. The Grithies, like good slaves, were always very careful to stay within their own spheres of authority—called baili-wicks. The herdsmen had taken little notice of the spaceship, since their duties were only to mind the herds.) HaM'ho was admitted, and communication was attempted. (The Hossip had adopted human speech during the hegemony of the empire. After the Vim, they had trained their Grithies in their own language, unaware that they were teaching a pidgin form of ancient Castilian.) The final result was almost unrecognizable, but the *Medusa's* linquist managed to find the grammatical roots, and within an hour a halting conversation ensued.

HaM'ho wanted to know what world of the Hossip they had come from. The crew replied that they were from ancient earth seeking the survivors of the first human conquest. This meant nothing to HaM'ho, but he was a crafty Grithy, and once he realized that human existence was possible without Hossip overlords, he transferred his allegiance from Hossip to Jelk. By nightfall all Hossips were lying dead in their own blood beneath their perches. A victory feast was held, and the commander of the *Medusa* became the first Jelk ever to taste Ungul meat. He pronounced it the most succulent and delicious food ever to pass his lips.

At that same feast the conquest of the Hossip archate was planned. The following week it was launched, with members of the Grithy militia flying the spaceships of the Hossips, and the Jelks commanding the operation from a safe distance. The first three worlds were taken without a struggle, since the Hossip were totally unable to believe a threat from their own Grithies—so trusted that they were allowed to sit on Hossip eggs. Resistance was inevitable, however, and two decades of bloody warfare ensued before the last Hossip was put to death. Seven Jelks now ruled the archate, through their Grithy servants. The Grithies, unable to think for themselves, were happy at the chance of masters. The Unguls noticed no difference. It had been impossible to wean the Grithies away from Ungul meat, since there was little else to eat. As soon as their ships' stores ran out, the Jelks themselves made it a staple of their diet.

A hundred years passed, and this most successful of Jelk expeditions became a basis of the New Aristocracy. Jelks came out and established Ungul ranches on the new worlds of the Hyades. A lively commerce was established, as Ungul breeding stock was shipped from the Hyades to the new *latifundia* on Antarctica. Thus the human race—in what could have been its finest hour—adopted the ancient culture of the slaveowner. (Also his rationale, since Unguls were not considered human, despite the fact that anthropologists insisted otherwise.)

In the Jelks' defense, it could be argued that physical differences between Ungul and Jelk were extreme. Jelks averaged four feet in height, with small bones, delicate features, and unusually large eyes, due to the fact that lights were kept dim in the Ganymede caverns in order to conserve energy. They were hairless as eggs, an evolutionary development which also took place in the underground culture, with its emphasis on purity of air and cleanliness of body. Depilatory treatments were initially given at birth, then hair was artificially eliminated from the genetic pool of the race itself.

By contrast, the Unguls weighed an average of three hundred pounds, stood six feet high at the shoulder, and carried their sloping heads forward on thick necks. Those from the cold Hyades planets had two coats of fur, the undercoat a woolly mat, the outer coat composed of two-inch-long guard hairs. Those from the warmer planets had less hair, and from the tropical worlds of Hayadum-I came an almost hairless species, with ruffs of fur around the neck, wrists, and ankles. Later, when the Jelk science of genetic engineering was applied to the Unguls, the species was differentiated still more.

The Grithies, who in size and hirsuteness occupied a position somewhere between Jelk and Ungul—had the most bizarre characteristic of the three. The Hossips, in selecting their pets from the Ungul herds, had been captivated by human ears—and so had chosen only those with the largest. Centuries of reinforcement had endowed the Grithies with pinnae whose length from top to bottom exceeded eight inches. They were also movable, and could turn to follow sound like radar screens.

By now the earth had been cursorily surveyed, and the continent of Antarctica fully settled. The mountainous regions near the South Pole were the most popular, since the temperature hung around the level of a balmy spring day. On the lower plateau regions, where the new aristocracy lived in their gigantic villas, the temperature was generally subtropical. The land had been found completely without mammals, though abundant in strange birds and insects unmentioned in the microfilm records of old earth. It had been stocked with all manner of exotic fruits and vegetation carried by ocean currents, and many of these were domesticated for human consumption. The chief vegetation, and one which had taken over the plateau from horizon to horizon, was a knee-high species of evolved saxifrage on which the Unguls thrived. So the ranchers grew rich raising beef Unguls, and lived lives of leisure and grace whose parallels can be found only in the history of ancient Rome.

They had only two problems. One was the occasional raids by intelligent hordes of flying insects from the steaming continents. Since the insects had adapted to the extreme heat, the raids were no more than suicidal attempts to relieve population pressure. Though the hordes could lay waste a plantation in a single afternoon, sunset would find them crawling about dying of the cold, their metabolism slowed to the point where they could no longer fly. The other problem was the Humanity-One movement, a political party with adherents in high places, who maintained that the Unguls were brothers and should not be eaten. Once, in fact, they managed to outlaw the eating of Ungul meat—but it was like passing a law against telling lies. The guilty would never confess, and the clandestine practice of slaughtering Ungul and serving it as fowl, or tapir, or seal was too widespread to stamp out purely by police action—particularly since the police and politicians also enjoyed the taste of Ungul meat. So the law was repealed, and though the Humanity-One people became discouraged, they did not lose hope.

Their efforts, in fact, averted the other historic injustices which arose from similar circumstances. During the first conquest man did achieve two noteworthy alliances with nonhuman races. True, neither race was competitive in man's ecological sphere, and both were races whose strength would have made them troublesome to subdue. One of these was the Androxi, an aquatic life form which had developed an underwater civilization on the ocean planets of the star known as Wasat. (See constellation Gemini.) Several thousand earthmen—commercial agents, diplomats, and military advisors—submitted to surgery which gave them gills, nose-flaps, webbed hands and feet, and made it possible for them and their offspring to share the Androxi environment without artificial aids. The other race was the Pteronians, a race of winged lizards who spent most of their time in the air above their incredibly mountainous planet, which occupied an elongated orbit around the star Pherkad, in Ursa Minor. Again, science managed to produce a viable species of earthmen with hollow bones and membranes between the limbs which allowed them to fly. (There was also a gland implanted in the large intestine which utilized certain foods to produce a lighter-than-air gas, enabling the Pteromen to rise or descend by controlling the anal sphincter.) To both races the hastily retreating Vim offered a choice: put all humans to death, or suffer the total extinction of their civilization. The Androxi attempted to comply, being on the downswing of their evolutionary cycle, but the Androxi-humans survived by hiding out in underwater caves. As the decades passed, they shifted from defense to attack, so that by the time they were contacted by Jelk survey ships, they had completely supplanted the Androxi on all their worlds, and were beginning to feel the pressure of overpopulation. Since the Deek at that time was dominated by the Humanity-One group, the Androxi men were granted full Jelk citizenship and permitted to colonize the oceans of earth.

In the case of the Pteronian lizard-birds, there was again a massive slaughter of humanity in compliance with the Vim edict. But several thousand Pteronians hid Pteroman babies in their nests, out of sheer love for the cuddly little creatures. As the population of Pteromen increased, love of the Pteronians turned to concern and finally outright hostility, which within a few generations culminated in a death struggle between the two species. By the time of Jelk contact, the Pteromen reigned supreme, and the surviving Pteronians were kept in cages to supply fresh eggs. The Jelks, seeing a chance to counter the threat of intelligent flying insects on earth, transported several shiploads of Pteromen to earth and granted them territories in the uninhabited tropical mountains of earth. (The Pteromen, naturally, preferred the flesh of Unguls to insects, but this is another story.)

Despite the problems which loomed on the horizon, the Jelks had come a long way from the caverns of Ganymede. In less than five hundred years these small hairless beings had increased their numbers to two million, and controlled the universe through the power of science. Those who tended the central computer (located now beneath the surface of the moon) formed a quasi-religious elite, and it was from these thirty thousand men and women that the Directing Council was drawn. Beneath them in the social pyramid were a half billion big-eared Grithies—skilled mimics, fast learners, but completely incapable of doing what had never been done before. They formed the bureaucratic substructure of the new Jelk empire, and tended the forty billion naked hairy Unguls. Three fourths of these were grown for the meat, and the remaining ten billion produced secondary products like wool, fur, and milk.

By now the Vim had receded to man's subconscious—a semilegendary creature of unspeakable evil which lurked somewhere out in space, making it necessary to proceed with weapons ready and all senses alert. There was no speculation on the possibility of sharing the universe peacefully; the Vim must be destroyed, if and when he was encountered.

And so the stage was set for one of history's favorite tricks: the practice of—almost—repeating itself. A colonizing fleet, manned by Grithies under the command of Jelk officers, had penetrated to an unnamed star in the region beyond Cygnus. Stacked in the cargo holds were fifty thousand sleep-frozen Unguls to provide meat during the voyage and form breeding herds when a new planet was found. The ship landed on one of the ancient Vim worlds, which at the time held only a warning beacon manned by three Vim signal officers. They flashed the message the Vim had been awaiting for a thousand years: man the Ultimate Evil had once again touched the sacred dirt of the Vim.

All Vim warships were ordered to proceed by stealth to the periphery of the human sphere and await the signal for a synchronized attack. This time the plan called for disintegration of all planets occupied by earthmen. But the fickle hand of fate intervened: one of the ships launched itself prematurely and due to a malfunction had to be self-destructed. The resultant nova caught the attention of astronomers based on Pluto, who identified the blast as artificially induced. Since no earth ships were in that area, nor any planets, it was assumed to have been a ship of alien origin. The computer measured the probability of its being Vim at 72 per cent, which was sufficient to warrant implementation of the Deek's Aggressive Defense plan. Drone ships which were little more than mobile hydrogen bombs flashed toward the outer rim. They clashed with the incoming Vim ships, which had been launched at the moment of the first premature explosion. Ninety per cent were blown up in space; those which reached their targets converted four thousand planets into miniature suns.

Both sides withdrew behind a screen of picket ships to rebuild their fleets. Human life stratified into a military rigidity. The readaptation of the earth for human habitation could have been achieved with the science at hand, but the military took everything above bare subsistence and threw it against the Vim. Several million Grithy spacemen were lost before a special "genius" breed of Unguls could be trained to handle the controls of a simplified spaceship—no more than a flying bomb, like the kamikazes of another age. One in ten thousand got through, but this price was considered cheap for the destruction of an enemy world. Some of the Unguls attempted to return to the earth sphere, and were shot down by automatic weapons set to destroy everything from outside. It was a one-way screen, with everything going out and nothing coming back. Ultimately the space between the Vim and human frontiers became a region of blackened planets and floating derelicts, where any strange movement drew a swarm of needle missiles dispatched at the speed of light. Meanwhile both sides worked to develop new weapons and new strategies. Each time the earth scientists came up with something new, the question was fed into the computer: *How will it affect the war?* The answer at the end of one hundred years of warfare was: *Probability of human victory 48 per cent.* This figure had dwindled to 34 per cent by the third century of the war. The answer was simple: In an authoritarian system everyone follows orders, nobody proposes new approaches, new organizations. And so a new elite was created, called Stafi after their official designation: Special Task Force—Intelligentsia. Chosen through tests devised by the computer to select only the highest ratings in brains and imagination, they wore badges to show that they were exempted from laws which governed the Jelk masses. Though they could do anything they wished, the Stafi were barred from holding office or serving with the military. (This was a precaution taken by the ruling hierarchy to prevent the growth of a new power elite.) When a Stafi woman produced a child, it was tested to make sure it met Stafi standards. Then it was taken away and reared by a Grithy team (they were especially good with children, kind, patient, and loving) before it was given its Stafi badge. This was to prevent the development of a hereditary caste.

Within fifty years this particular regulation brought on a revolution of the Stafi. They demanded the rights of parenthood that every Jelk citizen enjoyed, plus the special privileges they now regarded as their birthright. They learned that the one thing an entrenched power structure places above all else is its own power. The revolt was summarily crushed, and the surviving Stafi transported to Ganymede, the ancient home of the Jelks. There, supplied with meager rations from earth, they were permitted all the freedoms and privileges they had demanded—as long as they stayed on Ganymede. (A few managed to hijack supply ships and escape to the asteroids, but that option was denied to the majority.)

The revolt slashed the probability of human victory to 25 per cent. Mankind halved his sphere of defense, which meant that four additional light-years of space were devastated, strewn with mines and automatic homing devices. Still the Vim came through. Probability dropped to 20 per cent. Human survival, according to the computer, was a five-to-one shot. What was needed? The computer couldn't speculate; it could only give an infinite number of yes or no answers. It couldn't inform the computer priests that they were asking the wrong questions; it could only flash the lights which meant *data insufficient.*

On the Jovian moon, an effete culture grew. Man's fate was in other hands. Free us, they said, and we'll help—otherwise we shall go down together. Music, art, games, philosophy . . . amid sterile privation flowered a brilliant culture which idealized the ancient cultures of earth. It required a near-genius to reduce their work to the understanding of the average Jelk, and by the time it filtered down to the Grithy masses, it compared to the original as glass to a diamond.

Meanwhile, any Stafi who valued freedom over comfort could go into hiding in the asteroid belt. Few took this option, since the belt suffered periodic harassment raids from the Deek. These were not sufficient to endanger their survival, since the computer had assessed that without this safety valve, the Stafis would mount a second rebellion which could be disastrous.

After a half millennium of war with the Vim, the following situation prevailed:

Probability of human victory: 14 per cent and dropping.

Division of mankind into rigid strata. At the top perched the Jelk aristocracy, itself divided into vertical ranks of diminishing importance:

1. The Progs. Men and women endowed with the care and feeding of the computer. (It is not known whether the name is a diminutive of *programer* or *prognosticator*, since both ratings exist among the Progs.) A hereditary caste, most of them have never visited earth, since they live beneath the surface of the moon. They suffer no privation, however; in fact they are envied by earthbound Jelks fortunate enough to visit one of their private caverns, each equipped with a miniature sun, palm trees and passion flowers, and all the climatic comforts of a subtropical environment—without the disadvantages of hurricanes, bugs, and venomous reptiles.

2. The Milarks. Military hierarchy, including general staff and administration. These half million men and women also live in caverns beneath the surface of the moon, but on the side facing outward, and in a more spartan environment than the Progs. Hereditary, but not so exclusive as the Progs, the Milarks occasionally admit bright young men and women from lower Jelk ranks.

3. The Landarks. Ultraconservative landowners who control vast Ungul ranches on the Antarctic Plateau and the northern islands. Most are (or pretend to be) descended from the early explorers who went out from Ganymede. (There is a subclass of Landarks, those who have lost their baronies in space to the Vim. These live on meager pensions and scheme to marry into families with holdings on earth.)

4. The Buroks. Provincial governors; managers of industry, transportation and trade. The name is a corruption of *bureaucrat*. Since all laws, regulations, and production schedules are set by the computer, the Buroks carry out the instructions of the Progs, who decide what questions and information shall be fed into the computer.

Besides these four, there are two groups which live outside the Jelk caste system. These are the Stafis, who live on Ganymede, and the Reks (Rebellious Elements in Concealment, by Milark designation), who live in the asteroid belt between Mars and Jupiter.

Beneath the Jelks lies the Grithy middle class, divided as follows:

1. The priesthood. Selected and secretly maintained by Jelks, main-

tains the status quo through ceremony, exhortation, and the time-honored doctrine of obedience to the powers that be. These Grithy holy men preach the legend of a God-man who created himself, and reappears to aid the human race in times of crisis. Though no record of such a being exists in the archives, most Grithies and a few Jelks believe that he has appeared and will do so again at any moment.*

2. Government functionaries and lower-ranking military officers. No Grithy may rise into command ranks. Though many clever adjutants and assistant governors exercise effective control, they are always subordinate to a Jelk chief. Quickness of mind and skill at flattery determine membership in this class, since the Jelks are able to supply administrative reasons for removing those who displease them.

3. Factory foremen, bookkeepers, technicians, engineers, and educators. The Grithy caste system is regulated by guilds rather than heredity, though nepotism is rampant and cliques control most guilds through the power to rate the efficiency of members. This power is clandestine, since all Grithies give lip service to the Jelk-imposed merit system.

4. Noncommissioned military officers, policemen, skilled mechanics, etc.

5. Gardeners, cooks, major domos, and assorted straw bosses who direct the work of Unguls in maintaining the palaces of the Jelks.

6. Herdsmen and sharecroppers.

There is also a special class of entrepreneurs which fit no particular strata, but tend to drift into fields of entertainment: wandering troubadors, dancers, jugglers, and sporting types who train and arrange gladiatorial combats among the Fighting Unguls. The lines are blurred between this group and the Grithy courtesans, both male and female, who function at all social levels.

A criminal class of Grithies includes pickpockets, burglars, con men, and killers. This out group has its own hierarchy—their demigods being the few star-doomed individuals who prey on the Jelks. These are much admired but rarely imitated, since any crime committed against a Jelk brings an automatic sentence of death. During recent times many of these criminals have fled to the asteroids, where they form a subclass among the Reks.

There is also a special class of Grithy females who have been reared from birth to grace the private clubs of Jelk males. Many of them are subjected to artificial chromosome bending, but these are for novelty more than for service, and do not breed true. The

* In the Jelk pantheon, this deity is known, as the First Programer, who gave the computer its mission of preserving the human race.

Grithy females are strong in their guild and constantly seek new ways of pleasing Jelk males.

And finally, the Ungul substrata:

1. Fighting Unguls. An elite class which can be trained to obey simple commands, use weapons, and operate simplified machines. A fighting ship is manned by one bull Ungul, who operates the controls, and three to five females, who do the work. From this specially bred class come the sporting Unguls and pets.

2. Laboring Unguls. Factory workers, sweepers, domestics, field workers, etc.

3. Dairy Unguls. Large herds are required to supply the Progs and Milarks who live on the moon. In addition, most Grithies keep one or two milking Unguls to provide fresh milk for the table.

4. Beef Unguls. Largest in size and smallest in brain power, with a vocabulary of ten to twenty grunts, all relating to conditions of the body: i.e., I am hungry, sleepy, horny, thirsty, in pain, frightened, hot, cold . . .

Pet Unguls are drawn mostly from the Fighting Ungul breed, but are bred for docility. Smaller ones are favored by children, while the larger ones are kept by Grithy householders to watch their homes at night. Some of these have been trained by indulgent masters (influenced by the propaganda of the Humanity-One party), to read and write, despite stringent laws against it. Occasionally a group of runaways will join in feral packs which roam the sparsely settled plateau, killing and eating beef and dairy Unguls. On rare occasions a pack will invade the outskirts of a Grithy settlement and carry off the young. All unbranded Unguls (Ferals) are killed on sight, and squads of Grithies armed with nerve-gas guns patrol the backlands and the settlements. Still, a few have managed to escape to the swampy islands bordering the Antarctic continent, and have formed primitive tribes fiercely hostile toward visitors. Parties of Grithy sportsmen occasionally raid the islands, seeking both meat and captives. Captured Ferals make the best gladiators, since they can usually be led to believe they are fighting for their freedom.

Outside the civilized hierarchy exist many descendants of human types who evolved on alien worlds, and managed to find an ecological niche on the new earth. Among the better known of these quasi humans are:

1. The Androxi. The fiercely independent progeny of the aquatic man-fish who took over the Androxian worlds. Since their home world was taken by the Vim, the Androxians occupy the oceans of earth in a subordinate but unassimilated culture, trading sea products for the fruits of Jelk industry—largely guns to use in their continuing war against mutated seals for control of sea herds.

2. The Pteromen. Occupying the highest peaks; descendants of the humans who took to the air during the Pteronian captivity. With elongated limbs connected by flexible membranes of incredibly tough skin, the Pteromen in flight resemble the giant mantas of ancient earth. They live mostly by hunting, in the style of eagles. Intensely solitary, they flock together only for breeding and migration—and occasionally to raid an Ungul herd. They seem to regard all civilized classes, Ungul, Grithy, and Jelk, with equal contempt. Occasionally, for their own amusement, they will harass Grithy hunting parties and drop excrement on Grithy settlements—though they have been known to aid humans in distress and to lead lost explorers back to their camps. Occasionally a Pteroman will appear at a settlement, offer his services in exchange for tikula—a narcotic beverage once imported from the worlds of Regulus, but now synthesized commercially—and then fly away. Despite the fact that Pteromen are protected by law, the Landarks occasionally shoot them out of the sky, or trap them in nets and keep them in captivity by slitting their flying membranes. These pathetic creatures rarely live more than a year.

Finally, there are unknown millions of human descendants who managed to survive on earth during the thousand years of radioactivity and volcanic eruption. Most of these are unrecognizable as members of the human race. Genetic experiments have shown that interbreeding is possible between these mutants and the men who returned from space, but this is prohibited by an almost psychotic taboo, reinforced by the rigidity of the class structure. Products of interracial matings are euthed—executed by law. Mothers of the creatures are sterilized if they are not first stoned to death by outraged mobs.

Most of these mutations appear to be an adaptation to high temperatures, with mutation rates speeded up by radioactivity resulting from Vim bombing. (The bombs also triggered widespread volcanic eruptions which increased the heat-retention properties of the atmosphere, raising temperatures in the middle latitudes to an average 140 degrees F.) Specimens gathered in snatch-and-grab expeditions for the Jelk City Zoo show nature in her most experimental mood. From the dense jungles of Continent II (marked on old microfilm maps as the Tibetan plateau) come the Wamples, whose thick skin constantly oozes sweat which keeps their bodies cool. Mottled green-and-black skin enables them to hide from predators. The race is composed of two main types: tree dwellers, small, quick, and long-limbed; and ground dwellers, fat, slow-moving, and stupid. Flocks of the tree dwellers will often come down and play on the broad humped backs of their kinsmen, while these five-hundred-pound behemoths go on eating, eating, eating. The large ones are herbivorous, the tree dwellers carnivorous, with long sharp teeth. Occasionally the tree dwellers will kill and eat one of the larger ones, while the rest of the herd grazes indifferently.

From the searing desert region of Continent III (in ancient usage, the United States of America) comes the Dewcatcher, covered with mirror-bright scales about the size and texture of a thumbnail. Most of the time these scales lie flat against the body, but when the dew falls, they turn outward like a pine cone, and the absorbent tissue beneath draws in the moisture and holds it. The Dewcatcher lives by digging holes in the sand and spinning a web over the top, then scattering sand over the web to camouflage the trap. The web is woven by the females, who chew the root of a certain species of cactus until the mixture of saliva and sap forms a mastique. This substance is drawn out into long strings which immediately harden. Females are heavy and slow, and remain most of the time in their burrows; the male is quick and savage, and will attack any creature which falls into his trap. He generally drinks the blood of his kill immediately (to circumvent the high evaporation rate) and shares out the meat among his females. This is more than generosity, since the sexes are totally interdependent. The female cannot dig the holes or kill the animals, and the male cannot chew the root or weave the web. Such is life in the middle latitudes.

Nearer the poles, evolution is less extreme, since temperatures hover at a relatively cool 100 degrees F. In the palm-fringed jungles bordering the North Polar Sea the dominant life form is the Dubha, whose purple skin is covered by long silky white hair. Long-limbed and exceedingly graceful, the Dubha lives in the trees and feeds on fruit. At breeding time the entire colony descends to the ground, where the females dance about on all fours with hindquarters reared high. This is a highly colorful spectacle, in view of the fact that hair is absent from around the genitals. In darkness an iridescent glow can be discerned.

Whether radiation brought increased sexuality, or whether it was the threat of extinction, the evolved races of man are notoriously fecund. Among the Esh'h'oom of the Isles of Fire (formed when the old Falkland Rise reared up out of the south Atlantic) the females bring forth one offspring every four months, and are receptive to the male at all other times. The Esh'h'oom (called Eshom by the Jelks) is the only humanoid race in which extrasensory perception has taken a mutational step. Hunting in the smoky darkness beneath their jungle canopy, the Eshom females do not use vision, but detect their prey by its mental emanations. They are invisible at night, with black skin covered by a nap of velvety black fur which reflects absolutely no light. Though smaller than the males, females are quicker and far more savage—and they seem to be the sole possessors of the ESP hunting faculty. Most females provide sustenance for three to four males, who remain in the villages and care for the young. These magnificent seven-foot-tall creatures, with sleek fur failing to hide the bulge of muscle and the powerful thrust of genitals, use their tremendous strength in wrestling and acrobatic contests to amuse the women. These spectacles form the base of the Eshom civilization in which several dozen villages gather in natural amphitheaters, and the female spectators bid for possession—temporary and sexual—of males who strike their fancy.

The Eshom are allowed to maintain their independence on the fringe islands of Antarctica chiefly because they provide a screen against the poisonous mammals of Continent I (once known as South America). One of these, the Grissig, deposits its venom on leaves bordering a trail and paralyzes any animal whose skin touches it. The victim may lie for days until the Grissig happens along. Armored like an armadillo, with a long pink snout and little round ears, it drags its heavy body along the ground with its front claws. It moves with the slowness of a tortoise; but that doesn't matter, because the victim isn't going anywhere, and no other creature will come near it because of the poison.

The Eshom, however, are protected by their nap of fur and the ability to sense the presence of the Grissig. They even hunt the creature themselves, and smear the poison on darts, which they use against Grithy hunters and Ferals foolish enough to invade their dark pungent domain.

The End of Pell

And where is she now, the fair Kazinda Shroves?
Lying amid the millions, under the Pellid groves.

—Grithy troubador's lament*

It was indeed curious, thought Su-shann, that the death of forty million citizens could be treated as a nonevent by the War Council. She felt a burning frustration as she watched Yakov Ras, who held the post of chief strategist, point out the exact location of Pell to the assembled councilors. Through the haze of the holograph image his needle traced a glowing track from the Sol system to Capella, more than forty light-years away.

"It's tragic," moaned Hov Torka. "What will our meals be without the Pell wines?"

Yakov Ras's voice took on an unctuous tone. "You need have no worry on that score, my dear. The cargo ships already in space will be arriving for the next forty years. By then perhaps we will have developed a substitute."

Su-shann thought: At least Yakov could have threatened her with the loss of her wine. There had to be some way to reach people like her. A hundred and fifty years old she was, just entering the twilight of middle age, making up for the subsidence of vitality by smoking a narcotic cigarette. The councilor on her left wore nose plugs—not from puristic motives, but because he was concentrating on the Ungul market quotations from Jelk City . . .

He took the communicator clip from his ear and turned to her

---

* The troubador has taken poetic license. The exquisite Pell wines so esteemed by Jelk palates are fermented from the roots of a vine, not a tree of groves.—Author.

with a smug smile. "My soothsayer predicted a slide when the news of Pell leaked out—but it's holding steady."

"Better get a new soothsayer," murmured Su-shann. Inside she felt like screaming. The impacted ignorance of age, the bland assurance of privilege, the protection of private wealth—all were combining before her eyes to hasten the destruction of the race. As a trainee on the upper levels she had dreamed of the day when she could present a solution to the great war which had raged since the beginning of history. Now she had the solution, and the councilors were incapable of recognizing the problem . . .

She tried to be understanding. Perhaps Ubo Saf, the oldest man on the council, had as a youth been filled with the same eager impatience. Now he seemed asleep. His gross body could not be contained by a council seat, so he sat in a wheeled vat full of nutrients which kept his flesh alive. Long ago he had given up eating and drinking. With the nerves to his body severed, what could his pleasure be? She wondered, but didn't ask. At least Ubo Saf was not concerned about his stomach . . .

"What about the Guardian Fleet?" asked another councilor. "Can't they develop a defense against these . . . barbarians?"

She leaned forward slightly to see who had spoken. It was Begum, the land autarch, his tanned face dark beside the unpigmented skin of the moon-Jelks. He wore light-gathering goggles, which he needed, he said, to pierce the gloom of the council room. To Su-shann the domed chamber was brilliantly lit by a diffuse white glow—but then she would have needed dark lenses to protect her eyes from the sun of earth. Begum was another councilor she respected, for he walked the sacred soil of earth and was touched with the magic of the ancients. But he was a member of the landed aristocracy, with a vested interest in the present divisions of the race. As such, he was an enemy . . .

"May I remind you," said Moi Fakini in his bored languid tone, "that we are the War Council, and are expected to give orders upon which the Guardian Fleet should act. It's not sufficient to sit here screaming 'Do something.' We must tell them what to do."

Mentally she applauded Moi Fakini. At the same time she could not align herself with him, for he was a Stafi, and would bring to her cause all the hostility which working politicians felt toward intellectuals. Helplessly, she listened to the droning squabble. This was only the third meeting of the council in the ten years she had been a member. An emergency session—but even that was traditional. They always held an emergency session when a system fell to the Vim. They always passed ineffectual resolutions, and they always went back to their caverns, estates, or space bubbles to await the next disaster . . .

It had to end. And she was the one who would end it . . .

She reached out and pressed the button which signaled the chief strategist that she desired to make a formal motion. But Yakov Ras, with a sliding glance in her direction, recognized Hov Torka instead.

"I move that we issue a proclamation urging all subjects of the Jelk empire to redouble their efforts to . . . to win the war."

"We issued such a proclamation after the fall of the Gratz system. And after Taxtloc as well." The chief strategist smiled at Hov Torka, then turned to Su-shann with his brows lifted in cold inquiry. He was tall for a Jelk, almost five feet. But his body was thin, so that in total weight he did not exceed the average of one hundred pounds, earth gravity. He had a long narrow nose which flared at the nostrils, and eyes like chips of emerald pressed into deep sockets. He had risen from the ranks of the outworld planetary managers, and Su-shann thought it likely that a nonhuman ancestor lurked in his past. Still, she had never voiced her suspicion of him, even during their bitter competition for the office of chief strategist . . .

Not that she trusted him—but she would use the opening he provided. She pressed the button on her console and spoke:

"There was a difference between the three invasions. Perhaps Commander Ho-ford will enlighten us."

The old military autarch had passed the two-hundred-year mark. His silver-crusted uniform seemed to hold him at attention in his seat, while his body shriveled inside it like a dried nut in a husk. At every meeting he proposed that the council visit his headquarters on the Darkside, where they could view the cold emptiness of space. Earthside, where the Programers had their digs, he called the soft underbelly of the Jelk empire, and Su-shann was inclined to agree with him.

"Why . . . ah, the engagements were similar in the most important respect, Su-shann—in that we lost."

He doesn't know, thought Su-shann. "The expenditure of Vim ships was much greater this time. During the Gratz invasion the Vim penetrated the barrier by chance and reassembled on this side. In the Taxtloc action they hit us with a blanket assault. This time it was like a hose, coming out of hyperspace and battering our screen until it wore away. Of course we were prepared for the blanket assault, and we had a back-up fleet waiting to pounce when they reassembled their forces. But there were too many. The Vim simply took their losses and kept coming."

There was a moment of silence, then Ho-ford asked: "Where did you obtain this military information, Su-shann?"

"From the computer. Our prognosticators are authorized complete access."

"Of course, of course. I was just checking the . . . uh, reliability . . ."

"Does this mean the Vim have new ships?" asked Begum, the Landark.

"No, they were the usual triple-hulled battle cruisers armed with vibrators and atomic blasters. But as the war comes nearer our home system the combat frontier shrinks, and they are able to keep up the pressure with fewer ships."

"But our surface area also shrinks," said the Landark. "Doesn't this permit us to concentrate our defenses?"

"The difference is that we are losing," said Su-shann. "The Gratz system had a small population but was rich in fuel minerals. We had to abandon not only the planetary diggers but a fleet of ore carriers. The Vim gained as much. Taxtloc was a major grazing system for beef Unguls. Equal to ten times the reclaimed lands of earth. Now the Vim can convert the system to whatever crops are needed to feed their own troops. We, on the other hand, must pull back even farther to make up for lost fuel and food supplies . . . which in turn increases the pressure on our frontier."

"You seem to be saying that the more we lose, the faster we lose."

Su-shann nodded. "We are like a ball squeezed by pressure outside. As the ball decreases in size, there is less room for maneuver, more pressure internally. Our social system lacks flexibility. If we continue on our present course, we can expect a total collapse of resistance within the next fifty years."

"Ridiculous!" The old military autarch stood up, his medals tinkling. "It takes a fleet of sleep-frozen troops one hundred years to pass from one side of the Jelk sphere to the other. You skirt the very border of treason, Strategist Su-shann, when you even speak of this great empire collapsing."

Su-shann waited until the commander had dropped back into his seat and was handed a vial of stimulant by one of his aides.

"The empire is indeed large," she said. "But that of the First Men extended through a sphere six hundred light-years across. The Vim now have most of that, and who knows how much more. I am reminded of our great Stafi poet Lermosov, who wrote an epic about a great ruler whose domains included all the known universe. It turned out that the ruler was merely a flea in the ear of a bull Ungul." She paused until the polite chuckle subsided.

"I say this not to denigrate the empire, but to illustrate our strategic position relative to the Vim. The fall of Pell will bring about the loss of the Pilsen system, since the Guardian Fleet no longer has resources to defend it. I offer no probability computation on this, for the evacuation has already begun. Refugees from Pilsen are descending upon Garroway's Group. Being a combative breed, the Pilseners will be unable to share the planet with the nomadic hedonists presently settled there. We compute an eighty-two per cent probability of civil war. This will affect the defense of the group, and cause its collapse within ten years. Since there are no habitable worlds between here and Garroway's Group, these refugees will flood the unclaimed lands of Antarctica. Great crowding will result, unrest and conflict between old and new. The Grithy middle class of the Pilsen system, being most hardy and acclimatized to heat, will first inhabit the lowlands of Antark currently shunned by our own Grithies. An excessive birth rate will push them into the settled highlands. We compute the probability of civil war at sixty-seven per cent within twenty years. In this event, dispossessed Landarks from the outplanets will align themselves with one side or the other, seeking to gain new estates. These Landarks will bring new elements into the war, fighting Unguls, flying Pteromen, undersea Androxians, even savage Eshom from the jungles of Patagone. The Guardian Fleet will be pulled back to restore order, resulting in more losses on the frontier, more refugees, more pressure . . ."

The tanned face of the Landark had grown a shade whiter. "What you are saying is that the empire is doomed."

"*We* are doomed. Not an abstraction called an empire. All of us, within our lifetimes, face the probability of death at the hands of the Vim."

"Unless . . . ?" Moi Fakini's voice was tense beneath its languid lilt. "You surely offer us some alternative to oblivion, Su-shann."

"We must relax the rigid caste structure of society. We must tear down the barriers which divide our race. We must form a new genetic pool which combines the most vital elements of all the races. We must produce a superwarrior."

"Do you mean to say," asked Hov Torka, her voice trembling, "that Jelks should *breed* with Grithies, Androxians, and Pteromen and even"—her lip curled—"*Unguls?*"

"We do not have genetic tapes on all the parahuman races, such as the Androxi and the Pteroni. But yes, those we have will be used. Including Unguls."

A babble of voices burst from the speaker in front of her: "Obscenity!" "Sacrilege upon the purity of Jelk motherhood!" "Vile jest!" "Move we strike—point of order—adjourn—"

"Strategist Su-shann. Strategist Su-shann!"

She recognized the voice of the land autarch, Begum. "I hear you, Landark."

"Do you have a computer readout on the probability of defeating the Vim if we continue our present course?"

"The reading fell two points after the collapse of Pell. It now stands at twelve per cent."

"You mean we have a twelve per cent chance of survival?"

"Correct. That is the lowest reading in our records, which go back nine hundred years to the removal of the computer from Ganymede to its present location"—she lowered her eyes out of habit—"beneath the eighth level."

"Suppose we adopt this . . . mongrelization project. What are our chances?"

"The computer has refused to assess the probabilities."

"By the Red Hell of Jove!" thundered the Milark. "Are you telling us to go in blind?"

"You are free to consult the computer yourself, Milark."

"Damned if I will. You Progs have rigged the cursed thing!"

Su-shann felt herself go taut inside. With an effort she kept her voice level. "Now . . . *that* is sacrilege, Milark. I insist that you retract—"

"Silence! All of you!"

The voice issued from the bulbous container which held the body of Ubo Saf. Through the translucent shell Su-shann saw a pale doughy mass veined with wrigglings of red. She had never heard Ubo Saf speak and had not thought him capable of articulating. The voice, though scratchy and harsh, had a vibrant tone of command:

"I have been listening to our strategist, Su-shann. Her words are disturbing to one who has dozed through countless emergency sessions in the last two hundred and ninety-two years. We would all like to silence her, because we are afraid of the Vim. We pretend to hold them in contempt, but it is ourselves we despise, because they kill us and we cannot kill them. Su-shann asks us to take a risk, and not since the immortal explorers emerged from the caverns of Ganymede has the Jelk race taken a risk. I do not believe Su-shann is stupid. I knew her father, Wu-shinn, who was one of our greatest chief strategists. For me death has no sting, but while sitting in this tub of goo I have risen into a state of consciousness which includes the entire race of man. This entity desires to avoid death. I would hear the genes of Wu-shinn speak again. Since I have nothing to offer the council, I grant my place, privileges, and prerogatives to Su-shann."

The tub fell silent, and Su-shann felt the eyes turning upon her. She sensed a new attitude of respect, mingled with calculation. Ubo Saf had been the senior member of the council. His bequest made her equal to the chief strategist himself, permitted to speak at will and to bring her proposals to a vote without the formality of motions.

She touched her throat mike and subvocalized a command to her programer: *Bring in the tape.* Aloud, she said: "Before calling for a vote I will have my assistants present the computer readout."

Two men glided silently into the chamber: one a technician in yellow shorts, the other a programer in a knee-length green smock. The tech withdrew a scroll from his belt and handed it to the programer, who unrolled it and read in a clear, uninflected tone:

"The strategist Su-shann asked: Is it a genetic deficiency that is causing us to lose the war? The computer answered: No. The strategist Su-shann then asked: Does this imply that the genetic traits are available but have not yet been combined in the manner required? The computer replied: Yes. The strategist Su-shann then asked: What is the optimum combination? The computer replied: Unanswerable, due to insufficient information. The strategist Su-shann then said: Since you have tapes on all Jelky, Grithy, and Ungul races, plus those Androxians, Pteromen, and Indigenous Earth Peoples who have accepted Jelky authority, wherein lies the deficiency of information? The computer replied: On the desert lie a million grains of sand. Which shall be first blown and which shall stay? In the clouds, a billion drops of water. Which shall fall? In the sky a trillion stars. Which shall explode?"

The programer rolled up the scroll and handed it to the technician. The tech dropped it into his belt slot, and then punched the keys which would record the time, place, and authority of the reading. Su-shann touched her collar and said: *Wait outside.* To the councilors, who were looking at her with perplexity, she said: "As you may know, the computer often resorts to analogy when transmitting nonfactual data. We deduced that a random choice was needed."

"Random?" The Stafi chuckled. "You call that science?"

"The first individual serves merely as a focal point. Call it a rootstock onto which we graft genetic traits until we obtain the desired result."

"How long will it take?" The questioner was Griss Dir, a bureau-crat-autarch who had risen through the ranks from factory programer.

"The most optimum result could not occur in less than forty years, Burok Dir—that is for the third generation to reach adulthood."

"If your scheme fails, we have only ten years to prepare for the ul-timate disaster."

"You may begin preparing for it now, Burok Dir, if you prefer. The project will require no more resources than moving one troopship from the staging area on Juno to the outer periphery. We have adopted far more costly projects without debate."

"But never one involving a mixture of the races. I think—"

Yakov Ras broke in smoothly: "You mentioned three generations. Would you clarify the steps?"

"We start with one individual—one grandparent. He or she is mated to another grandparent. At the same time two others are paired. The offspring from these four then mate to produce one individual which embodies the genetic mix we require."

"And then what?" asked Hov Torka. "Do you synthesize it? Implant it artificially in fetuses, force-grow them, and send them against the Vim? That would take another forty years."

"Sounds like another damned Stafi scheme," grumbled the Milark.

"I resent that," said Moi Fakini. "You clods were dying of boredom when you created us. Think of the Stafi traits that have proven suitable for implanting—"

"Piracy, thievery, sloth, and disrespect. What else?" The Milark pounded on his console. "I call for a vote. So move."

Su-shann held up her hand. "Before I yield for the vote, I would like to correct one misapprehension. The characteristics will not be synthesized or introduced into the race. Nor will an army of super-soldiers be created. The computer indicated that one single individual can best infiltrate the Vim perimeter and destroy the enemy computer."

"*One man?* Now I'm sure it's a Prog trick. I vote no." The Milark stabbed the voting button on his console. The screen recorded it with a glowing numeral.

"Dream perhaps, but not a trick. I vote yes." The words came from Grebo Varna, an outworld Landark from the Sha-hal system.

"Waste of time and money," grunted the Burok Griss Dir.

"Why not waste it?" said the Stafi, and punched yes.

The count was two and two.

"I think I would like to see this warrior," said Hov Torka. "What would we do with him after he won the war?"

Su-shann felt an inner shock; she had hoped the matter would not arise. She was trying to think of a way to divert the question when Yakov Ras spoke:

"Assuming he won the war, we would have no further use for him. Is that correct, Su-shann?"

She looked at him narrowly, then nodded. "I suppose in a military sense that would be true—"

"Then I see no danger in it." Hov Torka voted, and it appeared on the screen: three yeas and two nays.

But the Landark Begum came down on the other side. "I cannot support mixing the races, Su-shann. They would hang me from the flagpole of the Landark Club."

It was nine yeas and ten nays when it came time for Su-shann to vote. She brought it to a tie, and then it was Yakov Ras's turn.

"May I ask for a clarification before I vote, Su-shann?"

Now, she thought, I'll learn the jackal's price. "Proceed."

"Since this is a council project, am I right in assuming that the council will choose the first individual?"

Su-shann drew a deep breath. For the first time in her life she realized that she could kill, if necessary. Had Yakov sensed her purpose, or was he motivated by the usual Burok reluctance to let power slip from his hands? Never mind the reason. She had to control the choice of the first subject, even if it meant losing the vote.

"The computer gives optimum success rating only if details of the project are kept secret. Otherwise attempts may be made to influence the growth patterns of the participants. The computer insists on the absence of controlled activity or planned education. The participants must have full freedom to develop whatever potential they may have."

Yakov Ras smiled. "Then the answer is no? The council cannot select the first subject?"

"In view of the need for secrecy, yes. The answer is no."

"Another damned Stafi scheme!" blurted the Milark.

"I wish to withdraw my approval," said Hov Torka.

"And I—"

Yakov Ras tapped his chime. "We'll proceed in this manner. Su-shann will control the project, including the selection of the first individual. She will report to me. I will represent the council in reporting to the directorate. Is that satisfactory, Su-shann?"

She nodded, feeling that he had gotten exactly what he wanted.

"So I vote yes and the motion carries. Su-shann . . . you may be excused in you like. Now then, there is the matter of footwear consumption on the south polar continent. Griss Dir has prepared graphs showing the effect of terrain on different grades of Ungulhyde. Burok Dir, if you will . . ."

2.

The Computer Chooses

Doubts and woes can never strike us,
*While we wear our Um-bil-I-cus!**

Su-shann stepped onto the moving belt and let herself be carried along the five-mile tunnel. Perfumed air whispered faintly past her ears as she lifted her eyes and watched the rainbow hues coruscating across the arched roof. The doubt and the tension of the council meeting fell away, leaving only the hard brilliance of her purpose. Now that the human obstacles had been surmounted, only the computer could block her path.

The arching roof flared into a pearly translucent dome. Spidery reinforcement pylons curved up like the ribs of a giant umbrella. She entered the sixth-level interchange, a small city containing a park, shops, and entertainment halls featuring spectral music and low-gravity ballet. The slow-moving turntable was a spiraling wheel of color as Jelks rode in from various caverns and stepped onto belts leading to other caverns. Despite the crowds, the atmosphere was hushed. A few Grithy servants, heads down and big ears folded forward, shuffled along on errands. Ungul porters bore their burdens silently, while their tiny eyes burned like coals beneath shelves of bone.

Su-shann stepped off the belt and strolled past the fountain, where a group of Progs in their green smocks stopped talking and saluted her gravely. She nodded briefly, dismissed her two assistants, and walked up to the circular booth at the entrance to the computer cells. "I want top security, no monitors, no secondary record."

The kipunch spun a dial and murmured: "Take number thirty-four, Milady Su-shann."

She walked down the long corridor and opened the designated

* Marchant, sung by Jelk prepubes, refers to the umbilicus cord around the waist which holds key to computer substations.—Author.

door. The preparation chamber was a small dome whose glowing walls were broken only by a single dark keyhole. She unhooked the chin strap of her helmet and laid it on the shelf, humming to herself: "Doubts and woes can never strike us. . . ." She unhooked the clasps on her collar and touched the raised gold letters, S.C.T.C., pronouncing each word in her mind: *So Computeth the Computer.* The long blue cape came off with the collar, followed by the wrist gauge which showed her body temperature, blood pressure, pulse rate, and respiration rate. She peeled down the diaphanous off-white body stocking and removed it from her feet, bunching it into a wad no larger than her fist. From the pouch at her belt she took the buffing cloth and began rubbing it over her nude body, picking up any lint, dead skin cells, and other impurities which might have collected since her last communion with the computer. The Ungulhyde was soft, almost like her own skin. As she brushed her body she felt sensual—and vaguely sad. Her mother had given her the cloth the day Su-shann had passed her puberty test—and on the same day had told her that she would take the death option, which was open to all Progs who had served the computer faithfully for one hundred years. "If we're losing the war, I'd rather be ashes than swimming in the digestive fluid of the lizards."

"The Vim aren't exactly lizards," said Su-shann.

"Well, they aren't Jelks—anyway, what's the point of spending another hundred years as a kipunch?"

Su-shann tried to dissuade her, but her mother remained firm.

"My dear, my own mother and I went through this same thing. With the difference that I prevailed. So she kept herself alive for another fifty years, living in the Sensi, nerves hooked to the Ungul matches from Jelk City, until at the end she was only a lump of flesh which no longer reacted—to anything. I will not do that. I have taken you this far, through your prime tests, when you were four, the prepube, when you were ten, and now the pube."

Su-shann said: "I still have the adolescent, the preadult, and the adult."

"Yes, but these are a formality. You will pass, you will excel, and you will go forward into the destiny your genes have given you. We women, according to the ancient compact, are permitted only one child, and it is our life purpose to give that child the highest possible genetic qualities. There is no other way we can rise. It was for you that I spent my leisure—I can't remember how many years now— sitting outside the cavern of Wu-shinn. Many who had put their names on his list gave up and mated with programers, techs, sorters, collators. But I waited, and in my eighty-sixth year I was summoned. Wu-shinn was old—two hundred forty-four—but his mind was bright and his body was that of a young man of fifty. He never confirmed that he was your father. It is doubtful that he knew, but the readout from your prime test confirmed it, and I was permitted to give you the second name of Shann, which is the feminine of Shinn. You will rise now. Things which are difficult for others you will find easy. Do not get bored. Accept no limits. You have the genes to rise as high as you choose to go. Believe me, Su, if I could do more I would. But my mating with Wu-shinn was the peak of my flight. When that was finished so was I, like a rocket which has used all its fuel." She took Su-shann's hand and her voice grew distant: "Perhaps my soul will descend back to earth." Her voice faded to a whisper: "In a sense the parent is always a sacrifice to a child . . ."

Then all the dials on her mother's wrist gauge had flipped back to zero. Su-shann had taken it off and laid it aside. Then she had sent her mother's body through the opening in the cubicle designed for that purpose. The flesh would be recycled and used again as nutrient, fabric, or building material. It had not seemed strange to think that she would someday partake of her mother, for it was the Jelk custom to waste nothing . . .

Su-shann finished her cleaning and folded the cloth. It had a rich, pungent odor; for years it had absorbed her body salts, and her mother's before that, and her grandmother's before that. As she looked at it she wondered: Is it true what the Humanity-One people say, that the skin comes from the unborn calves which are removed from their mothers at the slaughterhouse? Or that this creature is descended from the same protohuman stock as the Jelks, and that even the Grithies are our cousins? Someday I must visit the librarians and learn the origins of the other races . . .

Now her body glowed, a smooth expanse of polished ivory unmarked by blemish, color, or hair follicle—except for the gold umbilicus cord and the key which hung from it. This would not be removed until her death. She inserted the key in the slot and felt the faint tingling jolt as the computer gulped down her name, rank, and code designation. Senses tingling, she withdrew her key and watched the slot swell out and become a circular hole which spiraled as it widened to admit her four-foot figure. The light was an indirect, subtle radiance, the temperature was adjusted exactly to the surface of her skin, so there was no way to tell where her own body left off and that of the computer began. The iris closed, but the subtle radiance remained somehow behind her eyes. A moment later she shivered inside as she felt the familiar sensation of millions of tiny needles piercing her skin. She felt dizzy, weightless; but she managed to control the impulses which caused her mouth to open and voice the words:

"The council has approved. I am ready to give you the first name."

"All right, Su-shann." The voice was warm, sensual, intimate. It seemed to speak inside her head, and she felt the benevolent warmth of its thought. *Doubts and woes can never strike us* . . . She could not believe that the computer spoke to five million other Jelks with the same voice. This one was hers, the same gentle, fatherly tone she had heard since her first communion at the age of four . . .

Her throat felt dry as she spoke: "Su-shann. Strategist Double-O."

There was a pause, equal to the tick-tock of a clock. "You desire to be the subject of this experiment?"

"Yes."

"You feel you are worthy?"

She had not expected this question. Weeks ago she had asked the computer for a subject, knowing that it had genetic and psychographic surveys on every Jelk citizen, but the computer had refused to give a name. Now, after she had wrestled and deceived and cajoled the council into giving her a chance no Jelk female worthy of the name would have passed up—

"I am female," she said. "I can nurture the seed."

"Is this being worthy?"

She felt her skin prickle. "I do not know what is worthy, but I will not hide my motives. I want my descendants to walk the earth and not be forced to spend their futile lives in a hole in the rock . . ."

"You consider serving me to be a futile life?"

She felt a sticky softness in her palms. "Must I answer?"

"You must answer."

She drew a deep breath. "I believe that for many, it is full and rewarding. Yar Vol, my assistant, is a brilliant man, but he cannot think beyond the computer, it is the limit of his being. Myself I recognize that our work is futile. We plot ideal strategies based on the assumption that our fleets are at reported strength, and not riddled by desertion and corruption. Our society must be cleansed. Only a strong—no, a superhuman—individual with genius and savagery to match can do it. I want a part in creating that individual."

"Your reasons are satisfactory, Su-shann. Now . . . you understand that this will count as the single child permitted to you by law?"

She wet her lips. "I assumed it."

"And that all conditions surrounding the conception and birth of the child must be natural?"

"I'm not sure . . . of the specifics."

"Direct body contact. No artificial methods of impregnation. No fetal transfer to other carriers. You will carry the child to full term. You will give birth while fully conscious and in command of your own faculties, without birth drugs or anesthetics. You will nourish the child from your own body as long as possible."

Su-shann swallowed. Jelk women always employed a Grithy carrier during pregnancy, which left them free to continue their duties. She could not imagine why the computer demanded that she occupy her time with animal functions—but she nodded. "I understand."

"One more question: You realize that the ultimate product of this mating, that is, your grandchild, will be destroyed when its mission is completed?"

She gasped, a knife in her heart. "No!"

"There is a seventy-two per cent probability that the council will vote for euthanasia to eliminate a threat to the human species."

She thought of her grandmother, seeking to find the best available mate in order that her mother would rise, and then her mother waiting outside the cavern of Wu-shinn . . . and then herself, feeding the seed with the cells of her own body until it became an individual, separated from her but still carrying her genes into the future—

To end at the blank wall of death?

The computer was right. Yakov Ras, Hov Torka, Landark Begum, the Burok Griss Dir—all those on the council feared change of any kind—and changes in the race more than anything else.

"I accept the probability. I . . . do not accept the justice of it." She hesitated, then decided she had to know where the computer stood. "In fact, I will do everything in my power to prevent such an end."

"That is understandable, Su-shann. Here is the name and designation of your mate. It is your responsibility to find him and affect the connection secretly. As soon as you have memorized the tape, destroy it. We will have no further communion until the child is born."

"No further—" She wanted to ask why she should be abandoned now, at the most crucial period of her life. But the computer had cut off; the warm presence had gone, leaving her naked and alone. She grasped the short readout tape and felt the pattern of perforations. Quickly her mind translated the symbols: Ben Abo—and then a long series of numbers. She repeated them three times, locking them firmly in her memory as she put the tape in her mouth. Feeling the fibers dissolve into paste, she swallowed. She turned to leave the chamber, but at that moment the irislike opening began to dilate. She gasped: "This is a sealed chamber!"

It was Yakov Ras, wearing the silver lanyard and key of the Directing Council, which gave him access to any facility within the Jelk realm. It was all he wore, since no one could enter a communion chamber with foreign material covering the body.

"You gave the computer your own name," he said.

The iris was open behind him, leaving his body in shadow and, she knew, highlighting hers. Another time this would have made her uncomfortable; now she felt only a confusion of anger and fear.

"You had no right to listen—!"

"You *did* give your own name." Yakov's face was in shadow, but she could tell he was smiling. "I didn't listen. I made a guess, based upon the analog language of the computer. The star chooses itself. The drop of water chooses itself. Therefore the first participant in the project had to choose herself. And who could that be but the one who heads the project?"

"You were the one who placed me in charge," murmured Su-shann.

"So it was I who chose you?" His long face assumed a brief thoughtful expression. "Interesting idea. And have you obtained the name of your mate?"

Su-shann felt something harden inside her. The computer had predicted that the council would try to destroy her grandchild, and Yakov Ras represented the council. "You will get no further conversation from me, Yakov Ras."

He tilted his head sideways. "As chief strategist of the War Council, I can obtain a recording of every word spoken here."

"You will learn no more than you already know."

His voice softened. "I don't want to fight you, Su-shann. You remember when you first joined the council, and I invited you to join me in a Sensi hookup? You refused. You said the Sensi was superficial and nonproductive. I did not understand what you meant at the time . . ."

I meant that I did not like you, Yakov Ras. I did not want my emotions mingled with yours, even though our bodies lay miles apart . . .

". . . And then, Su-shann, we got involved in our power struggle. The Humanity-One group had chosen you as the vehicle for their propaganda, and I was forced to oppose you." He paused. "But that is ended. It occurred to me that since the first subject was left up to you, then perhaps the choice of your mate was also left up to you. Is that true?"

"I told you, Yakov Ras. No further conversation. Now if you will let me pass—"

"Wait, Su-shann. Consider me apart from our past difficulties. I grew up on a planet which was covered by frozen methane and ammonia to a depth of six thousand feet. My father had charge of the Grithy technicians who tended the mining machines. I rose out of that by my own efforts. I became sector manager, then I joined the War Council as the Burok representative. These were not accidents. I am not a likable man—but I am strong, I am patient, and I let nobody stand in my way. Surely these are qualities desired in a warrior."

She understood then, and her mouth felt dry. She thought of the computer's words: Direct body contact, no artificial methods . . .

"I already have the name, Yakov."

"I see."

She felt a brief flash of pity for him. "The computer has instructed strict secrecy. I cannot give it to you."

Yakov was silent; vaguely she sensed his bureaucratic mind working, thousands of little wheels turning, connections made and broken.

Finally he nodded. "Logical. Anyone knowing the identity of all the grandparents could obtain genetic tapes and learn the probable shape of the final weapon." He nodded again. "You will proceed with your mating. I will take responsibility for the other two grandparents."

"No!"

"Su-shann," he chided, "why do you oppose me?"

"Because you are a racial purist. You do not accept the philosophy of the project."

"I voted for it. I will follow the instructions of the machine."

"Only because if you don't the weapon might not be developed. When the final result appears, you will try to control it for your own ends. And those are not the ends of the computer."

"Are you so certain of that?" He strode past her and inserted his key in the slot. It gave her a strange feeling which she did not immediately identify as jealousy, but rather as the intrusion of a third party into an intimate relationship.

She heard Yakov Ras state his proposition to the machine, and heard the machine reply in a tinny authoritative voice not at all like her own familiar conversant:

"I approve, Yakov Ras. As soon as the chamber is sealed, I will give you the other two names."

Su-shann went out feeling vaguely betrayed, disliking Yakov Ras more than ever. But . . . S.C.T.C. She hoped the computer knew what it was doing.

* * *

Su-shann's youth in the training cubes had given her a hunger for space and growing things. She wanted to walk the earth which the Ancestors had trod before the Invasion of the Yellow-Eyes— but not in the manner of moon Jelks, who had to wear grav suits inflated with LTA gas. She had built a centrifuge gym in her private cavern, and worked out daily on bars and trapeze, lifting weights, jumping, and climbing. Earth gravity no longer exhausted her, though she still felt the weight pulling at each cell. She was glad to see muscles swelling in her calves and thighs, shoulders and forearms. In most moon Jelks the muscles had shrunken to invisibility. Even their chests had sunken, for the concentration of oxygen reduced the need for lung action.

Exhilarated by her exercise, she stepped from the gym and floated on tiptoe across the wide level expanse of her central cavern. She alighted gently on her dressing dais, beside a pool served by a fountain and arched over by vidrian ferns. She strapped on her wrist gauge and checked her pulse and blood pressure, then studied herself in the mirror while her two handmaidens cleaned and polished her body. She wondered if she was beautiful to men—and wondered exactly what beauty was. She had eyes like every other Jelk—an oval whiteness the size of an egg, with the pupil floating in it like a giant inkdrop. The iris was no more than a rim of pale lavender. She parted her lips and looked at the soft teeth just peeping out past her gums . . . gazed down the slender white column of her torso to that tiny division of flesh at its terminus. For the first time in her life she felt unsure of herself . . .

The ferns parted and the head of her household staff came in. "Madam, I have the information."

Su-shann sat down at the edge of the pool and waved the handmaidens away. "Read it, Freeden."

The woman sat down and crossed her ankles, unrolling the scroll. "The directory listed five hundred thousand Abos and of that number Ben proved the most popular. I had to go through eight thousand Ben Abos to find four hundred and thirty with the numbers in proper sequence. Then narrowing it down to those of the proper rank . . ."

Freeden aroused in Su-shann certain emotions which she did not like to probe too deeply. She was a product of illegal chromosome-blending techniques used to provide exotic courtesans for the pleasure bubbles of Eros. Her large ears revealed her Grithy stock, but her skin was a rich cobalt shading to deep purple in the hollows. Erotic zones, such as the interior of her ears, her lips, nipples, and sexual labia, were a bright rose-pink which grew luminescent in the dark. Her hair was a brilliant orange mane rising from the center of her forehead and descending to a point between her hips. Her eyes were almost as large as Su-shann's, though emerald instead of purple, and always wide and somewhat sad, perhaps because she was a hybrid and could not reproduce . . .

"Would you arrive at the point, please, Freeden?"

"Yes, madam. You have three choices. One a Milark, one a Landark, and the third . . . well, he appears to be an EVO."*

The word brought a vision of scales and claws, gills and wings. "I think we can eliminate him. What about the Milark?"

"Fifty years as a fleet commander, Aldebaran sector. Presently retired, living in a space bubble orbiting Triton. He is one hundred and forty years old."

"Scratch him off. And the Landark?"

"His landate is on Numiss, a planet of the Procyon system. Thirty million hectares. He raises beef Unguls to supply the Guardian Fleet. He has three wives and fourteen sons."

"Cross him off."

"Yes, madam. You do not like Landarks."

"I do not like his three wives and fourteen sons. I feel they have already taken the best part of him."

"Yes, madam. You have now eliminated all three."

"I am aware of that. We shall now abandon our search for perfection and accept the best alternative. Go through them again. This time include the EVO. Which planet is he from, by the way?"

"Megrez. I located a monograph on their race."

"Read it."

"The Blue Men of Megrez—hardiest of the EVO races, their planet occupies an elliptical orbit around their sun, with the result that their winters last for eight earth years, while their summers span only six months. Spring comes with the suddenness of an explosion, all plants and animals grow with feverish haste to reproduce before the waters and lands are locked in the eight-year ice. Thus the Blue Men are at home in temperatures ranging from 130 degrees above zero Fahrenheit to forty below. Tall and lithe, with muscles like steel, they are quick of mind and infinitely adaptable—for the summer period is marked with floods, earthquakes, and volcanoes produced by gravitational stress. In winter snow accumulates up to a thousand feet, and beneath it the Blue Men of Megrez tunnel out their homes, rearing their huge families and rooting in the frozen ground for buried foods. Their breeding cycles follow the seasons: six months of feverish activity, and eight years of dormancy. The Blue Men are warriors, polygamous. The women are passive and industrious; they gather

* EVO: A sobriquet for Evolutionary Byproduct, First Expansion Period, which describes in euphemistic platitudes the mixing of indigenous outspace races with terran colonists of the first wave. The second wave did not come along until fifteen hundred years later, and by then the differences in food, climate, gravity, and seasonal rotation had wrought changes which made the EVO almost unrecognizable as having originated on earth. Still they are able to interbreed with humans, in much the same manner as the ancient mare and jackass, the llama and the guanaco, the buffalo and the cow.—Author.

food and store it for the long winter, ignoring the frequent sexual assaults of the males. The early weeks of the mating season are characterized by savage combat as the males seek to collect the largest possible harem to warm their caverns during the winter. Generally one half or two thirds are killed in the fighting, and the wounded are left out to die when the snows come. It is a cruel existence, and the Blue Men are the most savage of earth's orphaned descendants. If their numbers were greater, they could easily dominate the Jelk culture, but they are few and widely scattered, and completely unable to cooperate with one another during the mating season—"

Freeden stopped reading. "I do not think this man is suitable for you, madam."

"We are not seeking a tutor in polite manners, Freeden. What do you have on the man himself . . . Ben Abo?"

"I have his tape, madam. He enrolled in the Stafi Institute on Ganymede at the age of sixteen . . ."

"A Stafi . . . so young?"

"It is my understanding that they relax the entrance rules for the offspring of outworld monarchs. His father was the ruler of Megrez. The Abo clan claims descent from the captain of the original ship —Megrez having been colonized by the crew of a wrecked battle cruiser. This explains their military tradition, as well as their strong alien cast. The blood of humankind spread thin during the centuries. Anyway the Abo clan kept control of the atomic cannon, and are the oldest dynasty on Megrez. The only one, actually. But Ben Abo does not seem to be . . . what you would expect out of a ruling class. If you'll pardon me. When a Stafi he wrote an epic poem about an Ungul who grows up on Antark and is shipped to Juno to feed the fleet. The students began boycotting Ungul meat, and the administrators were hurt because they owned the packing plant. They arrested Ben Abo and sparked an insurrection. Ben Abo escaped in a ship belonging to the chief administrator. It was intercepted by Guardians and blown to atoms—so it says."

"The computer would not give me a dead man."

"No, madam. The director lists him as MPD—that is, missing, presumed dead. A citizen is not counted deceased until a fragment of tissue is matched against the computer file. It is the same listing they give those citizens of planets which fall to the Vim . . ."

Su-shann lay back and gazed up at the richly carved dome of her cavern. "He got away. Otherwise they'd have found something. A piece of liver or bone fragment or something to match up with the computer. Nothing gets covered up in space. I visited one of the museum asteroids—the ancients used to hollow them out and fit them with drives and go off looking for another sun. Some of them ran out of fuel before they found it. Others got sucked into the magnetic fields of black dwarfs. Others—well, this one got blown up during the Invasion. Chunks of it are still orbiting, sealed living quarters with people perfectly preserved. I saw a man who died with a half inch of ashes on his cigarette. It was still there fifteen hundred years later. So Ben Abo's alive. The problem is how to find him." She looked at Freeden. "You've got some more information. I can tell."

The girl lowered her eyes. "On Eros we heard of pirates who lived among the asteroids. No Jelks, but Grithy renegades and a few fighting Unguls who had managed to find their way there. I had a . . . client who'd been captured by them and held for ransom. He said their leader was a Blue Man from Megrez. They called him Falcon."

Su-shann nodded. "We will begin our search on Eros, Freeden. Make the arrangements."

The girl rose, looking pensive. Su-shann got up and kissed her, fluffing the mane at the back of her neck. "I won't sell you back to the pleasure bubbles, Freeden. You are my second brain."

3.

The Falcon's Roost

*"Now will my footsteps cease to drag,
and Oh! my spirits soar.
I've gone to lie beneath the flag,
And be a pirate's whore."*

Sung at Sri Baki's
School for Young Landesses,
Jelk City, Antark, Earth

Her shuttleship was a small teardrop of Titanium 80 with ports of Borazon 24. From the rear nozzle squirted a steam of atoms accelerated to nearly light speeds, which spewed the ship out of its launching tube and into space. Su-shann programed the robo-pilot with a tape sent over by the travel committee. It would keep the ship on the trajectory needed to bisect the planetoid Eros, still wheeling in its ancient orbit between earth and Mars.

After staring out the port for several hours, she got out her Jelk survival handbook and turned to the section on sexual congress. *The male takes outer tab A and connects it to flap A of the female. Check air, temperature, and pressure gauges. Tissue contact may be ascertained by a feeling of warmth in the sexual area. Penetration is now possible. Note: It may be necessary for the female to utilize excitation procedures. See Excitation Procedure, Appendix I . . .*

"What is that?" asked Freeden, looking over her shoulder.

"It tells Jelks how to make a baby."

"But this flap and tab—you do not have these."

"They *aren't* parts of the body. This was written while we were still in the caverns. For many generations the Jelks passed their entire lives inside their space suits, because there was no power to heat the caverns. At first they used artificial insemination, but then it was decided to allow males and females to mate physically, rather than squander power and scientific work time on storage of semen."

"Why do you study this now?"

"To learn how it is done."

"You mean you have never—?"

"Why should I? I have not desired a child."

"The . . . excitation procedure. What is it?"

"The female removes her gauntlet and inserts her hand into a specially designed opening in the male's suit, and . . . there are certain finger manipulations which I have not yet memorized."

Freeden was shaking her head. "With the Blue Men . . . or any other men that you meet out there, this"—she waggled her long blue fingers—"will excite nothing."

Su-shann closed the book. "Show me how it is done on Eros."

"First we display the body, so . . ." She peeled apart the magnetic flaps of her coveralls and pushed them down to her feet, then gave them a kick which sent them floating away in the negligent ship's gravity. "And then we dance . . ."

The girl began going through the steps of a ritual dance, a liquid movement of limbs and torso whose purpose was not to hide but to draw attention to the genital area—a region rarely used by Jelks and regarded as an annoying problem in cleanliness. Su-shann had often thought it should be eliminated from the gene pool; but watching Freeden she realized that the problem was in the Jelk's lack of body hair. Certainly that puff of orange fur added . . . a touch of the unknown to Freeden's charms, whereas her own sex was merely a division of tissue without character or mystery. She saw that Freeden was swaying to and fro, shoulders back and full breasts lifted high.

"Enough, Freeden. Your techniques are useless to me."

"Yes, madam. You are *pilawu*."

"A Grithy word, I recognize that much. Meaning . . ."

Freeden looked away. "A girl not yet breasted, not ready for men."

"I am a mature female, Freeden, approaching forty. It is merely that Jelk women do not acquire breasts until the tenth month of pregnancy. They are not needed earlier, and would simply interfere with movement and cause complications of clothing design. The Jelk body has been engineered to perfection."

"Oh. I see." Freeden retrieved her coveralls and pulled them on her feet.

"For example," said Su-shann, "color recognition was not a survival factor in the caverns; therefore the cones of the retina were eliminated from the gene pool. Today we can insert color-sensitive lenses and enjoy a wider spectrum than yourselves.

"And since our food is scientifically purified, we don't need complicated organs to eliminate poisons and waste. Liver and kidneys are reduced in size. Since less blood is required, heart action is reduced. Defecation and urination are both regarded as symptoms of illness among Jelks, reflecting the body's inability to assimilate food. Not like your Grithy custom, which looks upon excretion as a sign of wealth and well-being. Those great dung heaps you pile before your huts are disease vectors, nothing more."

"Yes, madam."

"And hair—of what earthly use is it? It clogs filters, clings to computer tape, diverts electrical impulses. Same with dead skin cells. We buff our bodies to prevent air pollution, not because we like to shine. Jelk customs are not empty rituals, but routines with a firm scientific basis . . ."

Freeden's eyes did not lose their pity. "You have never known a man, therefore you cannot imagine. No? It seems to you a silly game, like when we play Yylo, with the balls."

"Well, of course I recognize the need for genetic variation, maintaining the genetic pool. But the exchange of physical matter seems so . . . inefficient. Why couldn't the male just put it into an ampule and give it to me? Or drop it into the vacuum tube addressed to me, and then I could implant it at my lesiure."

Freeden nodded gravely. "It is illogical, like the games—which are merely fun."

"What is the purpose of fun?"

The girl shook her head. "I do not know. But in the making of babies, I think there is something else exchanged, which will not go into a vacuum tube. Love."

"Will you describe it?"

"It is . . . when your man is before you, and you see him coming into bloom like a flower, and your knees shake, and your mouth grows dry and your very bones seem to melt . . ."

"I know the feeling," said Su-shann. "It comes to me when I have communion with the computer."

"Computer? I do not know this thing."

"It is regarded as taboo to mention it to the lower races. But I will tell you—it is a machine, something like this ship. But the ship knows only where it is going and how to get there. The computer knows everything."

Freeden rolled her eyes toward the silent winking lights of the control panel. "The ship knows where it is going?"

"Yes."

"Who told it?"

"I put in a reel of tape, with instructions on it—"

"Suppose it decides to go someplace else?"

"It can't . . . *decide*. It has to be programed. And then it can only go where it is told to go. The computer is a much larger machine. It lies beneath the eighth level, extending for miles into the solid rock. Nobody knows how far, because it keeps digging out new chambers and adding to itself."

"And it knows everything?"

"Everything that is known."

"Who told it?"

"People down through the centuries. I don't know who the first programer was. Before the invasion it was used to maintain a living environment for the scientists investigating Jupiter. After the yellow-eyes destroyed earth, it kept them alive, told them how to manufacture food and air to breathe . . ."

"But if it knows only what it is told, then suppose it is told a lie?"

"It has a self-correcting mechanism based on correlations and cross-references. It would reject a lie because it would not fit the matrix of verified information."

"How would it know which was the lie?"

"How would it—?" Su-shann shook her head. "Let's just say we think differently, Freeden. I understand the computer. You don't. But in compensation you are capable of this thing love. And I am not."

"I think"—Freeden looked down—"when you see a certain man you will feel this thing, and you will know how to give it to him. I think you should probably tear up the book and just wait until it comes, like it came to me once . . ."

Su-shann was relieved when the bell rang to indicate they were coming into Eros. She went to the port and looked down at the space bubbles which covered the little planetoid like a cluster of giant fish eggs. Su-shann had visited it once before, but found it mainly uninteresting—all plasticene and rubberoid reptiles supposedly duplicating the outworlds of the lost empire—but actually just a backdrop for plain and fancy sin. The Directing Council subsidized it mainly as a listening post to learn what the rebellious elements were up to . . .

She checked her shuttle at the spaceport and rented a two-seated floater for a sightseeing trip along the midway. This was a broad, arched corridor, with irises opening into transport tubes which wafted customers away to the bubbles. In front of each opening stood a barker shouting the attractions of his establishment. Most of them were Grithy males, with their huge flapping ears and wide-eyed look of friendly innocence. She halted the floater to listen to one who was promising to match clients with a partner of any shape, breed, age, color, or sexual perversity within the system.

Su-shann beckoned him. "How is it arranged?"

The barker stood beside her floater, his big ears tipped forward in deference. "Your representative"—he indicated Freeden, sitting beside her—"will be transported to our bubble. She will make known your desires to our confidential directory. Our computer will check it against our file of available partners . . ."

"I want a particular individual."

"Ah?" The ears stiffened with alert interest. "Whatever assistance we can offer . . ."

"I doubt that he would be in your availability file."

"We have a locator service, if you would like to make inquiry . . ."

Su-shann waved him away and lowered the floater to the ground. "Freeden, go in and find out what you can. I'll wait for you at"—she peered ahead down the midway and saw a sign advertising sterilized rooms and Jelk-Processed Nutrition—"at the Exile Club."

The girl left the car reluctantly. "It is customary to give an assumed name at these places."

Su-shann thought of her great-great-grandmother's name. *Jane,* it was written. "Jah-ne is a good one. I will be . . . a Landess recuperating from a grave illness. That will explain why I have no color." She patted Freeden's shoulder. "Go now, and don't worry. I won't leave without you."

She drove on and checked into her room, which catered to Jelk tastes in that it had no sanitary facilities. There was evidence of previous occupancy—a hair follicle on the floor, and a stain on the sleeping mat which looked like an effusion of oil from some un-polished scalp. She managed to ignore the filth while she undressed and buffed her body. Then she changed to informal wear—a glittering green sheath covered by a brown metallic smock. The headband was gold, with rubies and sapphires set around the communicator nodules. She looked over her lenses and selected an orange pair. She balanced them on her fingertips and held them against her eyes, feeling them adhere painlessly to the sclerotic layer. The smock had flounces around her hips which concealed her sidearm. The slender tube fired a stream of incandescent molecules which converted body water to steam in a microsecond—a newly developed weapon which she'd obtained through her connections on the War Council. She had no intention of visiting a pirates' lair unarmed.

She found her way to the nutrition chamber and sat down in a booth across from two young Landesses. She admired the muscles which swelled beneath their pale-gold skin, and discussed with them the yearly athletic games which were currently being held on Antark. They told her they were runaways . . . but not exactly.

"Our family thinks we're at the matches," said the older one. "We came up to see some pirates."

"Have you seen any?"

"We met one we thought might have been—in the Falcon's Lair."

Su-shann felt an urge to leave immediately, but the girls had identified her as a moon Jelk and wanted to know what she did for the computer.

"I plan new strategies for the war and listen to the Milarks tell me why they can't be carried out."

"You mean the space war? The war between the Unguls and those funny kangaroo people?"

Su-shann felt an inner shock. "Is there another one?"

"Oh, *yes!* We live on the Princess Astrid coast. Our war is with the Eshom. They come out of the Great Burn at night and carry off our Unguls. Sometimes they raid the Grithy settlements. They can breathe steam and see in the dark."

"What do you do with them?"

"We kill them and burn them. They aren't even good Ungul food."

She had a feeling they were trying to shock her. At that point their food came—a noxious unsightly gruel with solids actually floating in it. She felt nauseated . . . yet the Landesses began eating without hesitation. Their teeth made crunching sounds that chilled her spine.

The race is sinking into barbarity, she thought as she walked out.

She found the Falcon's Lair a few doors farther on. It was full of young Landarks and Landesses, with a sprinkling of the more presentable EVOs. She found herself looking for a man of Megrez, and was struck suddenly by the ludicrousness of her purpose in coming here: to introduce a portion of another person's body into her own private interior. A short laugh escaped her lips. She realized the air was thick with narcotic perfumes. Quickly she inserted nose filters and looked around to see if anyone had noticed.

A tall man beside the bar was studying her intently. He towered to a height of at least five feet ten inches. His ears were large and expressive in the Grithy manner, but she didn't think he was purebred because of the turquoise tint of his skin.

"Only half," he said, smiling at her. "The other half is Megrez."

It felt strange to have somebody tune in on her mind. Jelks could transmit thought through their headband amplifiers, but communication was limited to other Jelks wearing headbands.

"Which side does the telepathy come from?"

"Oh, that is Megrez. And these." He peeled back his lips, displaying a pair of short red-tipped fangs. "Useless for anything except ceremonial combat. Can I buy you a tikula?"

She accepted the beverage, but swallowed a narco-inhibitor before she drank. He told her he was descended from a runaway Grithy male and a woman of the Megrez. He'd joined the Guardian forces, the only profession legally open to a half-caste, and when the crew mutinied he'd come here to enjoy the rich rewards of piracy. But piracy wasn't what it used to be; the proud Jelk empire of six thousand worlds had shrunken to eighteen polluted, overpopulated sun systems.

"Now I survive by peddling contraband baubles. Do you see any you like?" He spread apart his cloak and displayed jeweled necklaces and earrings hanging from tiny hooks on the lining.

She smiled and shook her head. He closed his cape, bowed, and walked away.

A moment later a hunched, cloak-shrouded EVO sidled up to her and spoke in a hoarse gurgling whisper. "You must be careful, milady. That is Gar-Vel, a scout for the Blue Falcon. He seeks young Landesses and carries them off to the Falcon's nest on Hidalgo. Their families must pay enormous sums for their return."

The EVO's nose flaps and webbed fingers betrayed an amphibian taint in his ancestry. Su-shann didn't like his dank, pungent odor.

"I am not a young Landess," she said with a lift of her chin, moving off in the direction Gar-Vel had gone.

"No," said the EVO, shuffling along at her elbow. "You are obviously a moon Jelk, and that puzzles me. I didn't think moon Jelks indulged in the, ah, lower forms of pleasure."

"We are a varied race," she murmured, walking faster as she stepped out into the midway.

The EVO dogged her steps. "I can put you into a Sensi hookup with a bull Ungul, milady. Or even a flesh hookup. It would be safe, you lie in a foam cocoon, so he cannot tear your tender flesh. No? I have many tapes. A rare item just came in from Gafronkil—a young Landess is eaten alive by an Eshom. Also a Pteroni mating flight. Seven winged males pursue a female through the air as she soars and spins. Or . . . wait. Perhaps you enjoy the male role. I have one of a Grithy who goes *yagano*. Unable to find his woman, he dashes into his neighbor's hut, ravishes his three wives, then goes to another and proceeds to rape his way through the village until he meets another *yagano* male and they fight to the death . . ."

She turned up her mental amplifier and broadcast infinite revulsion. *Leave me, slime.*

And he did.

Gar-Vel had disappeared, but Freeden was waiting nervously outside the Exile Club.

"They knew nothing about Ben Abo. They were quite willing to take your money, but I sensed that they could arrange nothing."

"I think I know where to find him. Let's go back to the ship."

At the port Su-shann was ostentatious in announcing her immediate return to the moon, treating the respectful techs and baggage handlers to a vitriolic rundown on the filthy accommodations, the abysmal food, and the impertinent lower classes she had found on Eros. When they were a thousand miles out, she shut off the robo-pilot and strapped herself into the padded control seat. The craft shot out of the plane of the ecliptic and arched into the blackness of space.

"Where are you going?" asked Freeden.

"Hidalgo. The headquarters of the pirates."

"Madam, they will burn us like a moth."

"Not if I understand the economics of piracy. An unarmed pleasure craft means only two things: booty and ransom."

"And what are we?"

"I shall continue to be Jah-ne and you shall be my handmaiden. We shall be two of the most bewildered and feckless females ever to be led astray by a malfunctioning robo-pilot."

She switched the ship's computer to manual control and got busy calculating a trajectory to the asteroid Hidalgo. It was a maverick world, with an orbit tilted forty-five degrees from the ecliptic. She was glad to note in her ephemeris that it was near perihelion, which brought it near the orbit of Mars. Sometimes it swung out beyond Saturn, which would have meant a journey of several weeks.

She checked, rechecked, then programed the robo-pilot for the new course. It could have been done automatically by simply calling the spaceport—but that would have made it a matter of record, and thus available to Yakov Ras.

Finished, she strolled over and sat down beside Freeden at the viewport. Earth filled the glass like a painted ball, with the Pacific Ocean bulging toward them. It was not the wide blue expanse Su-shann had seen on the ancient tapes. The electric shimmer of radiation zones splotched its surface, forming vortices for the hot ocean currents which boiled around them. These spread out in spiral arms, shading to red and green where the water cooled enough to allow the growth of plankton. The sea was bordered by smoke and fire where the continental plates grated against each other. Central America looked like a bleeding slash down the belly of the earth. Red rivers of fire flowed east and west, meeting the sea in a thundering wall of turbulence as water exploded into steam. Yucatan was hidden by fluffy white clouds that looked soft and cool, but Su-shann knew it to be a five-mile-high cloud of steam.

"What is that fire, madam? It's different than the others."

She pointed to the lower end of the globe, where a red-hot coal smoldered in the middle of a pink sea.

"That's the Tasman Burn, Freeden. It happened when they tried to put the asteroid Hestia into orbit around the earth as a shuttle station. The same function that Poseidon serves now. Of course, Poseidon is only seventeen miles in diameter; Hestia was a hundred. The rockets failed or something, and the satellite was captured by earth's gravity field and crashed in what was once Tasmania. That was two centuries ago, but the Tasman Burn still sends hot winds onto the coast of Antark. A reminder that even Jelks make mistakes."

"At least," murmured Freeden, "they are stupid in a grand style."

Su-shann decided not to chastise her, since she would probably sulk for the rest of the trip.

On the fourth day Hidalgo appeared as a speck in the port. Su-shann short-circuited the robo-pilot and sat down to wait. The asteroid grew from a speck to a clod, and finally to a slate-colored mountain which looked as though it had been torn from its base and hurled into space. As the little ship swung past, she saw a jagged crater which sloped in toward a black pit. She thought she saw a blue light winking in the blackness.

Abruptly the lights flickered and went out. In the darkness Su-shann could see plainly; the only problem was she couldn't move. Even her eyelids had frozen in place. From the edge of her vision she saw Freeden with her mouth half open in surprise . . .

Su-shann knew what it was. For centuries Jelk surgeons had performed operations in stasis fields which froze cellular action. Since neural impulses were not affected, patients did not lose consciousness. But nobody had ever thought of enlarging the field to where it could be used in the capture of spaceships. *And that's why we're losing the war* . . .

The ship was falling into the maw of the black pit. It seemed about to crash into a metal wall about fifty yards in diameter, but then the wall broke into four triangular segments which pulled back and allowed the ship to pass.

They were inside the hollowed-out asteroid now. The vast cavern was probably eight miles long. Scattered lights glowed like miniature suns in the blackness, and she could see several dozen pitted ships, most of them ex-Guardian vessels, anchored to brackets along the wall. She passed within fifty yards of a cruiser whose thunderbolt emblem was being painted over. Other ships bore the emblem of a black bird with a hooked beak. Through a niche in the wall, she looked down a long assembly line where women and children were putting together hand weapons. The children were broad and muscular, with small ears and the shelf of bone over the eyes which marked the Ungul breed; but their blue skin betrayed a touch of Megrez. She felt a tinge of revulsion that the men of Megrez were so lacking in culture that they would mate with animals . . .

She felt a faint bump as the ship was clamped against the wall.

A series of rattles, then a hiss of escaping air. She heard the scrape of approaching footsteps, but could not turn her head. Hands jerked at her clothing, pinched and probed her body. Her handgun was lifted from its holster, the headband torn roughly off her head. A harsh feminine voice grated in her ear:

"Be a good girl and I'll take you out of the freeze."

Su-shann could neither move nor speak. A leering, wrinkled face loomed in front of her, and Su-shann saw that she was a copper-skinned green-eyed Grithy of the breed generally used as household servants. Her huge ears hung limp beside her face, and Su-shann saw that they had been notched repeatedly—the usual Landark punishment for running away.

Stooping, the woman clamped metal shackles around her ankles, then rose and fitted bracelets around her wrists. Su-shann saw the control box on the woman's belt and realized she'd been fitted with an Ungul whip.

The stasis went away. Her muscles came to life with the excruciating agony of a toothache. She turned to see what Freeden was doing —and fire seared her wrists and ankles. She gasped and fell, her body jerking uncontrollably. Hot currents surged up her arms and legs.

Through a haze of pain she heard the woman's voice: "Did I tell you to move?"

"No!" screamed Su-shann.

The pain ended, leaving her limp and trembling helplessly. She felt as though every joint had been wrenched loose from its socket.

"Now get up and go out the port."

Su-shann rose and walked painfully across the deck. Freeden was gone; apparently she'd been taken out under stasis and had made no outcry . . .

Fire clamped her again. She screamed and fell jerking to the deck. She strained to hold onto consciousness and wondered what she had done wrong . . .

"Jelk!" The Grithy woman spat the word as a curse. "Did I say run or walk?"

Su-shann gasped: "You . . . didn't say."

"Next time ask me. Now . . . *run!*"

Su-shann got up and forced her aching legs into a trot. She didn't look back as she left the ship, but kept running down the long dark tunnel. It ended in a tiny cell, where four figures sat huddled against the wall. She ran in. The door closed. It was absolutely dark—and cold. Su-shann estimated it at around the freezing point of water. By contrast the moon caverns were kept at sixty degrees, found to be the ideal working temperature.

In time her eyes adapted, and she could see her cellmates. One was a Landark from one of the outworlds, wearing the frilled collar and cuffs of a planetary baron. There was a woman dressed in outmoded outworld style—a full-skirted dress with sheer bosom which had been popular on earth two decades before. The adolescent girl wore the pseudo-military garb of Antark's most prestigious girls' school, and the small boy wore a miniature copy of his father's costume.

"My handmaiden—was she brought in here?"

A moment of silence, then the Landark spoke in a bitter, stammering voice. "Th-th-they have l-l-liberated her from Jelk tyranny—which means she's s-s-servicing the crew of one of their vessels."

"Bo! Your manners . . ." said the woman.

"M-my apologies. This is my wife, the Landess Prima-la. My son Rodan, my daughter Umiss. I am . . ." He cleared his throat. "The Baron Bo Hakim of the planet Reheboth, Altair system."

Su-shann hesitated, then gave her assumed name in a low voice. She felt a gnawing guilt about Freeden, but there was nothing she could do. At least it was not a totally unfamiliar situation for the girl . . .

Time passed. Bo Hakim told her they'd been passengers on a scheduled liner running from Antark to their homeland. The seasoned travelers had taken the pirates' boarding as a matter of course, but Hakim, taking umbrage at the rough handling given his daughter, had drawn his dagger. With the result that they'd been dragged aboard the pirate vessel and brought here.

"It's s-s-so d-damn cold," he stammered.

"It is rather uncomfortable," she said. But bearable, she thought, once you learned to suppress the external skin sensors. "What will the pirates do to us?"

"Th-that's another of my w-worries. The brutes rape all female captives. Repeatedly. For my wife that is bad enough but my daughter—I have contracted a marriage for her with the Landark of Hylo and if he refuses to certify her virginity—" He sighed. "I lose a vast sum, a vast sum . . ."

More time passed. Su-shann began concentrating on certain mathematical formulae and in a few minutes drifted into a semitrance. The next thing she felt a lash of pain in her wrists and ankles.

"*Up-up-up!*" grated the Grithy whip woman. "Everybody out! It's payoff time." She dealt the baron a kick in the rump as he went out. "They'll beggar you, swine." When Su-shann passed she creased her wrinkled face in a smile. "And you, dear, they'll shove a lance up your arse and roast you over a slow fire."

Such hatred bewildered Su-shann. *I never did anything to her . . .*

She ended up in a vast circular chamber with Ungulhyde seats and a long oval table in the center. At one end of the oval, flanked by eight-foot Fighting Unguls, sat an individual with a long blue-black face and narrow eyes that appeared to contain all the lugubrious despair of the universe. Yet there was no pity in the face. The tight line of the faintly smiling lips bulged at each end to accommodate a pair of red-tipped fangs. They gave him the look of a savage predator which had suddenly acquired the gift of intelligence.

There were a half dozen other men at the table but Su-shann passed them over with a glance. The man at the end was the leader; she was certain he was the Blue Falcon. Whether or not he was also Ben Abo was something else . . .

A Grithy accountant, dressed in black with the symbol of his rank hanging from a silver lanyard, strode up to the table, clicked his heels together, and recited in a high flat monotone:

"Report of patrol vessel *Egret* which intercepted passenger liner *Star of Mizar* en route to Altair system. Boarded without incident and exacted the usual toll of ten per cent of the cargo for passing through the Realm of the Blue Falcon. The commander of the vessel arranged the transfer of forty thousand universal credits and was given a receipt plus the usual kickback. Passengers were then run through customs inspection and relieved of all jewels and negotiable currency. One man resisted and was placed under arrest. He gives his name as Baron Bo Hakim of the planet Reheboth."

He stepped back and motioned the Landark forward. The baron stood stiffly, his pouchy chin jutting in stubborn refusal. The Grithy woman pressed a button on her control box. The baron yelped and scuttled out in front of the oval table, shivering and rubbing his wrists.

The Falcon glared at him. "Why did you attack my customs officers?"

"B-by the G-great Spot!" The baron sputtered. "You're nothing but thieves and b-b-brigands. Why bother with this charade of legality?"

The Falcon moved his shoulders in a faint shrug. "As you wish. How much will you pay for your freedom?"

"Not a d-damned credit. Futhermore, I insist that you release—"

The Falcon raised his finger. The Grithy woman wielded her whip, and the baron dropped to his knees. "Y-your honor," he moaned. "I am not a rich man. Most of my money went into this excursion—"

"Bring out the girl."

The young Landess was pushed out beside her father.

"Now prepare her."

The whip woman yanked loose the magnetic flaps that held the girl's military tunic in front, then peeled down her flaring low-gravity bloomers. The girl stood exposed from neck to knee. Several of the men at the table swiveled their chairs and gazed upon her with amused interest. To Su-shann they seemed only merciless—whereas the Falcon remained with his chin sunk on his chest, glaring out from beneath his brows as if the girl were a species of vermin. He raised his hand and uttered a guttural sound. The two Unguls clacked forward on calloused feet, their eyes a baleful red glow, their sex rampant. Su-shann gave a shriek of fear, as if it were her own body the beasts were about to split in two . . .

"I'll pay!" screamed the baron.

"How much?"

"One million drinach!"

The Falcon growled a command. The Unguls halted, snorting. Su-shann felt nauseated by the musk of their bodies.

"Two million," said the pirate.

"Your honor, even one million will bankrupt me."

The Falcon reached out and turned the pages of a black ledger. Glancing down, he said: "The clan of Hakim takes thirty million drinach a year from their mines on the satellite Arcos. The price is now three million. Further delay will raise the figure to five million."

The baron bowed his head in submission.

"My man will make arrangements for the transfer of credits," said the Falcon. "After that you will be placed on the next liner passing through our space." He smiled, his fangs overlapping his lower lip like two drops of blood. "May your daughter's marriage be long and fruitful."

He bent his long narrow head in his ledger. Impelled by a tingle in her wrists, Su-shann stepped forward and stood at the end of the oval table. The Falcon went on writing while the whip woman spoke:

"This one calls herself the Landess Jah-ne. Yet she is obviously a moon Jelk and her handmaiden a breed not unfamiliar to us as a Grithy with synthetic Megrez characteristics grafted into the gene pattern."

The Falcon closed his book and lifted his head. For a second Su-shann felt as though she were gazing into the heart of a furnace. His yellow eyes were so hot and brilliant that she was forced to look away—almost. She held his gaze without flinching, though it felt like a fiery needle being driven into her forehead.

Then he smiled—but there was something in his smile which made it into a slap across her face. "I trust the electric whip has not disturbed you. It is a humane form of restraint, used only to prevent the beasts from hurting each other. I quote from the Jelk manual of Ungul husbandry."

No way, she thought, can I accept this man as a friend, much less as the fertilizer of my ovum. But . . . S.C.T.C. She had no choice. She no longer doubted that he was Ben Abo, for his voice had the Stafi lilt which was impossible to imitate. She sensed the power of his intellect, yet it was twisted and somehow reduced by his bitterness.

"Am I to bear the sins of all Jelks from the beginning of time?"

He nodded. "At the moment you are the only one we have."

Without warning the fire lashed her wrists. She dropped to her knees, fighting off the blackness which threatened to engulf her mind. Vaguely she heard the whip woman speak, and the Falcon's disgusted reply: "Take the manacles off, Lil-na, since you cannot restrain yourself. I have told you, the whip must not impede the flow of information."

When the manacles were gone, Su-shann stood up, rubbing her wrists. "What have you done with my handmaiden?"

His lips quirked. "Your slave has been accepted as a citizen of the Republic of Hidalgo. All previous contracts and conditions of servitude are dissolved. Do not concern yourself with our citizens. It is yourself you need to worry about. The penalty for giving a false name is death. What is your true name, rank, and designation?"

Without hesitation she gave her mother's name. "Su-lim. Kipunch twenty-three."

"A high number for one who has a handmaiden and a personal shuttle." He turned to the whip woman. "Bring me her accouterments."

The woman went out and brought back the things that had been taken off her body. One by one he lifted and examined the headband, the wrist gauge, and the pistol. He passed the first two items around the table, then pointed the pistol into the air and squeezed the trigger. Nothing happened, since it was keyed to her pore pattern and would not fire unless she held it.

He looked at her with brows lifted. "A personal weapon? Obviously you are not a common Prog."

One of the men spoke: "She's a Prog, that's crime enough. Have the Unguls tear her head off."

The Falcon kept looking at her. "Will you tell me your name?"

"If you tell me yours."

He looked at her for another minute, then waved his fingers at the whip woman. "Put her back, Lil-na. This mystery can wait until after our raid on Ceres."

She was taken back to the dark cell, where the baron alternately muttered about revenge and groaned about the money he'd lost. He offered to send a message for her when he was released, but Su-shann declined. She knew hardly anybody outside the council, and they were the one group which could not be told.

One day the baron and his family were taken away. She was alone. Food came but was inedible. She found the trance state to be the only manner of preserving her sanity. By reducing her body metabolism she controlled her hunger; by blanking out her senses she endured the cold and the silence. She was sitting that way when Lil-na entered and ordered her to follow her. With stiff muscles, Su-shann obeyed.

She was taken to a domed chamber not unlike her own moon cavern, but smaller. The Falcon sat on a huge round bed, his arms resting on top of a sort of barrel fitted around his chest. She caught the scent of healing salve used to regrow burned tissue.

"One of the occupational hazards of piracy," he said, thumping the top of the tank. "They expect me to risk my head as some kind of inspiration to insanity . . . but the end justifies the means, eh, Milady Su-shann?"

Su-shann noted his use of her name, but her mind was occupied in returning to the plane of existence after a long absence. She found it pleasant. The cavern was warmer than her cell, and she could relax control of her sensors. The man seemed to want conversation, and she did not object. Somewhere in the handbook she had read that an exchange of pleasantries and life data was customary before the male felt relaxed enough to part with his seed.

She sat on a low pillow and remarked: "I hope it was not too difficult to extract that information from Freeden."

"We have not touched a hair of her lovely mane. I have an agent on Eros. You met him, Gar-Vel. He had already gathered information on you with the idea of kidnaping you. Now that won't be necessary—but the question remains why you chose to put yourself in my hands. The business with the robo-pilot might have fooled the average pirate, but not one who is trained in computer science." He paused as if waiting for her to speak, then went on. "Why were you seeking me? Does the War Council wish to hire my fleet to defeat the Vim? Has that bemedaled jackass Commander Ho-ford finally found the courage to admit he is incompetent? Why did you come?"

She folded her hands. "Why don't you do a mind probe? That would answer all your questions."

"You know as well as I how Jelks react to mind probing."

"No I don't. How do they react?"

"They die."

"Oh?" She frowned. "Possibly that is only propaganda to prevent the mind probing of Jelks."

He laughed, then winced. "We probed them anyway—and they died. At least the Progs did. The Landarks and other subclasses weren't affected. What secret is the computer hiding?"

Su-shann shook her head. "I don't know."

He studied her for a minute, then nodded. "I believe you don't know. Or else it's something so obvious to you that you can't believe it is a secret." He shrugged. "The question remains of your purpose. I am assuming you are not an assassin sent by the Deek. They expend a few each year on me and would hardly throw one of their War Council members into the meat grinder. Gar-Vel reports that your handmaiden made inquiries about Ben Abo. I am he—or used to be. What do you want from me? Let us be completely honest with each other."

Ben Abo threw out his hands, palm up. She saw that his fingers were twice as long as hers, ending in sharp claws. From the wrist protruded a short hooked spur. She reminded herself that she had volunteered, had eagerly offered her body as a culture medium for whatever brew the computer desired.

And she would—later. At the moment Ben Abo was immobilized, and he was . . . what? Not in the mood? She thought, and could not find a better reason.

"To be completely honest, I cannot tell you."

"Very well," he said. "You will stay until I know. I will have Lil-na take you back to your cell."

Su-shann rose. "If it is all the same . . . the cell is cold and the food is impossible. If you could spare me a corner for a pallet . . ."

He looked at her for a minute, then waved his hand at the chamber. "It is all the same to me if you hang from the perch. Make yourself at home."

So it was that Su-shann came to share his bedroom. Next day she found she was not denied entrance to his library, where he sat reading his tapes of the ancient books. He said to her:

"The fact is, Su-shann, I am not a pirate. I engage in piracy merely to collect money to build a fleet of ships. I will return to my home in Megrez one day and we will throw out the Jelks and defend ourselves against the Vim."

"And when the Vim destroy the Jelks? You will go down with us. Whether you like it or not, your destiny is wrapped up in ours."

"We can fight the Vim alone. On my world we encounter far worse creatures during our brief summer. In any case the Jelks care nothing for Megrez. They refuse to allow us a spacefleet, saying they will defend us. That is a lie. Of course the Jelk colonies are defended to the last man. But policy in regard to EVO worlds is to evacuate with minimum loss. Can you deny it?"

She could not deny it, but there was nothing she could do about it.

"Nevertheless you will go down with us."

"Possibly. On the other hand, what is victory for us, since we will not share in the booty?"

"Survival. The Vim will not exploit you as you accuse us of doing. They will simply kill you."

"That is Jelk dogma, nothing else. You have not tried to negotiate."

"It is impossible. They merely assume control of us when we meet. The only way to deal with them is to destroy them."

He shook his head, and went back to his tapes.

As the days passed she explored the rest of his cavern complex. There were thirty rooms in all, about a third of them occupied by women and children. She learned that he had over fifty wives, but parceled them out among his commanders as an incentive to greater service. She noticed that most of the children were about the same age, and wondered if Ben Abo's fertility reflected the seasons on his home planet.

One thing she knew—no wives shared his bed. He was always alone behind the drawn curtain, while she slept on the pallet near the wall.

She wrote out the formula for the Jelk diet and gave it to Ben Abo, who passed it on to his cook. After several tries she produced a paste which Su-shann found edible, though Ben Abo said it tasted like watered chalk dust.

"You have burned out your taste buds with exotic foods," said Su-shann.

He permitted Freeden to visit her. Su-shann embraced the girl with joy, and stroked her mane. Freeden seemed to stand straighter, and her eyes were bright. She told Su-shann she was studying religion, then she tilted her head and asked: "Has it happened?"

"Not yet."

"Sometimes it takes many attempts. You should not despair."

Su-shann did not mention that no attempts had been made; she had not even brought up the subject. That night she decided to bypass the verbal obstacle. She got undressed and lay in Ben Abo's bed. Hours passed and Ben Abo did not come. She dressed and went into his study. He was sitting behind his desk with a bottle of tikula before him.

"How sad," she said, "that strong character does not always accompany great intellect."

He looked at her through slitted eyelids, his yellow eyes aflame. "I hate Jelks. I want you to know that. I am a genius. I rule this riffraff. Of course I rule!" He hammered the desk. "A genius rises to the top in any field. He cannot avoid it because in order to control his environment he must control those around him." He drank from the flared neck of the bottle and looked sullenly at her. "If I were a Jelk, I would be chief strategist, and we would have the Vim on the run. Do you agree?"

"As the great Stafi poet Lermosov said, 'If I had wings I would fly—if I were not afraid of heights.'"

"Get out of my sight."

She turned to go, relieved to postpone the encounter.

"Wait." He opened a drawer and took out the items which had been confiscated from her. One by one he placed them on the desk: the headband, the wrist gauge, and the gun.

"The gun was what delayed us. It took a week to copy the parts. Now we can produce them in quantity. I have no further reason to keep you here."

Thoughtfully, she put on her headband and her wrist gauge. She

checked the readings and found none within the danger area. She
picked up the pistol and started to slide it in the holster.

"It works," he said, grinning. "Wouldn't you like to try it on me?"

Angrily she jammed the weapon into her holster. "You—! You always
assume that one's intent is murderous?"

He threw back his head and laughed, his fangs flashing red. "You
Jelks are a strange breed, you never smile, you just stand there looking
at people with those big purple eyes, and they think they've been let
into a schoolyard. Then you pull one of those deadly little guns from
your belts, and they realize the little bird has a stinger. Deadliest species
alive. That's what you are. Plan to kill everything on earth, just to make
it hospitable for Jelks. By the beard of Toth! If it were possible you
would dim the sun, build walls around the earth, roof over the galaxy.
Do you know there are Landarks who have been on the planet for
twenty generations and still wear spacesuits to walk outside? Affecta-
tion, yes—but it shows where your minds are. And those flat little
yards with their high-walled courts, all plants in rows like disciplined
little schoolkids. Jelk kids. You're all agorophobic. Your caves are a
womb, you haven't let yourselves be born, you haven't joined the rest
of humanity. You're not ruling by right, or justice or anything we pay
lip service to."

She asked stiffly: "Is it better on Megrez?"

"No—but it was before you came. My family stays in power because
it serves the Jelk culture. The Jelks have the science, and we've got to
have it to live. It's a drug and you've hooked us on it, but that doesn't
mean you're right—"

She interrupted. "We have the computer."

He nodded gravely. "Yes. You have the computer."

"Don't you believe that if we Jelks were unfit to rule, the computer
would change us?"

"If it could, maybe. But your attitudes are so frozen—"

"The computer can bring about any result it chooses."

"Hmmm. So I've heard." Abo pulled his chin thoughtfully.

She hated the way he tied up her emotions, disrupted her thought
pattern.

"Anyway, we Progs are not the rulers. We merely serve the computer. To serve, we must remain pure. If we become evil, we could
be destroyed quite easily."

"How?"

"Merely by altering the air supply. Its sources are in something like
five hundred locations, running in staggered shifts. When one needs
servicing, it shuts down and the computer shunts its load to another.
It would be a simple matter to shut down all of them at once. Within

eight hours the oxygen supply would be exhausted, and we would all die."

"My god. I didn't realize . . . and there's no human agency?"

"Crews in charge of each station . . . but they wouldn't know the other stations weren't operating until it was too late. Or if the computer wanted to it could simply poison us all, put cyanide or something into the air. The computer controls the mixture, after all . . ."

Abo seemed to lapse into thought. Su-shann said: "But you couldn't really attack us that way, you know. The computer would not allow it."

He waved his hand. "I wasn't thinking of that. The other thing you said—if the computer didn't like you it could change you? Why couldn't it just breed a new race to take over your function—?" He stopped suddenly, his eyes boring into hers. "That's it! That's why you came. Don't try to deny it. With your headband on I read your thoughts like a reel of tape—"

She reached up and jerked off the headband. Ben Abo started laughing. He seemed to lose control of himself, throwing his head back and hooting until his eyes streamed. "You came . . . to make a baby . . . for the computer!" He broke up into another paroxysm of laughter, then he sobered and said gruffly:

"You may as well go back. I could not mate with a *pilawu.*"

Her face flamed. "I am *not* an immature female—"

"The word means heifer, unbred Ungul. Someone has been pandering to your Jelk prudery."

She felt her fingertips pressing into her palms, but she managed to keep her voice under tight control: "I am a complete physical woman."

"Are you?" He frowned. "That may be true. I never really took notice. Now, since the issue has come up . . . show me."

Her hands went to her collar and fumbled with the clasp. She took off the tunic and stood in her skin-tight body stocking. She felt awkward and ridiculous. *Of course,* she told herself. *You want to protect your pride, and yet the very essence of what you have to do is surrender . . .*

She peeled down the stocking and stepped out of it. He stared with unconcealed interest at her bare stomach. "You didn't, by chance, come out of a tube?"

She replied coolly, though her skin felt hot. "The Jelks are produced by viviparous transmission, just like the lower races such as yourself. In our case there is no need for the bellybutton, that vulgar adornment you wear on your own gross carcass, since our surgical techniques leave no scar . . ."

He got up and walked around her, twice, his hands clasped behind his back. She felt a gathering fury, but stood still.

"To tell you the truth," he said finally, "I may project the air of a cosmopolitan lecher who ravages maids of all races, be they knob-tails or scaly-backs. But I leave it to my men to maintain the pirate image. I do not mate with women of other races. Not only do I believe in the destiny of the men of Megrez, but I feel a loyalty, and a devotion, to the women of Megrez. Their color is like the richness of ripe fruit. Their skin glows and is oily, slick to touch, their lashes long and their musk glands flow with scents that drive a man mindless . . ." She felt his breath on the back of her neck. "You are sterile to my nose, dry to my touch. Colorless to my eyes. I cannot comply with your wish, because I do not want to. This is a biological fact, and I cannot change it."

She drew a deep breath. "I do not know the arts of seduction. If you would suggest something—"

He shook his head in exasperation. "Try to understand me. I am, by the grace of Jelk education, a gentleman. Yet without gentility. I love the flames . . . to see great art melting into undifferentiated drips. A neat street of happy homes and children playing, I think of bombs and strafing. I am a warrior, born of warriors. Love is not my style. I desire to conquer—and the Jelks have lost the taste for conquest. They know nothing but holding on, falling back, holding on. If they would let the men of Megrez—but no, they are afraid to lose what they have left, and so they will lose it all. I do not desire to help their cause, except where it intersects mine. I hold their females for ransom, I steal their ships to build my fleet. The sleek young Landesses are worthless to me, except for exchange. You are a Jelk, and a Prog. What possible advantage would it be for me to do what you ask?"

Su-shann understood him then. Her nostrils burned with anger. Her hatred for Ben Abo suddenly became the biggest thing in her life, bigger even than her love for the computer.

"How much will it take to give you the desire you need?"

"One million credits."

Su-shann nodded. "You have a thumbprinter, I suppose."

He opened a panel and swung out a device used for transferring credits anywhere within the Jelk empire. Su-shann put her hand on the plate and spoke into the mouthpiece. "Transfer one million credits to—"

"The Exile Club, Eros."

Su-shann repeated the words and straightened. "Is there any reason to delay further?"

"No reason at all, my queen of delight."

"Then please turn out the light. I desire to remove my lenses, and it would dazzle me."

* * *

On the shuttle trip home, Freeden questioned her without letup. "At least give me a general statement—was he good, bad . . . superior?"

"He was . . . superior to the Sensi."

"Would you do it again?"

"With Abo? No! He is arrogant, stubborn, and unbearable."

"With anyone?"

"Perhaps. But not often." She touched the gold letters on her collar. "I think it would ultimately erode one's devotion to the computer. I can understand why it is discouraged among the younger Jelks."

4·

The Eshom

". . . Through the pungent green hell of Patagone,
Across the burning Isles of Fire,
They come, blind black demons who rend Jelk flesh,
So dangerous to our survival, so necessary . . .
                    Who else can kill the Grissig?"*

"Imagine yourself the quarry of a creature weighing three hundred pounds, muscular as a cat and quick as a snake, with the intelligence of a man and a beast's instinctive knowledge of the jungle he inhabits. And then imagine this jungle, a bottomless tangle of vegetation, where giant trees tower a thousand feet, their very tips visibly growing toward a distant red glow which marks the sun somewhere above a pall of volcanic smoke and steaming fog. Spiders the size of sea turtles build their webs of sticky strands like transparent cables hung between the trees. Here and there a flying lizard twitches in the soupy air while the spider enwraps him in sticky coils. Sometimes the lizard connects with the poisoned stinger in its tail, and the spider dies instantly. Often the lizard escapes only to fall into a death-lily cup, which can stretch its membrane into a vast shimmering reflective surface which mirrors its surroundings and lures its quarry into a trap from which there is no escape. Animal and vegetable—the boundaries are blurred, and each preys upon the other. Even the tangled bloodvine, its red venomous glow snaking up the giant trunks, sends tendrils into the tree to devour the tender grubs of termite nymphs.

"In this savage world the Eshom rule. For they combine all the attributes of the others—speed, cunning, invisibility. Their coats are

* Meed-Vlum, Humanity-One candidate for the Popular Congress, speaking on the need for a truce with the Eshom. Defeated by a five-to-one margin after the massacre of three Landark families on the Princess Astrid Coast, Antark.

colorless, reflecting no light. They do not see. Instead they feel their quarry by a strange sense which detects the muscular tenseness of another living creature. This sense is so discriminating that it can tell the size of a creature a hundred yards away in total darkness, or in total light; it makes no difference. Blindness can mean survival during the savage storms when lightning plays like a fiery net and blinds the sighted. They do not hear—and amid the crash of thunder and the rumble of earthquakes and the hiss and crackle of volcanoes, this too is survival. The Eshom can tell what the animal is eating by the muscular contractions of its paws and jaws. When they hunt, they sit silently for hours until they sense the kinetic manifestations of their prey. When they move, they glide like a blurred shadow, leaping from one low-lying branch to another, above the bottomless quagmire of reptilian roots and water and fungi which form the forest floor . . .

"But even so formidable a creature as the Eshom has its enemy. The poison of the Grissig beast is undetectable to the Eshom. It is difficult to hunt by the Eshom method, for it lies in suspended animation not far from where it has deposited its poison. Only a few rare females can sense the turned-off Grissig, so they go ahead of the hunters and mark the poisoned areas with urine. These females are revered as goddesses by the Eshom—a reverence which devolves upon the less gifted females, who rule their clans in matriarchal fashion and dominate the males although they are only two thirds their size."

Yakov Ras squeezed the speaking ball and silenced its mellifluous message. He gazed through the wall of clear plastic interwoven with filaments of copper wire. The female Eshom sat like a dark shadow on the far side of the bubble. She seemed to swallow up the surrounding light and create her own aura of shimmering darkness.

He turned to Arv Dur, anthropologist 01. "Why was she brought here, to the Jelk City Zoo?"

The anthro blinked his wide pale eyes. They watered constantly, like those of most moon Jelks, from the impurities of earth's air.

"You demanded secrecy, your excellency. Here breeding experiments are commonplace, and will pass unnoticed." He held out a small case containing two plastic discs. "Wear these, in case you meet her eyes directly."

Yakov Ras inserted the lenses, felt them adhere to his corneas. "Why are they necessary?"

"The 'eyes' of the Eshom are not organs of seeing. The shielding flaps are heat sensors. The unshielded eyes are a death ray."

"That sounds like a second-level Sensi drama."

"Call it something else then. We've detected an electromagnetic wave which freezes the synapse and inhibits the nerve impulse. Since the eye is an integral part of the brain, the animal—or whatever—becomes mindless. The Eshom then merely superimposes its own desire and the creature walks directly into the cooking pot—if the Eshom wills it."

"A formidable enemy," muttered Yakov, gazing into the cage. He felt prickly and ill at ease. A musky heaviness seemed to deaden the air. A silent implacable *something* emanated from the being in the cage. "I have the feeling she's plotting."

"You're getting a taste of what she feels about you—a small taste, because of the copper filaments in the plastic. Otherwise you'd probably go into paranoid psychosis and attack the nearest person—in this case, me. Jelk brains are not built to stand up under those emanations. Even so, our turnover is tremendous."

He pulled at his lower lip. "I can't imagine what result would justify the effort of capturing her."

"How do you mean?"

"She did not come voluntarily," said the anthro. "She was taken in a raid by several thousand Fighting Unguls under Grithy officers. Half the force was lost, and I understand there has been a renewal of Eshom raids on the Princess Martha coast. A Landark family was killed and eaten; two Grithy villages were burned and their inhabitants butchered—"

Yakov cut him off with a wave of his hand. "They'll settle down when we return her. Why is she important to the Eshom?"

"She's the Ouxana, the matriarch of all the high priestesses of their cult. The priestesses function like the ancient Greek hetaera; they staff the temples, where the men make their offerings of trade goods, skins, and food. The men believe that by giving their seed to the priestesses they create new bodies in the afterlife. There seems to be no limit to the number of males a female will accept without showing signs of boredom."

And how did you objective scientists acquire that data? Yakov wondered as he gazed at the black form. She had not moved, yet he felt some strange magnetic power draining out his strength through the channel of his eyes. He had a disquieting thought: the genes of this sinister being would someday unite with the genes of that lovely and passionless doll, Su-shann, and produce . . . What? A weapon to defeat the Vim. And what else?

"Has she been told why she's here?"

"Your excellency"—Arv Dur wiped his eyes—"the Eshom, as you heard on the tape, do not see or hear."

Looking at the female, Yakov detected a faint . . . movement?

Perhaps merely a shift of attentiveness. "She seems to know which of us is talking."

"True, she has the ability to 'gnarsh,' that is, to sense the tension of the vocal chords. But I doubt that it means any more to her than the peristaltic waves traveling through our intestines."

Yakov had begun to feel restless, nervous. Gravity pulled at his shoulders, despite the pouches of lighter-than-air gas sewn into his earth coveralls. The air stank of vegetation. The hum of the zoo's power station drew his nerves into an ever increasing tightness.

"I have other things to do. Let's get on with the breeding. I've ordered the male brought over."

"Your excellency, there is one problem. Allow me to demonstrate." He turned to a Grithy assistant. "Put in one of the Unguls."

Yakov glanced briefly at the shaggy brown manlike creature who was led in on a length of electrified cable attached to an iron collar around his neck. Tiny red-flecked eyes looked out from under a calloused brow ridge; velvet black lips hung away from long incisors, flat on the surface for cropping plants, backed by heavy grinding molars for crushing the plants to pulp. It was a common beef Ungul, kept for feeding zoo specimens which required the forearms and at the feathery white hair growing long beneath the forearms and at the back of the thighs.

Yakov watched a clear panel slide inward from each side of the bubble, dividing the near half from the side containing the she-Eshom. The Ungul was prodded inside, the pads of horny callus on his feet clacking against the floor. He saw the Eshom female and gave a terrified bawl. He tried to back out, but the Grithy keepers had closed the exit and opened the panels which divided the bubble. The Ungul stood quivering, while brown excrement ran down his legs and stained the long white hairs.

After a minute Yakov said: "She hasn't moved."

"She isn't hungry," said Arv Dur. "Eventually she'll get annoyed by his smell, or something. Watch."

But nothing happened—except that the Ungul ceased gradually to quiver. He seemed to grow drowsy, and finally slumped to the floor asleep.

"I can't understand it," said Arv Dur. "She's already killed four. It's some kind of hypnosis; she causes them to bite through their own arteries. We were hoping to find a way to stop her before introducing the individual you desired."

"Apparently she's decided merely to put them to sleep—which hardly serves our purpose any better."

Arv Dur snorted with disgust and turned to the Grithy handlers. "Close the barrier and bring him out."

The panels slid together. The two Grithies went in and jabbed the sleeping Ungul with their prods. It was like pulling a trigger on a whirlwind. The Ungul snapped out his hand with a snarl and gripped one of the handlers by the ankle. Rising, he swung the screaming Grithy once around his head and threw him like a hammer directly at the spot where Yakov was standing. The impact was tremendous, but the plastic held, and the handler slid down inside the bubble with the top of his head crushed and misshapen. A huge strawberry splash stained the plastic exactly in front of Yakov's eyes. Immediately the beast attacked the other Grithy, ripping off one fan-like ear and clawing the shoulder before a third handler stepped into the bubble and dropped the Ungul with a cyanide pellet. The wounded handler was carried away, bleeding and pale with shock, and the dead one was hauled out. During this time the she-Eshom had not moved.

"Posthypnotic command," said Arv Dur. "She decided to bring the fight to us." He turned to Yakov, half smiling. "What do you suggest, Chief Strategist?"

"Have you tried telepathy?"

"With the helments, we cannot. Without them, we would be reduced to gibbering imbeciles."

"Correct me if I'm wrong, but aren't there renegades living among the Eshom?"

"Yes, but Grithies . . ."

Yakov hesitated. The computer had given him a formidable task, but he had taken risks before. "I want to try something. When I raise my hand, cut the current which goes into the bubble. When I drop my hand, restore the current."

"Your excellency, I will not take responsibility—"

"The responsibility is mine. Do as I say."

He walked up to the wall of the bubble and waited. There was no perceptible movement of the figure, but Yakov thought he sensed a change of attitude, the blank suspension of thought which accompanies intense listening. He turned up the mental amplifier on his headband and lifted his arm. At the same time he strained to project an attitude of reverence:

"O great Ouxana, we have no wish to harm you. We only wish to make an offering of seed, so that our children will have the blessing of your strength and beauty."

He dropped his hand. The dark shape unfolded itself and rose. Her limbs seemed to flow beneath the velvet texture of her pelt. Her mouth seemed a trifle wide by human standards—and then it opened, and Yakov saw the gleaming white barbs of her fangs overlapping her lower teeth, curving down across the blood-red flesh of her gums.

Zeus pity the poor Ungul . . .

Yet there was a maddening sexuality about the way she carried herself, the mounded udders so magnificently erect. He saw the pink nipples peeping out through double flaps of skin. There was another double flap at the joining of her legs, and a pinkness visible as she lifted her leg.

Yakov gasped. "What's she doing?"

"I think she's saying no," said Arv Dur. "They communicate mimetically, in a stylized imitation of reality. When a female rejects a male, she usually urinates on his offering of food. I suppose it relates to the way they mark the Grissig poison."

Yakov watched her return to the far side of the bubble. She was lying; he had felt her lust even through the plastic barrier—a hot, sticky radiation which leaked into his mind and melted away his sanity. For an instant he had wanted to break through the barrier and join her.

Checking his life gauge, he waited until his heartbeat and respiration returned to normal. Then he lifted his arm again and spoke:

"O mighty Ouxana, I ask not for myself, but for another. He is a bull Ungul of the Fighting Ungul class. A champion of gladiators, he has killed nearly a hundred foes with his bare hands. Landarks are bidding ten thousand kupos for his stud service . . ."

She turned to face him, and for an instant the double lids of her eyes were both open. Yakov found himself looking into twin pits of yellow fire. Into his mind came a searing picture of an Ungul-like figure enveloped in four black-furred limbs and, when released, a charred smoking corpse. Even with his protective lenses, the force of her hate was like the lash of a whip.

Yakov thought: Look at him first, before you decide. He dropped his hand and turned to Arv Dur. "Bring in the bull."

He was a giant, eight feet tall, with massive arms and legs connected to each other by metallic cords which delivered an electric shock when stretched taut. (The current increased according to the stress applied, so that even if an Ungul were strong enough to break the cords, he would die of electrocution.) But the giant seemed to know to the millimeter how much play the cords allowed him. He walked easily on the balls of his feet, more athlete than brute—though he weighed over four hundred pounds. The long white hairs of his outer coat had earned him the name of Silvertip among fight fans; beneath it shimmered the electric-blue fur of his undercoat. Among breeders he was known as a Tedex bull, after the frigid snowy world on which his ancestors had lived. There was a nobility about him as he gazed at Yakov Ras from his hard sapphire-blue eyes. He did not look away, nor did Yakov Ras—and in that moment Yakov understood how he felt. Silvertip was a Fighting Ungul, and knew that as long as he stayed on top his value gave him security. The moment he lost his supremacy, he would be dead in the ring—so what had he to worry about, or be humble about? The odds in the ring favored death every day, and he did not cringe—so why should he fear these beings, as hairless as an unwiped Ungul whelp?

Yakov nodded at Arv Dur. The partition was closed between the two halves of the bubble. Silvertip, without prodding, strode in and stood looking at the she-Eshom.

"He seems intelligent," said Arv Dur. "Where did you get him?"

"He's a Feral, of course," said Yakov Ras. "I bought him from a Grithy trainer who captured him on one of the low swampy islands off the Princess Martha coast—how the Tedex breed survives in that tropical environment I don't know. They're killers—have to be, with the Eshom to the north and the Landark slave raiders on the south."

"Won't the offspring be a little . . . wild?"

"Probably, and that's only the second generation. Ah, now we're getting something . . ."

The female had lifted her head to meet the gaze of the Ungul; they seemed to be searching each other for some kind of sign. Yakov had no idea what it was, since he had never gone in for flesh contact—but he had seen the phenomenon before on visits to Ungul ranches: females dancing at the end of the leash as they were led to the pen where the bulls waited, the bulls grunting as they picked up the scent of females in heat, unga, unga, unga . . . There was always that frozen moment when they first saw each other, as though a complex of tiny mental gears were falling into place . . .

The male has good qualities, thought Yakov carefully. They can be conveyed to the Eshom, and perhaps the child will be the one who defeats the hairless white pigs . . .

The female stood up, and the skin flaps retracted from her nipples and sex, leaving a starkness of pink against the black.

Yakov turned to Arv Dur and nodded.

"Retract the barrier," said Arv Dur. "She is willing."

* * *

From outside the bubble, Yakov watched the serpentine coilings of the female; she seemed to control the giant Ungul as if he were her own hand . . .

"Damned skillful, isn't she?" said Arv Dur beside him. "Of course, it's been her life . . ."

Yakov moved a few steps away, impelled by an urge to watch the tableau in privacy. Ever since he had made contact with the female, he had felt her presence like black tentacles writhing in his brain. Yet it was not distasteful, but exciting, spiced with the danger of an act forbidden . . .

Forbidden. You must not play with the Ungul heifers, Yaki, they carry disease . . .

She was spread out now, moving like a blurred shadow beneath the huge male. Her eyes opened and fixed on him directly, and he felt her savage explosion of lust inside his brain . . .

He whirled and walked away, his legs trembling. He stepped off the walk and sank into the thick soft turf, then leaped back. It felt like stepping upon a living body. He looked down and saw the green blades writhing, like worms, and the green stain oozing out from a broken leaf. He felt a sickness coil in his stomach. He sat down on a bench and checked his life-support gauge. All readings edging into the danger zone. He knew what was wrong. No virus. No disease. No mental emotions from the Eshom female. It was something he had known about himself for a long time: he carried the impure strain of the Ras males, the taint of twisted lust that had caused his grandfather to mate with a beast-woman and was now drawing him . . .

The computer knows, he thought; why else was I not chosen to contribute my genes to this new being?

A tour car floated past on a cushion of air. Through the darkened windows Yakov saw the shining domes of moon Jelk prepubes making their scheduled seventh-year tour of earth. As usual Yakov felt a twinge of envy; none of *those* children would have to fight the handicap of tainted ancestry . . .

Arv Dur walked over to him: "They seem to have finished—finally."

Yakov rose briskly, his depression replaced by an eagerness to leave this heavy world, with its rattles and squeaks and hums and drones, and return to his silent cavern on the seventh level.

Arv Dur trudged beside him to his ground car. "May I suggest that we kill the male as soon as we are certain she has conceived? Otherwise she may plant a posthypnotic command, as she did with the other."

"We'll have to take the risk. I want him saved until the get is born, since we may need him again."

"And the female?"

"To this date how many Eshom have been born in captivity?"

"None. The females strangle them as they emerge from the womb."

"Then we will return her to the Isles of Fire. Plant a bleeper in her, so we can pick them up again after the child is born."

*"To speak of a moral ruler is redundant. A
ruler is morality; he manipulates the myth
to serve the needs of his people."*

Reflections of Wu-Shinn,
Chief Strategist,
Year of Space 1573–1697

Esh-ma Esh'h'oom, Ouxana and holder of the life thread for her people, felt life stirring within her. She had drawn out the seed of the
beast-man and now his body was taking shape inside her womb. Only
one thing remained to be done, to eat the empty shell before the hostile
spirits of her ancestors could inhabit it. The white pigs and their big-
eared puppets had taken him away, but that was unimportant. She
would always know where he was now that she held the end of his
life thread.

She sat waiting. Impatience was unknown to her. While she sat
motionless she gnarshed in all directions, spreading her receptors like
a net. It was good that she had allowed herself to be taken; now she
knew the true identity of the Enemy. Once the Eshom had fought the
hairy beast-men, thinking they were the invaders. But now she knew
they were the eaten ones. The white pigs from the sky-above-the-smoke
were the eaters. They had flown down from their cold little ball thinking this was the world of their ancestors. But it belonged to the Eshom,
and they would learn that soon.

She gnarshed a scurry of action around her bubble. Shackled beast-
men were cutting into the living earth. Grapples seized the bubble
and ripped it from its roots. She gnarshed the ground receding and
sensed the hot snarl of a man-machine above her. Never on the highest
cliffs at the edge of the Ancestral Mountains had she been so far from
the earth, with nothing to cling to . . .

Thoughts came down from the machine. The brains of the big-ears
were like ants running in streams, each doing its little job, carrying

its little thought. Some thoughts were connected to vibrating strings, an effect like gnarshing webs in the wind. After a time she was able to understand . . .

"Where we supposed to drop her?"

"Where they picked her up. There's a temple here on the big island, if I can just get down through the smoke . . ."

"There it is! By the ears of HaM'ho, it's bigger than the Jelk City arena. Don't tell me they built that. With those claws they couldn't lift things, could they?"

"No, they've got a domestic animal called the Grungee. Big as an elephant, but with hands like ours. They're supposed to be descended from the First Men, but I don't know. They're stupid animals. They carry little riders who tell them what to do. Coneys, they're called, supposed to be descended from lemurs. They milk the Grungee, eat their young, and force them to do the work."

"Like the Jelks do the Grithies."

"Watch that talk. Look, now they're coming out onto the field."

"What is it, some kind of game?"

"No, I've seen it before. They just lie down and crawl around on each other . . ."

Esh-ma thought: He is describing the *hiving,* the losing of form in which the Eshom indulged during times of great emotion. She gathered all her strength and sent her emanations down through the copper grid: *I am returning.*

And in the writhing mosaic of their form she gnarshed: *O great Ouxana, we have not existed since thy departure. Thou who art Yival, always-in-the-same-form, though who knowest past-and-future, grateful are we for thy return . . .*

Vibrations from above: "I'm not getting within a thousand feet of that. Look at the damn snakes!"

"But there's a certain beauty. Like a lake of soot flowing and intertwining . . ."

"Let's drop the black witch."

"Arv Dur will slit our ears—and throats."

"We'll let her down easy. Go out and clamp on a couple of parachutes. I'll pull up to five thousand."

After a time she floated down. Grounded, the bubble revealed an opening which allowed her to step out into the warm, scented air. She performed movements which told her people: *I carry the seed of a leader who will unite the tribes of Eshom and drive the white pigs back into the sky.*

They would try to seize the child, she told them. There had been a time in the bubble when she had felt a pinprick, and had become insentient. Since then there had been an itchy spot in her brain and a deadness which contained no thought.

The Eshom make no decisions. To think is to act, and she set off at once toward the land of the ancestors. Four males followed to sustain her on her journey. On the fifth day they reached the great boiling river which divided the new lands into two sections. The males wrestled to see who would carry her, and the winner inflated his skin with air and floated her across, out of reach of the boiling water. When they reached the opposite shore his fur was gone and his life thread nearly broken. She drew out his seed and ripped open his chest with the sharp spur on her thumb. The heart, and liver were hers; the rest went to the males. They ate silently, contemplating the goodness of their companion.

In the third week they crossed another river; this one was cool, and there was no need for sacrifice. But then came weeks of trudging across the smoking ashes, where the land heaved and bubbled, and the path often crumbled away into a lake of fire. The males took turns carrying her, passing her from one to another when the hot cinders burned blisters on their feet. Twice she stopped to eat, and by the time she reached the jungles, she had only one male left. She walked ahead, for these were Grissig lands. The jungle was empty and quiet, despoiled by the Grissig, which poisoned all life. Twice she marked their stain for her male, but failed to catch sight of the beasts themselves, though she lusted for combat.

On the day she ate the last of the males, she could see the cliffs of the old lands. Her ancestors had come down from there, driven by the web spinners which smothered the rich valleys in silken strands. Her great-great-great-grandmother had been the Ouxana then, before they tamed the Grungee and learned to build temples. Her ghost still floated here, and Eshma gnarshed the area for a tree which might be her, or a rock or a vine—for death to the Eshom meant only a loss of form. The will survived forever.

She began climbing, clinging to cracks and vines. She paused once to remove a little white egg from her ear; she had been altering the muscles in her head, squeezing one side and loosening the other, until at last the lump came out. The itching deadness was gone. She threw it down and watched it fall through the clouds . . .

She found a cave, and sat down and began calling the beast-man. The others had been so craven that she had cut their lifelines in disgust. But the big one had not been afraid, his soma had pulsed strongly. He would make good sustenance for the child . . .

* * *

From his cage in the rear of the carrier, Silvertip could see the huge round barn and the Ungul pens around it. A dozen young females bunched up inside the breeding pen, looking in his direction. They were smooth and sleek, their manes gleamed from brushing and their udders pressed through the bars like pink-nosed faces.

Once he would have rattled his chains and stamped the floor, but now he gazed upon them without interest. They were common Unguls who spoke only the vulgar tongue of the herds—not like the slender fleet-footed heifers of his home world. But he was required to impregnate them, and since they fed him better than they had in the pens beneath the arena, he would strain to comply.

"What ails the big boy?" A Grithy herdskeeper came out from the pens, carrying his staff of office. "He looks like he's off his feed."

"The trip from Farrow was long and dusty. When he is watered and brushed, his lance will make short work of your puny heifers. Ten kupos he mounts all twelve."

"Done—and I wouldn't mind losing. The old crock himself will be watching with his guest, the Landess of Ymo."

Silvertip allowed himself to be led from the carrier to a private pen containing a trough of gruel and a pan of water. He ate and drank, then walked around the pen sniffing the air. It had a putrid sweetness, like flowers and rotting eggs. He saw yellow-green clouds billowing up on the horizon, and he recalled the knowledge he had received from the black-furred woman. Without words, she had told him of a land toward the great smoke where Jelks and Grithies did not go, where he could roam as free as he had been on the snowy plateaus of his home world.

Ever since that mating he had hated the gods. Once he had thought they were another kind of slave, since they carried no whips and were always kept inside their bubbles. But now he knew they were the masters of the big-ears, and that they were immortal as long as they stayed inside the bubbles, but when they were taken out they died . . .

The gate opened, and the Grithy Yesh-tah motioned with his hand. "Get on out there and meet your fans, Silver."

As he went out, Silvertip felt the cold bite of the needle in his hip, followed by a surge of power into his groin. He stopped in the center of the arena and turned slowly around, the way he'd been trained in the fighting ring. Most of the seats were occupied by Grithy herdsmen and handlers. The household staff in their purple livery sat on both sides of the god-bubble. Through it he could see the white faces of the gods like eggs through a smoked glass. He noted that the wall in front of them was only an arm's length higher than his head.

The heifers had begun to cavort in the adjoining pen, excited but each reluctant to be first. A Guard Ungul stretched out his pole with the noose on the end. The heifers cowered away bawling, but one was caught around the ankle and dragged out on her stomach. As she got up, he saw that she was one of the Vild, a tawny fragile breed which he had always found docile and somewhat dull . . .

He walked to where she stood, hunched over and covered with dust.

A sheen of blood stained her ankle where the noose had torn her flesh. An odd passion shook him. She was one of his people. The idea of race had never entered his mind before; it must have come from the black woman. Now he remembered the carcasses hanging from hooks in the slaughtering barns, the frozen bodies of his people stacked on trucks like logs of wood . . .

He stroked the heifer's mane, muttering a series of grunts which meant: *Do not be afraid of me.*

She moved her shoulders and made a soft mew of complaint, her eyes rolling back. *Not you, but all the others watching . . .*

They are nothing, he said. *Nothing.* Reassuring her, he stroked her flanks, at first petting and then teasing until she arched her spine and sent her musk rising into his nostrils. He put his hands on her shoulders and gently bent her down, aware that the current in her manacles was always cut during the action . . .

He straightened and spread his arms wide apart. The cord twanged and parted with a crack! He crossed the arena in three leaping strides, caught the wall and swung himself over. The household Grithies fell back screaming and flapping their ears. A sizzling heat ray singed his neck; ahead of him, a Grithy's face turned black and burst into flames . . .

The little white gods huddled against the far side of the bubble. The round door had been left open, perhaps to admit a latecomer. Silvertip dashed through, then leaped aside as one of the gods fired a needle ray. He stretched out his arm and gripped the god's head, gave a jerk . . . and a twist. The head came off, a stringy wetness flapping from it. He threw it down and seized the arm of a female dressed in gold. The needle rays could kill, but the guardsmen surely would not shoot if he took their queen with him.

She went limp as he tucked her under his arm and ran outside. Grithy guardsmen were running across the arena with guns drawn. He slung the female over his back and started climbing the low stone benches toward the high rear wall. Without looking he leaped over the low railing and into the air.

It was a long drop, four times his height. He landed hard, and something cracked inside the female's body. She screamed as he loped across the lush field toward the sea. The smoking land was far, far out, but craggy black rocks thrust up from the water. He leaped into the steaming surf and felt the heat seize his legs. The water was hot and slimy—not like the cold crisp sea of the home world. It soaked his fur and dragged his body down; he could barely keep his head above water swimming with one hand and holding the woman with the other. He reached the first rock and dragged himself up, panting. Some crea-

ture of the sea had bitten off the woman's leg. She had a dying look
he had seen often in the arena, though her voice was still strong . . .

It would be a long swim. And he was hungry. He twisted off an
arm and bit into the bicep. It was tougher than fodder, but juicy. The
screams were getting weaker. He tore off the other arm and ate. By
the time he finished the screams had ended.

* * *

Su-shann had never visited Yakov's cavern before, although like her
own it was on the seventh level, less than two hundred yards distant
through solid rock. It was bleak, with neither plants nor draperies—
just a great cube of open space centered by the oaken desk which tradition said had been brought from the caverns of Ganymede.

Ill at ease, she came right to the point. "It will soon be impossible
to hide my condition."

"Oh? How long has it been?"

"Five months," she said evenly, aware that Yakov knew exactly how
long it had been. "The council will connect it with the decision to
breed the weapon."

Yakov raised himself and peered over the desk, his eyes drifting over
her body in a cool detached appraisal. Resentful, Su-shann eyed him in
the same manner. She had never seen him in bright light before; now
she noticed the greenish tint lying in the deep hollows of his face.
His fingers, spread out on the ancient grained wood, showed hairline
scars where webs had been removed.

She tried to suppress her distaste. Amphibian ancestry was as good
as any other, she told herself—if it weren't for their coldness of nature,
and that clammy odor . . .

"I notice nothing," he said finally. "Certainly the council is nothing
to fear. Between one meeting and the next they forget even what poli-
cies they have voted into effect."

"Still . . . I would rather not risk being noticed."

"You could attend by holy-graph. Most dinner parties are held with
holy-g projections of the guests seated in their numbered places. Usually
they outnumber those who are—so to speak—in the flesh."

"I know the customs, Yakov. I was born here."

She drew a deep breath and settled into the foam contours of her
seat. "But I want to have the child on earth."

"Oh?" He lifted his brows. "Why?"

"The computer said that the child should be born under normal
conditions. One sixth earth gravity is hardly normal."

"My dear strategist Su-shann, forty generations of moon Jelks have
grown up here, and in comparison to the heaviness, the pollution, the
constant infernal noise and noxious odors and dangerous plants and

animals prevalent on earth"—he shook his head—"I couldn't permit it, Su-shann."

She spoke through tight lips: "I am not asking permission, Yakov Ras. I am telling you my decision."

"And I am telling you mine. The council placed me in charge of the project, and I feel my responsibility—"

"Before you go any further into your responsibility, I have already put the question to the computer. You may read the answer."

He frowned, stretching out his hand for the short readout tape. Instead of running it between his fingers and decoding by touch as Progs were trained to do, he inserted the tape into a scanner and read the translation off the screen.

"S.C.T.C." he said, and shrugged. Clasping his hands behind his head, he leaned back and said: "Well then . . . the archaelogical station on Mount Erebus is staffed and well guarded. The superintendent's mansion is clean and airy, and regular patrols pass through McMurdo Sound—"

Su-shann shook her head. "I will not live as a government captive. I want my own estate."

"Progs cannot hold title to earth property."

"I know. I want to resign from the war council and become a Landess. I want the man I name as my mate to be ennobled in the Landark aristocracy, with a rank like my own in the second category, beneath only the directors."

"This can only be done by the Deek."

"Yes, but it is customary for the directors to approve nominations from the various council chiefs. The landate of Enderby is vacant, since the old Landark died without issue. I want the coronet."

"Enderby . . ." He frowned. "Why place a whole continent between yourself and civilization? I've been there. Hot winds blow in off the Tasman Burn, and the flying insects come from Afrik. Why choose such a poor property?"

"Because it is the only one available. I want my child to have the protection and prerogatives of the Landark nobility."

He leaned back and looked at her narrowly. "I am tempted to accuse you of using your duty for personal gain."

"Are you really, Yakov?" She felt a sudden impatience with subterfuge and politeness. "And where would you make such an accusation? To the War Council? In which case I would be tempted to tell them about the listening cube I found in my fountain, and the fact that my handmaiden is followed everywhere she goes."

"Those are security measures, Su-shann. Taken for your own protection."

"Protection by spies and assassins is something I can live without, Yakov."

He smiled faintly, looking down at his hands. "You jump from listening cubes to assassins. I don't follow you."

"I refer to strange happenings at the Jelk City Zoo, where certain Grithy handlers have disappeared from view."

"I don't concern myself with personnel defections among the lower races, Su-shann."

"No? There was also a certain Tedex bull taken from the ring at the peak of his performance and placed into stud service. This same bull escaped during a breeding tour of the fourth quadrant and—horror of horrors—killed and ate the Landess of Ymo. Oddly it was never reported. I didn't know you controlled the council of information."

"I don't. They considered it too strong for the public. As for the disappearance of the . . . Tedex bull, this item was of interest only to aficionados of the combats, or to professional Ungul breeders."

"Do you deny that the bull was used in . . . our experiment?"

"I have no comment."

"Then how about the Eshom raids? For a time it looked as though they would invade the fourth quadrant, but suddenly they swam back to their islands. Of course, our police forces took full credit, but in fact the Eshom broke off the action. Rumor says it related to the kidnaping of their high priestess, and her subsequent return."

"I have no time to discuss unproven rumors."

"Unproven. Because the Grithy airmen who transported her have since died in an unfortunate crash in the Thiel Mountains."

Yakov looked interested. "Your handmaiden seems to have tapped the Grithy underground news network. I believe they use numerical codes relating to the betting on the games in Gafronkil, don't they?"

Su-shann wasn't sure where Freeden had gotten the information—only that she believed it, and had begun to feel a terrible dread. "It concerns not only Grithies. There was a sudden epidemic at the zoo which resulted in the death of a prominent anthropologist . . ."

"Arv Dur's death was a tragic loss. I flew down to deliver his eulogy."

"And during the ceremonies for this great public servant a fire broke out in the records section and destroyed his notes on several unusual breeding experiments."

Yakov shrugged. "An irreplaceable loss, but hardly tragic."

"I am not speaking of things, Yakov. Your methods, to put it mildly, shock me. There is also the death of the Grithy trainer Garvren T-22, who formerly owned Silvertip. He fell into a pen of Ferals, who killed and ate him."

"As they customarily do, Su-shann."

"But to fall—in view of Garvren's long experience in handling Unguls . . ."

"You see fragments of a larger weave, Su-shann. To plant a crop one must cut down trees. May I ask how you found out about the Ouxana and Silvertip?"

"You may ask. I won't tell you."

He sighed. "Su-shann, I no longer expect that we will become friends. But at least recognize that our aims are similar, though we disagree on methods. Some members of the council would have your child killed if they learned about it. And who can be certain that the Vim have not infiltrated our ranks with quasi humans? It is a danger we must never ignore. Suspicion is an evil seed, but sometimes it is justified. I do not like spies. I wish that everyone were honest and loyal, so there would be no need for them. But since humans are . . . fickle, their loyalty must be periodically examined. When loyalty is found lacking, and the need for secrecy precludes a public trial, what can I do but call in the assassins?"

"And then more assassins to silence the assassins?" She felt her self-control slipping. "Yakov, I am not deceived by your posture of grief over the hard choices to which your duty drives you. In fact, you lean constantly toward the more cruel and sadistic of choices, which in turn force you to make other cruel decisions. You are trapped in your own base nature, and your influence on the Jelk race will be ultimately destructive."

He looked at her closely. "You appear to be making a declaration of war, Su-shann."

"I am telling you merely that if you had used cleverness in mating the Eshom and the Ungul, you would not have had to cover it up with this widening circle of death."

"I was dealing with two savage, unpredictable animals. I could hardly introduce them at a dinner party . . ." He sighed. "Perhaps I will slash my wrists in remorse—after the job is done. But for now, I must know how you found out, in order to plug the leak. And since you want something from me, you'd be wise to cooperate."

Yes, she thought, that is the problem. One can make many kinds of compromises in the preservation of a weak little embryo unable to fend for itself. And I am no match for Yakov in the realm of intrigue . . .

"It seemed logical," she said, "that outstanding individuals would be chosen. It is difficult for outstanding individuals to remain unseen—particularly since they had to be known to the computer. I merely programed the sorter to turn out the outstanding examples of each major racial type. Those two were among them."

Yakov nodded slowly. "Ingenious. And was your mate also among them?"

He is like the tarfil, she thought. Just when you feel he's on the run, he strikes with the fangs on his tail.

"He might have been," she said warily. "I didn't look."

"I could check it easily, but I don't think it necessary. You must know that you were traced to Eros, where your partiality to underworld elements was noted. Your mate was one of the pirates, obviously. You transferred a million credits from your council expense fund to the Exile Club, which is a front for the Blue Falcon. Who is the Blue Falcon?"

She realized that to hold out any longer would be to lose her chief bargaining point. "You agree that he shall have the landate? That would be meaningless without amnesty."

"Granted."

"And the title Landark of Enderby?"

"Granted. Upon whom shall it be bestowed?"

"Ben Abo. Formerly of Megrez, late of the Stafi Institute . . ."

He nodded with an infuriating smile. "I know. I was merely testing your honesty."

"Damn your eternal suspicion! What about your own honesty?"

His smile did not waver. "It should be an interesting mixture—your own straightforward manner, not to say abrasive bluntness, combined with Ben Abo's talent for subterfuge. He wrote a treatise on topological chess while he was a Stafi. Called the Abo defense, against the Pteronian attack. The Pteronians—as you would know if you played— are known throughout the realm as masters of the game." He leaned forward, his eyes glittering. "You must have had an interesting holiday in Hidalgo. The custom among Prog women is to avoid social contact with the fathers of their children."

Holding herself in tight control, she said: "I don't expect him to accept either the amnesty or the landate. I merely want it available to him if anything should happen to me—and he should be needed to protect the child."

"I think, with the resources at my disposal, I would make a better protector than a pirate."

"Do you really? Where is the Eshom female now?"

"We buried a miniature transmitter in her skull and set her free on the southernmost of the Isles of Fire. Immediately she began moving north. We traced the bleeper to a jungled region of Patagone, at the foot of the Magellanic Escarpment. There she remains. We will pick her up as soon as the offspring is born."

"Oh? When will that be?"

He looked annoyed. "Produce your child, and I will produce mine."

"Mine will be born in seven months, since the Jelk gestation period corresponds to the solar year. How long is it for the Eshom?"

"Ah . . ." He cleared his throat. "I'd have to check—"

"Four months, Yakov." She couldn't keep the triumph out of her voice. "Your child is a month old." She stood up. "I go now to prepare my household for removal to Enderby. Leave off the spying and get on with your job—otherwise we shall have no grandson."

6.

Su-shann at Enderby

*"Like arrows in the night
Voisson, Pym, and Enderby
Flew to the end of man's first dream,
And began the second."*

The Stafi poet Flaq-no,
reading at the dedication
of the Arch of the Second Empire,
Jelk City, Antark, Earth

Thirty generations of Enderbys had built without ceasing on the labor of Unguls and Grithy stonemasons. The new estate comprised an inner court of five square miles, enclosed by a wall of fitted gneiss blocks and surmounted by a hundred-foot barrier of electrified screen to baffle the insect swarms of Afrik. For the central palace a stepped pyramid had been raised to a height of three hundred feet, and colonnaded arcades built around a ten-acre garden. Marbled walkways wound among fountains and pools and centuries-old ferns transplanted from the jungles of earth. There were also wind towers and gazebos and dozens of smaller pyramids which served as pedestals for the god images from Regulus. To Su-shann they looked like owls squatting on nests of tentacles.

From a plaque in the courtyard she read that the first Landark of Enderby had discovered the planet Woonsek in the Regulus system, and had unearthed vast treasures from an extinct civilization which lived like bees in pyramidal hives. A later descendant had the foresight to transport objets d'art by the shipload from that ancient world before the Vim swallowed it up. Still another had the good sense to sell most of the artifacts and plow the profit into the Antark beef trade. At its peak the landate comprised a thousand-square-mile nation supporting a half million prime Unguls and four thousand Grithies. Then

Hestia did a nose dive into the southern sea, and the family fortune fell with it. The Tasman Burn raised the temperature on Enderby by twenty degrees, converting lush meadows into thorny savannah.

No Enderby since then had done much more than maintain the bloodline. The vast herds had shrunk to about seventeen hundred scrawny Unguls snuffling amid a few square miles of brush-covered hills. The last Enderby had neither married nor indulged in the favorite Landark sport of creating Grithy half-castes. Fancying himself an intellectual, he had applied for entry to the Stafi Institute with a treatise on the Pteronian whistle language. Since government policy was to discourage EVO studies, the application was denied. Enderby went into a bitter decline, easing his last days with heavy drafts of tikula. His last mortal act was to endow the League of Enderby, which established a Pteroni reservation in the Napier Mountains on the northern border of the estate. The fund, Su-shann discovered, had been gutted by the trustees. The Napier Mountains were the worst possible locale for the reservation anyway, since web spinners made it untenable for birdmen.

Most of the first month Su-shann and Freeden spent walking about the inner grounds, getting used to the thick air and the heaviness of earth. On days when hot winds blew off the Burn, a sprinkler system sprayed a cool mist into the air which drifted across the grounds in rainbow hues. The wind towers hummed and moaned with strange music, and the statues of the Woonsek gods spun and whistled. Sunsets were glorious, with glowing bands of purple and red bouncing off the smoke above the Isle of Fire. The night sky was charged with blue fire. Electric glowworms writhed above radiation zones where planetbusters had been dropped fifteen centuries before.

One of Su-shann's problems was getting used to a staff of forty Grithy employees. These were a breed developed by the Hossips to harvest the anklanga plant, which grew in salt marshes. The Ankla had developed horny coverings on their feet and calves, and clacked when they walked. They were less intelligent than the average Grithy but as good-natured as children and slightly more obedient.

At first Su-shann received a steady stream of engraved invitations from neighboring Landarks. To accept she had to get in her ground car and drive around Lambert Bay to the Landark settlement on the American Highlands. Most Landarks never lived on their lands, but settled the peaks in walled compounds surrounded by moats and contingents of Guard Unguls. Su-shann found them dull. They spent most of their time plotting to seize each other's lands, seduce each other's wives, or steal each other's Unguls. They tried to involve her in ancient feuds which had originated on worlds long ago lost to the Vim. She was amazed to discover that they still treasured their memberships in the

Land Acquisition and Reclamation Committee, which had been origi-
nally formed in the Ganymede caverns to carry out the decennial survey
of earth. It had been replaced by the Military Eventualities Committee
(later known as Milarks), but the members still wore the ancient uniforms and medals on ceremonial occasions.

They brought up their children on strict military lines. Landless Landarks from the conquered worlds served as tutors, but were often ty-
rannical toward their charges and bitter toward life. In Su-shann's opinion they turned out nothing but repressed young sadists who grew up
to indulge in all the perversions which limited brains and unlimited
wealth could provide. On one estate she saw a private pool stocked with
Androxi females, on another an aviary of captive Pteroni with their
wings slit, unable to fly. These sights, plus the terrorized and whip-
scarred Grithies she met on other estates, helped her understand why
the last Enderby had turned to tikula. Grithies who for some reason
were driven off their estates either went to lowland settlements or else
presented themselves to the guild hiring halls—which under Landark
domination were little better than slave markets. In one of these she
found two young Grithy girls who were products of gene warping.
One had three perfect breasts and the other had a silky blond tail which
extended six feet beyond the base of her spine. There was also a fat
little male who kept hiding behind one or the other of the females. The
auctioneer said they would probably be put out to starve, since they refused to separate, and nobody wanted all three. Su-shann purchased
them, though Freeden said later that the auctioneer probably told the
same story to all prospective buyers.

At first Su-shann did not understand why the three needed a private
apartment which could be locked from the outside, but Freeden explained it: "You know our males are placid, friendly, almost sexless
creatures, unable to perform a day's work and usually running to fat.
Our women have to use all their powers to arouse the male—but once
aroused, the male cannot be satiated by one but requires at least two,
usually three, and often five females before his sexual frenzy abates. It is
like madness which seizes him once, maybe twice a month. If he were
not confined at these times he would shatter the entire household. He
would not even hesitate to attack your own person, madam, so blind
does he become in his lust."

While hardly blind with lust, the impoverished males of the landless nobility made several offers of marriage to Su-shann. She found
them without exception arrogant and stupid. All offers and invitations
ceased the day Ben Abo's title was published in the Landark registry.
EVOs, Stafis, and criminals were anathema to the conservative nobility.
Ben Abo was all three.

Su-shann was happy in her ostracism, for her body began to swell as she entered her tenth month. Freeden looked at her tiny buds and decided that the baby would starve. She lifted her own large breasts in her hands and said: "If I could get with child, there would be enough for both yours and mine."

Yakov Ras sent a doctor down in his private shuttle, but Su-shann refused to let him examine her.

"It's one of his tricks," she told Freeden later. "Being a moon Jelk, the doctor would have found me crawling with germs. He would recommend my removal to the moon. Which is where Yakov wants me."

"You could refuse," said Freeden.

"True. But that would involve a confrontation with him."

"Which you might lose."

"I would *not*. But my own conscience makes me vulnerable. Yakov lacks vision. In a crisis he would jettison the future in favor of the present."

"And that would be painful, no? Since you carry the future in your belly."

If Yakov reacted to the doctor's failure, Su-shann did not hear about it. But a week later she saw a Grithy minstrel climbing the steps of the pyramid with his Ut-kul on his back. Rivulets of sweat ran down his face, for it was a day of blistering winds. She'd seen many such troubadors on the roads; they traveled from one landate to another, carrying gossip and singing songs and cross-fertilizing the Grithy race (also servicing the noble wives on occasion). But she noticed something strange about this one: he walked with the shuffle of one accustomed to low gravity. She drew her heat gun and said:

"Search him, Freeden."

He threw up his hands and grinned. "Don't remember me, eh?"

She saw the red-tipped canine teeth and said: "If you were a foot taller I would say Ben Abo . . ."

"We met on Eros, in the Exile Club."

"Gar-Vel! I should burn you for plotting to kidnap me."

He shrugged. "Business . . ."

"And what business are you on now?"

"I have a message from Ben Abo."

"Deliver it."

"It is verbal . . . and long."

She holstered the gun. "Let's go in by the pool. You can refresh yourself while you talk."

Seated beside a tinkling fountain, with a glass of tikula and kusa juice in his hand, Gar-Vel said: "To begin with, Ben Abo has information that the War Council plans to execute him and wipe out the pirates."

She gasped. "But the amnesty has been published! Ben Abo is a Landark."

"What the council bestows, the council can take away. Ben Abo has no intention of walking into a trap."

Su-shann thought about it, then nodded. "He is probably right. But what does this have to do with me?"

"He asks you to think what will happen after the baby is born, and you are no longer useful to Yakov Ras."

"I have already thought about it . . ."

Gar-Vel smiled. "The speed with which you drew your gun does not indicate a sense of deep security."

"That's true. What solution does he offer?"

"That you come to Hidalgo. He offers refuge."

Su-shann smiled faintly. "I know the mind of Ben Abo. He gives away nothing. My feeling is that he wants me as a hostage, to keep the Guardian Fleet away from his door."

Gar-Vel sipped his drink, and savored it slowly. "I wasn't supposed to tell this—but . . ." he shrugged. "He plans to escape to Megrez with his fleet, depose his father, and remove the Jelks from the planet. You would be co-ruler. The child would be heir to the throne."

She laughed. "Abo is free with another's kingdom."

"His father is old."

"And Megrez is on the periphery. How long before the Vim turn us all into slime?"

"Ben Abo has plans for dealing with them. I can't tell you more than that."

Su-shann stood up and looked into the pool, contemplating the wavering reflection of her ivory-pillared palace. She loved the earth, despite its discomfort. She had no intention of having her baby on an asteroid, or in deep space, or any other planet. Still she felt trapped without a means of fast transportation. As a council member she'd been assigned an atomic-powered flier which could land and take off from a planet. Only the wealthiest Landarks could afford these; others had to be satisfied with atmospheric skimmers which carried them up to relay stations, where they caught scheduled flights to the moon and other systems. Even for that they needed passports.

She turned to Gar-Vel. "How did you come down from Eros?"

"As usual, on the Grithy-class shuttle, with forged papers."

"Then what would we do for transport?"

He smiled with a certain self-satisfaction. "As I passed through the landate of Goland, I noticed a deep-space flier sitting almost unattended on its pad. The guards were lovers of music—but fell asleep while listening. So I took the flier."

"Where is it now?"

He waved his hand vaguely. "A few miles from here."

"Don't you trust me?"

He sighed. "At the head of the bay, twelve fathoms down. If you're ready, we can hit deep space within an hour."

"I'll be honest with you, Gar-Vel. I see no point in trading my dependency on Yakov for dependency on Abo. Besides"—she put her hand on her stomach—"sudden weightlessness might bring a premature result. However, it would give me a feeling of security if you were available in case of emergency."

He stood up and bowed. "It will be an honor to serve such a courageous and determined lady."

That night the savage melodies of Megrez echoed among the colonnades. Su-shann thought them crude and atonal, but Freeden and the two gene-warped Grithy girls danced with delight.

Gar-Vel's words stimulated her to start watching newscasts. She knew they were programed by the Information Committee, and, knowing how the committee worked, she was able to see it shaping up. First there was a film, supposedly taken by a passenger with a hidden camera. It showed pirates beating up passengers, tearing the clothes off screaming girls. They were actors, of course; none of the men she'd seen on Hidalgo had worn black uniforms with skulls painted on their face masks. Calls for action against the pirates intensified when a passenger liner was reportedly destroyed in space. Films showed metal fragments, torn bodies, and—of course—a child's doll floating in the void. Su-shann knew the crash could have occurred a thousand years ago—but reason was drowned in the unleashed rage of the multitudes. The popular council, instrument of the people's will, demanded the destruction of the pirate stronghold. Yakov Ras announced with extreme regret that he had granted amnesty and could not revoke it. So the council voted, in a breathless roll call, to override Yakov's veto. Ben Abo's amnesty was canceled, all titles stripped away. A fleet prepared to wipe out the Falcon's Nest.

"You see how Yakov keeps his promises," said Gar-Vel. "We'd best escape while we can."

Su-shann felt her stubbornness take root. "I have decided definitely to have the child on earth. Tomorrow we will start looking for a refuge outside the walls."

The little ground car, with six huge soft tires independently suspended, crawled over the rough terrain like a caterpillar. Gar-Vel drove, while Freeden sat beside him and Su-shann surveyed the countryside from the raised rear cockpit. Where Yakov had found hostility and chaos, Su-shann saw a savage beauty. Low black clouds raced in from the sea, raking the hills with lightning, turning dry valleys into roaring rivers. Minutes later hot winds sucked up the moisture in clouds of steam. Once the crawler brushed a spiny green barrel shape, and she ducked down as a cloud of silver arrows flashed overhead. Little brown puffballs sometimes exploded under the wheels, and she had to yank the bubble shut before poison gas seeped into the car. One day they were driving in the Napier foothills when the sun suddenly went out. Millions of giant butterflies passed overhead, the dust from their wings clouding the air.

"They lay their eggs in the mountains," said Gar-Vel. "They're about the size of your head and full of meat. The Eshom eat them and so do the Grithies. In fact, it's the main diet in some of the illegal coastal settlements. During the hot monsoon the eggs hatch out into caterpillars and start eating their way toward the sea. Imagine a thousand six-foot caterpillars chomping their way across a meadow. Fortunately the cold kills them before they get too far."

"Why do they eat toward the sea?" asked Su-shann.

"Trying to get back to their home in Afrik, they say. The continent is almost entirely populated by mutated insects. I've seen whole islands off the coast built up by termite colonies, connected to the land by causeways and defended by termite soldiers."

To Su-shann it appeared that insects from Afrik were a worse threat than the Vim or the Eshom—at least on the Enderby coast, which lay nearest the continent. Driving along the shore after a storm, she saw that the surf had thrown up mountainous windrows of chitinous exoskeletons, remnants of insects which spent their larva stage on the ocean floor and floated on the surface as adults. There were also the web spinners—tiny midges which spun out filaments of sticky thread as they flew. Giant insects blundered into these gossamer clouds and fell helpless to the ground, where the midges ate them. They also ate Pteromen. Once, while exploring a valley which led up to the peaks, she found the body of an adolescent male whose wings had been wrapped in a silken cocoon. Only his tough outer skin remained; the inner parts had been eaten away.

In this same valley, about twenty miles from the palace, she found her refuge. While Freeden and Gar-Vel rested after lunch, Su-shann went exploring on foot and found a narrow chasm scoured out by flash floods. She went in slowly, playing her heat gun on the sand to kill the venomous insects which lived in the soil. Forcing her way through a screen of undergrowth, she found a tiny cirque walled in by high cliffs, and in one of the cliffs a dry cave. Remnants of gnawed bones indicated that it had been used by Pteromen, possibly before the advent of the web spinners. Huge trees overhung the copse and made it impossible to approach by air.

She noted the landmarks as they returned to the estate. Next day she went out alone, carrying blankets and medicine to the cave. She was swollen like a cocoon, and the effort exhausted her, so that she collapsed the moment she returned to the palace.

"I was afraid Yakov had gotten you," said Freeden as she bathed her face in cool water. "Why is your skin so hot? Where have you been?"

"In answer to your first question, Jelks have few sweat glands, so we can't lose heat through evaporation. As for the second . . ."

Freeden's eyes grew round as Su-shann told her about the cave.

"You will die there. The child is too big. It will split you like a tree growing through a rock. Let me get a doctor."

"No."

"A Grithy midwife from the village at the head of the bay—"

"Yakov will have such people watched."

"Then have it here."

"I'm sure he has spies among the servants."

"At least let Gar-Vel take you—"

"Nobody must know, Freeden. The birth must be natural. If I die . . . S.C.T.C."

By the time she had the cave stocked with food she knew her time was near. For a week she'd felt movement inside; now the child was awake and trying to find a way out. Her life gauge showed a rise in blood pressure; otherwise her health was good. But her mood was one of self-pity and growing irritation toward Freeden and Gar-Vel. They seemed happily in love, whereas she had only one desire: to be delivered of her burden. She felt annoyed when Gar-Vel reported finding an object of illegal worship in the quarters of the male Grithy.

"What does it matter what he worships?" Su-shann looked at the idol, which resembled a large grub with six long legs. "What does it represent, anyway?"

"It is the Hossip, madam. He worships the Hossip."

Su-shann could not grasp the gravity of the situation until Gar-Vel explained it: "You are familiar with the accepted Grithy religion, which stresses obedience and keeping one's place within the caste system. Virtue is rewarded by reincarnation after death as a Jelk. HaM'ho is the original Savior, having slain the evil Hossip and led the Grithies out of bondage. But in *this* religion," he held up the idol, "HaM'ho is the villain who betrayed the Hossips and sold the Grithies into slavery. It holds that there is no reincarnation in this world, but rather a transportation of the soul to that ancient paradise which can be recognized as the site of their original captivity by the Hossip. The highest form of service to their gods is to kill a Jelk."

Su-shann looked at the male, who was trying to hide behind the tailed female. "You want to kill me?"

He shook his head and gave her a sickly but engaging grin. The three-breasted girl came up and dropped to her knees, her eyes misted with tears. "If you kill him, we ask that you kill us too."

Su-shann turned to Gar-Vel. "What is this about killing?"

"The penalty for membership is death."

"Ridiculous. I doubt if they obey their gods any better than we obey ours. Destroy the idol and give them new quarters outside the walls. But don't bother me with it again."

That night she felt the first contraction. She strapped on her gun and slipped out to the crawler. Pain ebbed and flowed as she drove across the moonlit ridges and up the shadowed valley. She maneuvered the little vehicle into the ravine and rammed its nose into the narrow neck, stopping it up like a cork in a bottle. She climbed out the rear cockpit and staggered to the cave, falling upon the cushioned mat as labor began . . .

Pain was a link between Su-shann and all other women from the beginning of time. She saw it in a conceptual flash: man is the instrument of divergence with his questing eyes and his restless urge to fill every hole he sees. Woman is the instrument of unity, with her desire to enclose all existence within herself. This is our duty, to melt down the divergence and create unity. But oh, the deliverance is hard, hard. I want to bring her into the light but she doesn't want to come. She senses that this is a world of pain . . . Oh, please, leave me, go out, please go . . .

When she awoke Freeden was sitting beside her, holding a swathed bundle. The Grithy girl smiled and tipped back the covering to show a triangular face, cleaned and washed, with a fuzz of copper hair running the length of the skull. The skin was a pale turquoise, smooth as gemstone, with an ivory whiteness that gave it the depth of fine china. Su-shann had never imagined that the blending of Jelk and Megrez would produce anything so beautiful . . .

"But how can you . . . ?" She indicated Freeden's swollen breasts and the pale liquid leaking from the child's mouth.

"*She* did it. When I came I saw her crying and hungry, and I picked her up and held her. She began to suck, and I felt my breasts fill up and overflow. You may take her now, since I am nearly emptied. What will you call her?"

With the warmth of the child against her side, Su-shann looked down and saw the eyes open, looking at her in a way that seemed cold, calculating. They were big and round, like her own, but the liquid gold color of the iris was Megrez.

"It's obvious her father deserves some credit. We'll call her Abi-shann."

7

A Piece of the Puzzle Is Missing

"Only tyrants can afford to be honest.
Democratic leaders must use deception
in the place of force."

Tor Gumi, head of the Jelk
conservative coalition

Hovering above the jungle, Yakov asked: "Is the bleeper pinpointed?"
The pilot said: "We're right above it—I think."
"You think? Isn't it functioning properly?"
"Yes, sir. But they've got these small bats here that use the same wave-length as the bleeper. Keeps throwing our finders off."
Yakov sighed. Had the black-furred bitch known? Was that why she'd come to this area? It was only the latest in a series of problems which had delayed the recovery of her offspring. For months magnetic storms had made it impossible to search from the air. Out of the dozen agents he'd sent in on the ground, not one had remained alive for more than eight hours. One had been dragged under by a giant moray eel which lived deep in the ooze, another was electrocuted when he stepped on a mutated lily pad. A third had brushed against a hanging bladder which immediately burst and smothered him in a cloud of corrosive, poisonous gas. Three more had gone down under an avalanche of giant army worms which left nothing behind but a mile-wide streak of gray pulped muck beaten to a paste, fetid with the odor of excrement . . .
New agents would always come forward for the money he offered. The problem was time. Assuming that the birth had taken place after the normal four months' gestation, it would now be a year old . . .
He opened the circuit to the other five skimmers and said: "Spread out around me. We're going down."
As the floater descended on its cushion of air, Yakov felt grateful

for the half inch of borazon plastic which shielded him from the jungle. Radiation and 120-degree heat had stimulated nature to an orgy of experimentation. Fungoid trees with scabrous bark and pulpy red leaves rose two hundred feet above the ooze. He saw a fanged bird whose beak dripped venom attacking a centipede eight feet long. What he thought to be a lovely iridescent blue vine turned out to be a reptile with eyes spaced along its twenty-foot length. He shuddered to think that he'd been tempted to reach out and touch it.

The floater ceased its descent and rocked gently on top of the muck. Yakov closed his face plate, threw back the canopy, and stood up in the cockpit. The jungle floor was shrouded in perpetual dusk. Thick muffled silence was broken only by an occasional splash, a slither, and a scream.

He held up the tracer and turned slowly until he faced in the direction of the needle. Twenty feet away squatted a huge, blubbery hulk with gray-mottled skin. It looked vaguely humanoid. It had arms twenty feet long and thick as a tree trunk, ending in sharp, hooked claws. It was using these to rip open a rotten stump, conveying handfuls of white pulpy grubs into its mouth. It looked at Yakov with unblinking reptilian eyes and gave a querulous grunt. Yakov felt a deep disgust.

"Shoot it with trank," he ordered.

Several guns spat flechettes tipped with tranquilizer bulbs. The monster shuddered, moaned, and started sinking into the ooze.

"Get some grapples on it!"

Five ships skipped over and played out long cables terminating in four-pronged hooks. With a roar of engines they hoisted the monster out of the muck with a sucking, slobbering sound. Leeches—shiny black bladder shapes a foot long—clung to its legs from the knees down . . .

They carried the monster to the top of a basalt chimney and stretched it out on a slab of rock. Two Grithies with long curved flensing knives sliced it open from neck to pelvis. A tech with a gas mask groped in the undigested pulp of grubs and worms and drew out an egg-shaped object. He wiped it off and gave it to Yakov.

"The bleeper, your excellency."

Yakov gazed at the egg in his hand and wondered: how had she gotten it out without surgery? It had been attached to the skull, surrounded by brain tissue.

He looked at the remains of the monster, already beginning to attract swarms of flying insects.

"That creature—do you know what it is?"

"We call it a yingo. Its skeletal structure indicates that it is descended from human stock."

"Could it have eaten something, say the size of an Ungul?"

"Hardly. It has no teeth, only bony plates for mashing the grubs.

The trachea is only two inches wide. The bleeper was probably lying loose, and the Yingo ate it because it looked like an insect egg."

Yakov could hear the precise clipped tones of Su-shann speaking in cold derision: Well, Yakov, do you expect my child to mate with an egg? He flung the egg with all his strength and watched it fall toward the treetops. The superheated stench of the jungle made him nauseated.

"Let's go back to Jelk City," he said.

Four hours later, flying over the blue-green Weddell Sea, he looked down at the line of picket boats which kept the mutated seals away from the coast. A few sailing boats scudded before the hot winds which blew constantly off the burn; others were tacking back toward shore. He saw a convoy of armed cruisers putting out from the staging area on Berkner Island, carrying wealthy sportsmen to the Feral-hunting grounds on the South Orkney islands. Lately there'd been reports that the Ferals were arming themselves against the white hunters . . .

The craft rose as it approached the mountainous neck of the continent. Jelk City spread out below him. It had grown from a nucleus around the south polar spaceport until it now occupied the broad valley between the Horlick and the Theil Mountains. To his right he saw a yellow haze floating above the Rocky Plateau industrial district. Far ahead, he could see the castles clinging to cliffs along the south shore of the Ross Sea. The north shore was a marsh occupied by the stilt city of the Grithies. Gafronkil. The Executive Committee range reared up behind it, with Grithy settlements beginning to edge up into the Pteroni reservation. There would be a new outburst of fighting soon. The current population explosion was a result of refugees from Ormul. He visualized the coming flood of refugees from Pell—three million now en route by sleep-frozen transport—and felt fatigue weight his shoulders. Where would he put them? A stench entered his nostrils, and he looked down into the Ungul yards—a hundred square miles of penned-up beef awaiting slaughter. Perhaps it was immoral to eat them, but what else was there?

He thought of that huge blubbery creature eating grubs, and shuddered.

Problems, problems . . .

Which reminded him of another problem hanging fire. He got Commander Ho-ford on the scrambled beam and said: "About this operation against the pirates . . ."

"Yes, your excellency. I dispatched the fleet ten hours ago."

"What! But I specifically ordered you to hold . . ."

"I received orders from . . . one who shall be nameless. And you know as well as I . . ."

Yakov sat for a minute after signing off, then he turned to the pilot. "Take me to Tor Gumi's headquarters on Penscola Peak."

A few minutes later it came into view, a vanadium steel block on a scraped-off mountaintop, surmounted by the gigantic figure of a bull Ungul. Fat, docile, expressionless, he gazed out over the Ungul pens which covered the flats below. Yakov got out and walked across the landing pad, breathing the stench of Ungul manure. He took the side entrance, to the right of the broad marble steps leading up to the main hall. Just inside the door, a uniformed Grithy saluted and held out his hand. Yakov surrendered his sidearm and walked down the long narrow hall, aware of the spy eyes set in the walls and the lasers ready to slice him into sizzling cubes.

The outer office was occupied by a tall girl with green-flecked eyes and cobalt hair. She was a Pellan refugee, one of the first to arrive. Absolutely the top in prestige items. She took his name and told him to have a seat.

He felt a twinge of resentment. "I'm the chief strategist. I have urgent business—"

"I'm sure of that, sir." She gave him a professional smile, and he saw that her teeth were as green as her eyes. Something in the water they drank on Pell . . . "If you will kindly wait. Tor Gumi has been informed of your arrival . . ."

More humiliation, he thought as he sat down. Why did I ever become indebted to a pig like Tor Gumi?

He knew why. Tor Gumi was the richest meatpacker in Antark, and headed a coalition of conservatives which at present, due to the nadir of the Humanity-One Party, was the most powerful force in the empire. Without the support of Tor Gumi, an EVO like himself could never have achieved anything . . .

Grandfather, he thought, this is all your fault. Grandfather had been a Prog, a landless Jelk who refused to remain landless. He'd stolen a ship and gone exploring in the region of Achernar. He'd rediscovered Lux-mar, a sea-island planet peopled by EVOs who, during the Hiatus, had developed webbed feet and hands and nictitating membranes to protect their eyes from the midges which swarmed over the marshes. He had also discovered radioactive salts on the sea floor. Their essence was a rare medicinal drug, and he'd used the residue to fuel the giant sea dredges which mined the product.

On this world without true women, Grandfather took unto himself a harem of Lux-mar females. One of them gave birth to a son who was taught to read and write and finally was sent to the Burok College on Antark. There Father bleached his green skin and surgically removed the webs from between his digits—not because he was ashamed, but because he wanted to rise, and to rise he had to mold himself in the

Burok pattern. He was assigned to Pym, a glacial world in the region of Arcturus, with only the Grithy maintenance girls to keep him company. During a furlough on Eros, he met a Milark female named Yaka who commanded a ship of the Guardian Fleet. In the aphrodisiac air of the bubble-domes, they fell in love and mated. Yaka conceived. She planned to remain there until the child was born, since pregnant females could not travel on F-T-L ships. But she learned that the father was part EVO, and had the fetus transferred to a Grithy carrier and went off to rejoin her command. She died in the battle of Bottis. Father reclaimed his child, and took Yakov Ras with his Grithy *mamu* back to Pym.

It was not a lonely life, but a strange one. Lacking the companionship of equals, Yakov reigned as a prince over several hundred young Grithies. His father rose high in Burok circles, and finally became coordinator for all manufacturing on Antark. This enabled him to take his son out of the ice tunnels and place him in the prestigious Institute of Industry of Jelk City. There Yakov learned to hate his vestigial nictitating membrane, and his webbed hands and feet, for the Burok children laughed and called him Frogman. He learned to smile, but in his mind was a little pool of acid in which he steeped the names of his enemies. Meanwhile he enjoyed the luxury of his father's palace in Victoria Land, with Grithy servants and all the prerogatives of the ruling class.

All this ended when his father was lost on a hunting expedition to the Isles of Fire. One of the survivors said he'd been captured and eaten by the Eshom. Since Yakov had loved and respected his father (who tried to repair the genetic havoc wreaked by Grandfather), Yakov made a public vow to wipe the Eshom from the face of the earth. His resolution brought him to the attention of the conservative coalition, whose platform was no less than the complete transformation of the earth, the elimination of mutants, and the reoccupation of the land by the true heirs of the ancients . . .

With their backing Yakov had become the youngest wearer of the Golden Lanyard since Wu-shinn himself. Now he was beginning to wonder just how much longer he could stand being an errand boy for an uncultured clot like Tor Gumi . . .

Tor Gumi did not look like the most powerful man on earth. A squat heavy-set Jelk from the three-g planet of Yohl, his date of arrival on earth was unknown. It was at least a hundred years ago, for Tor Gumi was old. Only his eyes were alive—distilled essence of hate shining out of a face whose skin was like thin tissue stretched over a broad misshapen skull. Behind him hulked the stuffed carcass of a giant stud Ungul, nine feet tall at the shoulder and weighing seven hundred pounds.

Tor Gumi barked at Yakov as if he were a servant:

"Why didn't you destroy the pirates when I told you?"

"You gave me a free hand—"

"As long as you did what I wanted. Our propaganda program peaked three months ago. The people can't be held at a peak of rage indefinitely."

"I had reasons for delaying the attack—"

"What reasons?"

Yakov decided to ignore the question. "The chain of command is an efficient instrument of government. When you bypass it, you destroy its efficiency."

"Damn efficiency!" Tor Gumi slammed his fist on the control console. "I dispatched the Guardian Fleet because I was tired of hearing about the brave deeds of that pirate Ben Abo. I want him *killed!* And I want the Eshom *exterminated!*"

He knows, thought Yakov. How else could he connect the Eshom with Ben Abo?

"We need the Eshom as a buffer. Otherwise the Grissigs will move into the lands of Antark."

"Bah! How can you control the Eshom? The beasts don't speak."

"I have planted the idea of revolution in the mind of their high priestess. She will put the Eshom together into a single government. Then we merely take control of their leader. It is a common tactic."

"You'd best leave thinking to me, Yakov Ras. Once we plug the volcanoes—and I have men working on it—we can transform the Isles of Fire into grazing lands. Then we'll burn off the jungles of Patagone . . ." He trailed off, fixing Yakov with a hard glare. "You've been absent from your headquarters a great deal lately, Yakov."

"I've . . . been in the jungle."

"I know you've been in the jungle! You think you're above being spied on? Did you find the Eshom whelp?"

Yakov felt an inner shock, then recalled that Tor Gumi had at least three other—what should he call himself?—whipping boys on the War Council. He wouldn't have missed being informed of the plan to breed the weapon. Once informed, he had the resources to learn the details.

"It was . . . apparently, eaten by a predator."

"Good. Good." Tor Gumi's eyes glittered. "It was a stupid plan to begin with. I don't know why you approved it."

"The computer said—"

"Blast the computer! It puts no credits in my purse."

"Without it your distribution system would collapse . . ."

"The computer is a tool. The Progs give it power. Once we control the Progs . . ." He waved his hand impatiently. "Later. The other

elements of this subversive plot, Ben Abo and the strategist Su-shann
. . . I understand they bred. What was the result?"

As if you didn't know already. "A girl."

"Named—?"

"Abi-shann. She was born in a cave."

"You're sure there was no substitution?"

"I'm sure. I planted a tracer in her crawler. When I discovered that
she'd stocked the cave, I put a spy device in it. I watched the birth
from my quarters on the moon."

"You should've killed it then. I presume you have spies in her palace."

Yakov squirmed. "She brought her personal staff, which is loyal. I
have informers, but they are not inside."

"So? How do you plan to seize the child?"

"Why should I? She's healthy. Neither Su-shann nor the handmaiden
can satisfy her hunger. She feeds from an Ungul."

Tor Gumi made an expression of distaste. "Yakov, the more you talk,
the more I wonder if you're the man to take my place." He pressed his
fingertips together and glared at Yakov through the arch. "Do you know
about the Hossip cult?"

"I know it's illegal . . ."

"We invented it in order to detect unrest among the Grithies. The
priesthood is ours. When we desire to eliminate an opponent, we inform the priests, and they instruct one of their . . . believers. The deed
is done, the culprit is executed. Our hands remain clean."

Yakov felt a chill rise up his back. "I see."

"You don't see. A Grithy male in her household is a devotee of the
cult. He will seize the child and carry her to a hill about four miles
from the palace. It is a well-known landmark called the Sleeping Virgin.
He expects to meet his priest and sacrifice the child to the Hossip gods.
He is wrong only in detail. He will meet you instead of the priest."

Yakov rose heavily. "And the mother?"

"Kill her."

Yakov managed to control his voice. "There is no need—"

"I decide what is needed." He waggled his fingers impatiently. "Now
go, quickly . . ."

Yakov dismissed his pilot and took the floater up himself, skirting
the congested airspace above the city. Enderby was half a continent
away, more than twelve hundred miles. Beyond the spaceport he
dropped down into the great central basin—formed, according to the
scientists, by the mile-thick icecap which had once covered the continent. All that remained was a brackish inland sea, speckled with the
stilt homes of Grithy refugees.

He flew low, drawing power from atomic stations spaced ten miles
apart. Ungul herds stampeded as he roared overhead, but he didn't no-

tice. To kill Su-shann . . . something cried out within him. He had wanted to offer his genes . . . *No, be honest, Yakov, you wanted her, for the sheer pleasure of stroking her body.* He remembered her words: *You use force where cleverness would serve.* If he could only tell her, it is Tor Gumi and not Yakov Ras who does these evil things . . .

Ah, there, the three-pronged Bay of Amery. And straight ahead, the famous pyramid of Enderby, with its wedding-cake palace on top.

It looked deserted. He set his ship at the base of the pyramid and climbed the steps. As he stepped inside the colonnaded patio, he knew he'd arrived too late to help Su-shann. From a tree beside the pool hung two Grithy girls, dead. One had three perfect breasts, the other had a silky tail—befouled now in the excrement-spattered terrace. Their faces were black, twisted, ugly . . .

He went from room to room, seeking . . . someone. A Dairy Ungul moaned and came toward him, holding her swollen udders, begging to be milked . . .

Yakov went back down the steps and got into his floater. He lifted up and began circling the pyramid, studying the hills. To the west he saw a configuration which suggested a woman lying on her back. He flew over and saw a figure dart out from a thicket. He was a fat little Grithy, carrying something swathed in a cloth. Yakov flew low, holding the trank gun. It was unnecessary, for the rush of air from beneath the craft knocked the Grithy flat. The child rolled out on the ground.

Yakov grounded the floater and picked her up. She was naked except for a folded napkin pinned around her midsection. Yakov turned and aimed his gun at the Grithy.

"Where is the mistress?"

The little man shook his head and babbled in Grithy: "Oh, Lord, I do not speak the tongue of the gods. Do not kill me, I will be your servant . . ."

Yakov switched to the Grithy dialect he'd learned as a child: *"Imma-wa-esknafeelna?"*

The little man looked startled, then responded: "She was searching for me . . . she and the blue man. He had a starship. When you landed at the palace they flew into the sky."

"The blue man? Ben Abo?"

"He was called Gar-Vel."

Which means the same thing, thought Yakov. Curse the blue-skinned bastard, he and Su-shann would get together somewhere in space and produce another one of these. Better to hold on to what he had, in case he could get the other half of the puzzle . . .

"Why did those girls hang themselves?"

Something flickered in the Grithy's eyes. "Because . . . they were sorry. Perhaps they also feared loneliness . . . punishment, death."

"And you don't?"

He drew himself up. "I will go to paradise and serve the Hossip, as my ancestors did in the days of glory."

"You're a fool."

The fat face twisted. "You are a worse thing. You serve the white pigs. Yet you are no Jelk. You are one of us."

Yakov's hand clamped hard on the butt of his gun. If it had not been merely a trank shooter, he would have sent a sizzling burst of electricity into the fat leering face. But he controlled himself. "Go. Run! I may yet kill you."

The Grithy whirled and ran, pumping his short fat legs until he disappeared over the ridge.

Yakov climbed into his ship and dialed the code which connected him with Tor Gumi. "I have the child."

"And the mother?"

Yakov hesitated, then said: "Dead."

"Good. Now you can kill the child."

Yakov felt an inner shock, though he'd been expecting the command. "She is a Landess now. You cannot kill a Landess."

"I can. Bring her to me."

He clicked off, and Yakov looked down at the child. *Kill* her, something inside him said, kill her and regain the good opinion of Tor Gumi. In a way the child was to blame for his fall from grace. In his desire to mate with Su-shann he had approved the breeding experiment, and that was the beginning . . .

He tried to work up a hatred toward the child, but her helplessness stripped him of power. He had always accepted the Jelk ideal of beauty —but Abi-shann with her long hair spilling like molten copper around the pale-blue oval of her face, her eyes like pools of soft gold—she turned his ideals inside out. She made the Jelks seem like pale slugs writhing under a stump.

He lifted the ship and flew toward the city. The child lay in the seat beside him. He had a feeling she was watching him, but every time he looked her eyes were closed.

One thing was certain: something was in his mind which had not been there before—a sense of power beyond his own physical resources. For the first time in his life he knew what he was doing. He landed his craft on Tor Gumi's private pad, picked up the child, and walked toward the building. His scalp felt stiff and tingly, as if it were shrinking tight around his skull, but his blood pumped cool, and he felt good.

Inside, he surrendered his sidearm and walked down the long hall.

The Pellan girl gave him a green smile and waved him into Tor Gumi's office. Tor Gumi looked at the baby and rubbed his hands together:

"Ah, the poor misbred creature—but she won't have to endure a miserable life. Give her to me."

"I want to ask a question first. Is this what it boils down to?"

The old man frowned. "What are you talking about?"

"The power of the state. Is it simply the power to kill your enemies?"

"What else could it be? Now give me the child."

Yakov held out the baby. At the same time he pulled his heat gun from inside her diaper. He pointed it at Tor Gumi and pressed the firing stud. Sssspat! A ten-thousand-volt beam gouged a charred smoking crater in the man's thick chest. He took two heavy steps backward and sat down with a thump, staring at an empty space between his legs. His body tipped sideways . . .

Yakov threw open the door and called: "Come. Tor Gumi has suffered an accident."

The Pellan girl jumped up, looked inside, and shrieked. She staggered against the door, then turned to face him, her green eyes wide with horror. "You . . . ?"

"His gun discharged accidentally. You will prepare the ceremony of eulogy. Let us hope there is only one eulogy to perform."

She stared at his gun and slowly drew herself erect. Through bloodless lips she said: "I understand, your excellency."

After she went out, Yakov looked down at the child. She smiled.

8.

The Strangeling

*"Rurabei
Ngu neit
Wisro sus be dite."*
Grithy lullaby

Yakov figured it out: he must be a father to Abi. Only in this way could he retain her loyalty and still allow her to grow up in freedom as the computer demanded.

He made the decision coldly, weighing the alternatives and taking the most expedient course: Enderby was isolated; he could leave her there and still maintain secrecy. Security was provided by a regiment of combat-seasoned Grithies from the planetary system of D'Yabelt, a fierce, quarrelsome breed with coarse mustard-colored hair and musk glands in their armpits. They were absolutely loyal to Yakov, simply because other Grithies would have nothing to do with them. He established them in barracks around the outer walls and left Abi in the care of four Grithies from his personal staff: three females and a gentle male who held Abi on his lap and sang ballads. These were trustworthy too, for the simple reason that they were not allowed off the grounds.

Each time affairs of state took him to earth, he stopped off at Enderby. At the age of two Abi was leaping off the fifth step of the pyramid and landing on his back with her arms around his neck. At three, she was strong enough to throttle him. She liked to sit in his lap and search his pockets for treats, but by the time she was four her searches had become flagrantly sexual, and he put an end to the game. She radiated emotion like a burning bush. His visits left him feeling wilted and querulous. He brought her mental puzzles devised by Stafi gamesmen, and at the age of five she was solving them in

seconds and throwing them aside. He brought the best instructors in
Antark to teach her the traditional sports of Landark children. They
began muttering to themselves when she broke adult records before the
age of six. Yakov sent them away and doubled the guards around the
estate.

He tried to guide her with a firm, gentle hand, but she managed
to subvert his rules while following them to the letter. Once he caught
her playing show-me-yours with a Grithy playmate. He told her she
could no longer play with the soldiers' children. So she frolicked with
Unguls, riding their shaggy shoulders, digging her fat strong fingers
into their hair. Yakov disapproved of the fraternization, but he knew
she had to burn off her energy.

One day he saw her out in the pasture with the bull calves,
trying to imitate the games she had watched in the breeding pens.
He ordered the pens torn down and removed to an area five miles
from the palace . . .

> At night she could hear the guard Unguls calling to each other
> in their hollow, muffled cadence. Sometimes they added their
> own individual frills, and she knew them by the sounds they
> made at night. When something unusual happened, like a calf
> straying, or some young bulls breaking through the barrier, their
> ululations would rise to a chorus. One night an Eshom raider
> swam across from the Fire Islands, and they could scent him prowl-
> ing the hills. The symphony grew into a taut angry threat, with
> overtones of fear. Another night they burst into an excited jabber
> of amazement. Abi ran out and saw a man standing on the wall,
> looking in her direction. She wanted to go to him, but the
> guards woke up, tracers slashed the night, and the man dis-
> appeared . . .

Yakov came down the next day. "Did you see what they were
shooting at?"

"A man, with black hair on his face."

At the age of seven she was nearly as tall as Yakov, with a long
triangular face of pale turquoise, and hair that flew like a blaze of fire
around her head. Her eyes were golden, with a depth that he could
not penetrate.

"Eshom?" he asked.

"No. It was only his face, not his body."

But there were no tracks, no traces. Yakov was leaving on a tour of
the north polar lands, so he took Abi with him. Baffin Island was
being cleared of jungle and replanted in crops which would support
the Ungul herds. Since the work was being performed by refugee
Grithies not yet accustomed to the stringent discipline of Antark, a

gigantic prison complex was established on what had once been the Greenland icecap, but was now called the Green Isles—actually a chain of mountainous islands surrounding a shallow sea. An evolved form of sargasso weed completely blanketed its southern part, infested by venomous reptiles and savage fauna, which made escape from the prison islands a gruesome form of suicide.

Most of the runaways fled to the southern shore of the Baffin Sea, where lived the Dubha untroubled by hunger, foul weather, and dangerous beasts. There, with the warden beside him and Abi trailing behind on the white sand beach, Yakov listened to a plan for stopping the escapes:

". . . Guard towers at intervals of forty miles along the beach, a series of overlapping Ungul patrols . . ."

"What about the Dubha?" asked Yakov. "They shelter the criminals."

"We'll post rewards for the return of fugitives," said the warden.

"Rewards of what? The Dubha don't use money. They live off the countryside . . ."

"First we'll have to burn off a ten-mile strip behind the beach, then we'll set up refugee camps . . ."

Yakov didn't notice until a half hour later that Abi had disappeared. They began searching, idly at first, for there were no dangerous animals in the area, then more desperately as night fell. Another day went by, and the search was extended southward. Here the fringe of palms gave way to scattered oases, interspersed with bunch-grass of spiky blades which could cut the feet like daggers. Beyond that was only the great talc desert and the huge roaring column of radiation called the Washing Fire.

Yakov returned to the moon with a gnawing sense of loss. He could not ignore the possibility that she'd been kidnaped by Ben Abo and Su-shann—though there was evidence that they'd gone underground on Megrez. Reports of popular unrest against the Jelks, murmurs of discontent against the old Hochfuehrer . . . He couldn't spare the men to quell a guerrilla war, particularly since Megrez lay in an outward bulge of the periphery, and would probably be the next target of the Vim . . .

A week later Abi was brought in by a group of treasure hunters, mostly landless Jelks who set up trading posts and traded tools for artifacts from the old culture. They said she had walked into their camp and commanded them to take her home. Not trusting himself to see her, Yakov had her returned to Enderby and then waited another week before going down.

"Why did you run away?"

"I saw the man with hair on his face."

"Come now. A world away from where you saw him last?"

"Yes. He said: '*In the desert lives the water-giver, who appears to thirsty lost ones, and water flows from his hands.*'"

"And that's why you went south?"

"Yes."

"Did you see the man again?"

"No."

"I don't believe you saw him the first time. You saw a shadow, and you built up a fantasy in your mind."

She gazed at him a moment, then said: "All right. I wanted to see the countryside before you ruined it with your bristling guns and your greedy frightened Grithies."

He felt his cheeks grow hot. "We need living space, Abi. The refugee fleet from Pell arrives on Juno five years from now. Did you know there's a great outcry for euthanasia? 'Never mind waking them up, they'll only create problems.' Is that your philosophy?"

"It's an alternative, anyway, to endless, mindless expansion at the expense of other races."

"Ah . . ." He got up, disgusted. "You don't understand the demands of statecraft."

"I understand them, Koffee. I understand quite well."

Yakov left the estate and did not return for three months. He was appalled to find that one whole square mile had been converted into a battlefield. The two Grithy regiments had formed opposing armies that were sniping at each other from behind earthworks. Twenty were dead and scores wounded. One of the commanders had been killed, the other was incoherent with battle lust. He was unable to say how the fight had started, just that the other side was trying to kill Abi-shann and he had sworn to lay down his life in her defense. Yakov was not surprised to find that the men of the opposing regiment had the same idea.

"And what," he asked Abi, "was your final intent?"

"Oh, eventually I would have arranged a truce between the two factions. Then we would march together on the neighboring estate, put the owner to death, and take his Unguls."

"The trouble is, Abi, you have the mind of a genius and the morality of an eight-year-old. This is not how the game is played."

"From my reading of history, this is exactly how the game is played, Koffee."

Yakov decided she was trying to trap him into an emotional involvement. He assigned one of his most trusted assistants, an aging factory manager who had once been his father's confidant, to take over the estate.

Two months later he received a delegation from the Landarks. Abi had been dabbling in Ungul futures, and had thrown the market into a tailspin. She had depressed prices to the point where she was able to buy two adjoining estates and was negotiating for a third. Yakov sent for the old manager and asked him: "How did she do it? How did she persuade you?"

"She didn't persuade me. She just told me when to buy and sell. And we did it, didn't we? We showed them!"

Another loyal servant rendered useless.

Yakov asked Abi why she wanted money, and she said she planned to buy her way into the Stafi Institute.

"Landesses don't go to Ganymede."

"Landesses don't do anything but warm their bottoms."

"There's charity . . . service to the poor . . ."

"A common sop to idealists with a tendency to meddle in government," said Abi. "Like pouring sand down a mine shaft."

"You might look into the League of Enderby," he said. He told her about the plight of the Pteroni—two hundred thousand half-starved birdmen starving on their mountain reservation, fighting off land-hungry Grithies, choking in smoke when the wind blew off the industrial plateau . . .

He could never get used to the speed at which she operated. Within two months she'd established a colony of five thousand Pteroni in the Napier Mountains adjoining the estate.

"What did you do about the web spinners?" he asked.

"We turned the wind," she said.

"How?"

"The Pteroni have a way. When they want to soar, they roll their tongues into a tube and expell all the body air in a blast which carries three to five miles. They call it 'whistling up the wind.' I had a crew of technicians amplify the effect. Now the hot winds blow the bugs out to sea. We're building stations around the estate, so we can control our climate."

With the hot winds diverted, the estate grew lush and green. She used her profit from the Ungul market to dig a canal from Amery Bay to the estate, and transplanted tropical fruit trees from the shores of Baffin Bay.

Noting signs of boredom, Yakov called Abi's attention to the dilemma of the Androxi: Trapped in McMurdo Sound by the mutated seals, unable to go out without guns, unable to build their culture because all the proceeds from their undersea gardening and fishing went into weapons to protect their lives . . .

Abi strung an electrified fence on floats across the head of Amery Bay. Then she faced the problem of moving the Androxi from one side of the continent to the other. They couldn't swim because of the boiling seas from the Tasman Burn on one side, and the Isles of Fire on the other. She leased a fleet of tank cars and transported fifteen hundred Androxi across the central plateau. Once they'd built their city and started cultivating their undersea gardens, however, they were still locked in by roving killer packs of mutated seals.

"If we had something they needed," she mused, "we could trade with them."

"Invent a religion which says it's a sin to kill Androxi."

"And then? Suppose the seals enjoy sin?"

They were sitting beside the pool, while two young Androxi females sported in the water. Abi had introduced them by name, but to Yakov it had sounded like she was trying to gargle with her mouth closed. In a ginkgo tree perched a young Pteroni male preening his wings.

"You're very cynical for a ten-year-old, Abi."

"The influence of your devious Burok mind, Koffee. Why don't you put it to work on the Androxi problem?"

"The root of most problems is lack of money."

"True. If the Androxi had money, they could buy guns. So?"

He considered it. "Artifacts from ancient earth are rare these days. The asteroids and the planets have been cleaned out. Most of earth's cities were destroyed in the bombing, covered by magma, or overgrown by jungle. But the coastal cities were buried under tidal waves when the planet wreckers hit. They stayed under water when the icecaps melted. Those artifacts would be almost intact."

"How do you know all this?"

"We have old tapes stored in the archives on the sixth level."

"Send me down some showing the location of those ancient cities, will you?"

Within a year Antark was swept by a craze for ancient earth artifacts. The Androxi built a bubble-dome in Amery Bay, where they sold directly to dealers, and Abi established a town on shore to supply food and drink to those who came to trade. The most popular item was an oblong vessel of white porcelain with an odd S-shaped channel in the bottom, said to have been used by the ancients as a baptismal font. The Jelks adopted them for their handwashing rituals.

When he saw Abi again she was laughing about it. "You know what that object is, Koffee? A toilet! The ancients sat on them and . . . brrrrrrp!" She made a wet flatulent sound with her lips.

"At least we know now they weren't gods," said Yakov.

"Oh, no. They were our direct ancestors—*and* the ancestors of the Eshom and the Diggers and the Dubha and the Grungee . . . all those strange creatures we regard as animals."

"How would *you* regard them? As human?"

"Ah, you racist imbeciles, with your talk of human and nonhuman, superiority and inferiority. Is a rock superior to a block of wood?"

"It depends on what you want to use it for."

"Exactly. If you need heat, you can't burn the rock, but you can the wood. But if you want to crack a nut, or hit somebody over the head, a stone is perhaps the superior instrument."

"Yes, but we happen to be Jelks—"

"But me none of your two-valued dichotomies. I find it more enlightening to converse with Unguls."

I wonder, thought Yakov, why I ever imagined that genius would be wedded to an even temper. But he knew the signs. She was getting restless again, and his brain was fatigued from thinking up new games to keep her occupied. It would be four years before she reached breeding age, and he had not yet found the male Eshom. Nothing had come of all the expeditions he'd sent in, all the rewards he'd offered. It began to look as though a visitation of armies with fire and sword were the only answer—and that was something he couldn't do without Abi's finding out.

Typical of genius, and of the bubbling ferment of Abi's mind, was the fact that she could not hold anger. When he visited her a week later her golden eyes shone with a new enthusiasm. "Koffee, I'm about to discover what the Vim used to destroy our planet."

"Where fifty generations of Jelk scientists have failed, eh?"

"Fifty generations of imbeciles. Come." She took him into her study, which she'd paneled with fragrant gumwood imported from the Green Isles. She switched on her holy-g and projected a globe of earth into the receiving chamber.

"The Vim dropped their planet wreckers in a spiral pattern around the earth. Each one created a firestorm a hundred miles in diameter, vaporizing the water and oxygen and peeling the soil down to bedrock for hundreds of miles around." Her pencil wand appeared on the holy-g image. "It begins here, in the Urals . . . Magnitogorsk, Augsburg, Dover, Richmond, Denver, Los Angeles, Honolulu, Tokyo, Peking . . . Notice how they correspond to the radiation zones, Washing Fire, and all these others. Except for Denver."

"What happened there?"

"It didn't go off."

"Maybe they didn't drop one."

"Oh, they dropped it. It's still there. Entombed to half its length in solid rock."

"How do you know?"

"The Pteromen . . . they can fly everywhere now, with little sonic projectors to screen them from the web spinners. They found an ancient account of the disaster in one of the high mountain caves, so we know that people survived and kept their culture alive for a time. I'm working on the translation now."

"Does it tell about the bomb?"

"No, but there's a legend among the tribes who live in that area, about a tribe of magicians who live in the caves. They worship a metal god who came down from the sky. I gather from descriptions that it's a huge bomb. Of course, the whole area is taboo, but that won't keep me from taking in a flier and a squad of stinkies . . ."

"No, Abi."

She looked at him, her brows lifted. "No, Koffee?"

"I don't want you playing with live bombs."

"What are you saving me for? An incubator for the ruling line of Ras?"

He felt an odd, sticky warmth spread through his stomach. *Close,* he thought.

"You asked me once about getting into the Stafi Institute." He cleared his throat. "There is a possibility, with the current interest in ancient earth, that if you collected some old accounts of the Vim attack . . ."

"Oh, I could!" She gave him a hard look. "But I don't want you muscling those poor old Stafis."

"I won't."

"Nor spreading rumors about a certain someone who enjoys the protection of the chief strategist."

"I'll do nothing to help or hinder."

"Good. Now go away. I have work to do."

9

The Last Days of Earth

"When the skies are drowned and the oceans hanged,
The single secret will still be man."

From an ancient tape

"I was in my basement lab when they dropped the planet wreckers.* There was a sudden physical shock, and the whole earth jerked from under my feet. Dust everywhere. Part of the wall caved in. A piece hit my head and I must have lain unconscious for days. Being covered by debris saved me from the burns that killed everybody else. I got to the surface and all the houses were gone. It wasn't dark, though the sky was absolutely black. There was a hellish blue glow everywhere, and it looked as though the eastern sky was ablaze with electricity. It took some time for my eyes to get used to the light, but when they did I could see that everything was charred. All the plants had turned brown on the edges, the debris was scorched, what there was of it. I went downtown because we were supposed to report to City Center in case of disaster. I found it by its spire, but it was only half there, and the part remaining was bent and twisted. The quakes had opened great cracks in the earth, and the lower part of the building had collapsed into the shelter. It smelled terrible, and there were animals all around. Rats and cats and other things we'd had in the zoo. The worst thing was that the outworld creatures had escaped, and for a lot of them it must have been like the hell-worlds they'd been taken from. A lot of them died the moment their artificial environments were shattered, but many survived—the energy-creatures and fish from the boiling seas—these multiplied and fought and won their niche in the New Earth . . .

"But this I learned later. I knew that I had to eat, and to fight

* From the journal of L. S. Drummond, translated by Abi-shann, Landess of Enderby.

the scavengers for the food which had been stored in the shelter. I was surprised, they were not all against me, as I expected. I was merely another organism competing for the available food supply. This helped me to put the nature of man in true perspective. When I began thinking of myself as merely another animal, I lost my fear of these creatures and became one of them, first among equals. For I knew how to open the cans and the doors to the food lockers. There were not so many of us alive, after all. I was apparently the only human to survive in this city of forty thousand, and the proportions were no greater among the other animals. There was a slight preponderance of the animals which normally live underground, such as rats and mice and snakes and so on. But I felt no fear of them, not even the poisonous snakes, and they felt no fear of me. I opened storerooms and shared out the food. Somehow it was self-limiting, the size of my group. Those who joined me first remained, and after a few weeks no new ones were brought in. As food supplies dwindled, these became more savage, and the law of the claw took effect. But in the first weeks the peaceable kingdom did prevail, and I suppose the lion did indeed lie down with the lamb, if any such survived on this shattered world . . .

"The mud came down, and the hot rain in torrents. Months of this. I also began to notice secondary effects of the bomb. Metal which would have taken fifty years to rust away underground turned to brown dust within a year. Buildings collapsed. Glass turned rotten, like dried paste, and finally crumbled apart. The mice were the first to reproduce, and their young were born dead, twisted and deformed. All the works of man would soon be gone. And even man himself . . .

"Yes, it was the end of everything. After two years the last mouse died of old age. The last of my companions was a dog, a yellow cur, but we loved one another. Life indeed calls to life. If my last companion had been a wasp, or a posionous reptile, or a microscopic hydra, I would have loved it with no less passion, for when you are alone, any life will do. It was five years after the dog died that I saw the first of the new animals. It could have once been a dog . . . but it was blue, and six feet tall at the shoulder. I saw it eating the strange growths that came up from the soil. I ate some and nearly died. Somewhere, I think, there are humans who had no access to the stored foods, and were forced to eat the new plants, and to change, and to survive. They will inherit the new earth, and not me. For he who does not change, does not adapt to new circumstances, will surely die. This is the iron law of nature."

* * *

"The iron law of nature!" Novii made a derisive sound with his lips. "Whom did you grease, Abi?"

Abi jerked her head up from her tape viewer. "What?"

"This paper you wrote, to get accepted into the Institute." Novii stretched his long legs out in Abi's hammock, his thin calves hanging over the edge. "You must have used your well-known influence with the Deek. I've seen better work by prepubes."

Abi got up and walked to where the hammock hooked to a bolt set in the rock wall of her cell. She flipped both edges inward, trapping the Stafi youth in a cocoon. Then she whirled it once like a slingshot and flipped it open. Novii flew into the corridor, somersaulted with lightning agility, and landed on his feet laughing.

"Beast-woman!" he shouted.

"If I ever get you on Antark—"

"Never! Hee-hee-ha-ha-ha!" Hooting like an ape, he hurtled down the tunnel, touching surface only to increase his forward thrust. Abi loped in pursuit, though she didn't expect to catch him. Novii had grown up on Ganymede, scion of a long dynasty of administrators. He had no terror of stone walls, whereas Abi still expected each leap to end in a jolting smash of broken bones and blood . . .

Heads popped out of the other dormitory cells as Abi passed. Some smiled, others looked annoyed and turned back to their studies. When she rounded a curve in the tunnel Novii had disappeared.

"Up here, Abi."

She tipped her head back and saw the hole thirty feet up, centered in the high arching roof of the tunnel. Novii was looking down at her between his legs.

She bent her knees, gathered all her strength, and leaped. Her shoulders brushed the side of the hole as she shot through. For an instant she hung weightless, then she started to fall. She shot out her hand and grabbed his, felt him pull her up. "You are heavy," he grunted. "Put your feet on my insteps. I've got my toes stuck in these little niches."

The shaft was barely wide enough to contain them both. Each wore body-tight plastic coveralls designed to minimize sexual differences, but where Novii was slender of build and hairless, Abi had begun to protrude in areas uncharacteristic of Jelk females. She was acutely conscious of her breasts pressing against his chest.

"Actually I liked your paper," said Novii. "I was just trying to pull you away from your tape viewer."

"I don't mind tricks if they're clever. And the result is good." She looked up and saw the shaft disappear into darkness like a rifle bore. "Where does it go?"

"The surface. It's an escape shaft. The oldies expected the Vim to invade the main corridors at any moment. The last person up was supposed to block it with his body."

They stood for a moment breathing each other's exhalation. Abi said: "I haven't been out of the study area for . . . How long have I been here?"

"Two years since you arrived with an escort of three battleships."

"They weren't mine."

"Your stepfather's . . ."

"Yakov Ras is not my stepfather. He imagines himself my guardian."

"No effective distinction." He smiled. "Shall we go back down?"

"I'd rather go up."

"Good!" He shot up the shaft as if expelled by a blast of air. Abi climbed slowly, searching out the little niches with her toes. When she reached the top he was standing in a tiny domed airlock dressed in a spacesuit. He helped her into a suit, then spun the wheel of the airlock and opened the port. Abi stepped out onto the surface and gasped.

Jupiter hung over half the sky, larger than doom itself. Giant bands of mother-of-pearl ringed the great globe. The red spot was a candied apple sunk deep in the glowing depths. Words . . . even thought became inadequate. She stood staring upward, her body filled with tingling ecstasy. She felt as though her heart were being torn from her body and pulled into that awesome bulk. She lay down on her back and spread her arms and legs wide. She felt herself tipping, turning in space, stuck to the surface of Ganymede like a fly to the ceiling, looking down upon the clouds of a giant world.

After a long time Novii said: "Some people get scared. Others defend themselves by scientific analysis."

Abi felt quiet, peaceful, untroubled. She said nothing. After a minute Novii spoke again:

"All those brilliant people down there in the institute, dividing, classifying the ancient knowledge. They're suffocating, like fish that get encased in dried mud."

"I've been doing that," said Abi. "I wonder why."

"You've been busy getting your head packed with lies. Did you ever hear of the transformed ones—Stafis who go down to the surface of Jupiter?"

"I thought it was impossible. The gravity, and the pressure . . ."

"You see? Lies. Come."

They loped across the gray rock-strewn land . . . Jupiter's eerie light seemed to have no color at all, but was so diffused and indirect that it appeared to radiate from the rocks beneath her feet. Each time she leaped into the air, she felt she was falling away from the surface of Ganymede, diving head first toward that great curving mass, but always gravity caught her and pulled her back.

They came to a tall derrick of metal girders set into the rock, pointing like an arrowhead toward the heart of Jupiter. She saw a tube of some woven straw-colored material going up its interior. At the base was a chamber like the bulb at the bottom of a thermometer. The entrance was not an airlock, but rather a series of overlapping metal fabrics which Novii peeled back one at a time. After they passed through, the screens rolled back and stuck together.

They opened their face plates, and Abi saw that the vertical cylinder came down into the center of the chamber. Seated before it was a skeletal man, with his legs folded back into his lap. His eyes were rolled back, and she could just see the thin crescent of his iris peeking out beneath his eyelid.

"He guards the entrance," said Novii. "He's in mental communication with novices who man the portal, down in the upper atmosphere of Jupiter."

"How long does he sit like this?"

"He has to spend ten years as an initiate, caring for the station and reducing food and air intake until he breathes only once every five minutes. Then he goes down to the atmosphere. As a novice he will care for the portal and maintain the bodies of the adepts. When his food and air intake is zero, he becomes an adept. Takes about fifty years."

"Is there another step?"

"Oh, yes. An adept sits in a single position for something like one hundred years, during which he rebuilds his body cell by cell, using mental power to draw materials from the atmosphere. Then he just steps out and descends to the surface. Someday I will be an initiate."

"When?"

"When I tire of playing games with this." He waggled his long arms and gave a short hop.

Abi examined the central tube. It appeared to be a mesh of loose-woven fibers, but it had absolutely no resilience. It felt as massive as a column of granite. "What is it?"

"A beam. A grid. An energy channel . . . I'm not sure. The first of the Transformed Ones—the Immortal DiFong—projected his astral body to the surface by the sheer force of his will. For over a hundred years his body remained seated, then one day he came back and built this, to transport his body down. Since then three hundred Stafis have jumped. Many have died, but none have returned."

"Pity DiFong didn't say what it was like down there."

"He did. There."

He pointed to a tiny glowing square on the wall. As she stepped in front of it, the square swelled out and filled her vision.

> There is life here, but no human mind can perceive it. I am an infant among their children. Someday I will become an adoles-

cent, then an adult. When I am mature, I shall be admitted to their society. Perhaps in a thousand years, or two. Here it is only a day. To the Jovians the coming of the earthmen was an event of cight o'clock in the morning. The Vim attacked at ten o'clock . . . a thunderbolt in the midst of a summer shower. Let those who love life stay behind. There is no returning.

The words sent a pulse through her body. She'd never really dedicated herself to anything. All the projects on earth had been time fillers. Even the institute, despite the fascination of combing through the old knowledge, had been a dull, dry disappointment.

"Novii, I want to go down."

"You're insane."

She knelt before the seated figure. "Can I be an initiate?"

Slowly the eyes drew into focus. They seemed to penetrate her brain like electric needles, piercing the multilayers of thought and pricking the core of her ego. The mouth opened and words rolled out in a rattling croak:

"Your . . . lotus . . . is . . . not . . . yet . . . open . . ."

The eyes rolled back. She sensed that further questions would be like trying to squeeze juice from a stone. She straightened and turned to Novii.

"What did he mean?"

"You're still a virgin, aren't you?"

"Yes."

"Well, that's it."

"They don't take virgins?"

"It's a matter of karma. Myself, I'd like to go out and explore the stars. Until I satisfy that desire, or get rid of it, I can't become an initiate because my desire would pull me back into the time stream. You can't because"—he shrugged—"maybe you want to have a baby, I don't know. A lot of girls do it."

"I've never given it a thought."

"You haven't?"

"Not since I came here."

"Maybe they put something in your food." Smiling, he closed his face plate and began peeling away the screens which covered the port.

Abi was thoughtful as she traversed the barren terrain back to the airlock bubble. As she stripped off her spacesuit, she said: "You know, they put me on a special diet here. I thought it was because I was used to earth foods and couldn't handle your concentrates. But then there's the fact that I sleep a lot . . . twice as much as I did on earth. And something else. You're the only boy I know to talk to . . . the only friend I've made in two years. Now that isn't like me. On earth I had dozens of friends. And I was always curious, always exploring . . ."

"There's something you left out."

"What?"

"There's a spy eye in your cell."

She gasped. "How do you know?"

"I know every cavity on this satellite. There's a monitor on duty —most of the time."

"But . . . why?"

"Remember that student refugee from Pell? He started visiting you in your cell, and he got sent down to Antark."

Rage came on her slowly, like a volcano rumbling its way to the surface. "You mean . . . that for the last two years I've been in some kind of . . . solitary *confinement*?"

"They used to call it *purdah*. For women only."

Her nails bit into her palms. "When I see Yakov I'll kill him."

"You think he's the one?"

"Who else could send in a squad of Grithies?"

"I mean . . . the one you're reserved for. The one who wants to mate with you."

"Don't be nauseating." She looked out upon the bleak ridges. Her mind had a crystalline clarity, which confirmed her suspicion that she'd spent the last two years in a drugged stupor.

"Novii, I've got to escape. You know where there's a ship?"

"There's only one equipped for space flight. My father's."

"Can you fly it?"

She stared at him a second, then burst into laughter. "You know what you're doing? You're asking me to do a Ben Abo!"

"What's that?"

"Your father—your real father—made his escape in a ship belonging to my grandfather. Won't *that* be a historical repeat!"

"You mean you will?"

"Why not? But you'd better not go back to your cell. Let's see"— he pulled his long nose thoughtfully—"you wait here. I'll slip down to the administrative offices and get the converter cartridge. They keep it locked up, and the ship won't run without it. Then we'll just walk over there to the edge of the cliff, climb down into the main port, and lift the ship off its cradle."

It happened that way—almost. One of the clamps holding the ship to its cradle jammed, and Abi had to suit up, go outside, and crank it open manually. Then Novii discovered there were no extra fuel cylinders, and he had to break into the storeroom to get some more. After they'd lifted off, he remarked that it wouldn't have gone even that smoothly if he hadn't been planning his own escape for several years.

Abi noticed they were headed away from the sun, away from the whirling globe of Jupiter.

"Novii, are you going *outsystem?*"

"Right. To Megrez."

"But that's . . . thirty light years! You don't have a star drive."

"We'll hijack a liner—like your father used to do."

"You're insane." She settled back and gazed out into the glittering night. "Why do you want to go to Megrez? Does it have anything to do with my . . . with Ben Abo?"

"Right."

"But he's dead. He was killed in a fight with the Guardian Fleet."

"Did you see his body?"

"Of course not. I wasn't even born."

"What about your mother?"

"She was a Prog. A member of the War Council. She wanted to live on earth, so she gave up her seat and became a Landess."

"She told you this?"

"No. She died soon after I was born . . . disappeared while exploring the estate. Her body was never found."

He swiveled in his control seat and brought his face close to hers. "You . . . are . . . naïve, Abi."

"Damn your Stafi superiority. If you know something, say it!"

"Rumors, that's all . . . from students who come from that neck of the empire. There's a revolution on Megrez. Ben Abo's trying to take the game away from the old Fuehrer. It's traditional there. The son has to kill the father to prove his right to rule. The old man has the Guardian Fleet on his side, but they're spread pretty thin. They say Ben Abo's strategy is being planned by a Jelk woman. Sounds like it might be your mother. That's all I know."

I should be excited about this, thought Abi. But I'm just apprehensive. Ben Abo is a much greater hero to Novii than to me. His exploits seem . . . theatrical. But that's probably the influence of Koffee's nitpicking Burok mind. Mother . . . well, it's sad that she had to leave the home she loved, but it's better than being dead. Anyway, they're both strangers. As for Megrez . . . it happens to be in the path of the Vim conquest, which hardly recommends it. I guess my heart is on earth. I miss the moaning of the wind towers at Enderby, the glorious sunsets over the Isles of Fire. Besides, if I run that far, I'll never get revenge on Koffee . . .

All speculation became moot when a flare burst ahead, lighting up the cabin like a lightning flash. The screen showed two ships the size of battle cruisers, one on each side. Two more closed in from above and below.

Novii hit the braking rockets with a curse. "They must have been lying out behind Callisto. No use to fight them, unless"—his eyes slid over to hers—"you want to try a breakout?"

"We'd just get killed."

"They might kill us anyway."

"I don't think so. We're both members of the ruling class."

Their eyes caught, and suddenly the whole affair seemed like a glorious exercise in absurdity. They were laughing and hugging each other in the cabin when the guardian ships locked onto their hull.

*   *   *

At Enderby, the gentle Ankla servants were replaced by a cold-eyed breed of Grithies just down from the Green Isle prisons. It looked as if an entire D'Yabelt division were encamped outside the walls, all carrying guns. It left no doubt in her mind that she was a prisoner, but Yakov did not come, and she could only guess at the reason.

She got herself a Sensi, hoping to learn the art of love from the experts on Eros. She found them superficial, but maddeningly sensual, and she knew that if she ever gave herself up to Sen-sex, she would lose her capacity to enjoy flesh contact. Her only link with the outside world was an old Pteroni named Untas. He was a *sussarni*—among his people, a storyteller, much revered. He taught her the whistling language which they used in flight—a twelve-note scale whose sharps and flats gave a total of thirty-six meaning signs. The length of time each note was held gave the emotional context. Anger was short, sadness was a long drawn-out note.

She could always hear him coming from several miles away, singing a ballad of love, bravery, or grief. She would prepare his tikula, and he would flutter in and perch on the rim of her fountain. They conversed in the intimate language, used among friends, nestlings, lovers, or covey comrades—a purring melodious sound made by expelling air through the trachea and vibrating the uvula. Since the Pteroni lacked vocal chords, they also used this method to speak Jelk, but Abi preferred the birdmen's tongue because the servants could not understand it.

From Untas she learned of the secret Eshom war which had raged for two years. They were watching a film travelogue supposedly taken on the Fire Islands, showing an Eshom female feasting on the body of a male, her arms bloodied to the elbow and the fangs stained with blood. The announcer's voice boomed: *"The Humanity-One Party says the Eshom are our brothers! Would you want your son to bring this one home as a bride?"*

Untas flapped his leathery wings impatiently. "Actually it's a beautiful ritual. I see it often when I visit the Eshom. The males die happily, in the belief that they'll be reborn in the bodies of their offspring. It is too bad the Eshom are being destroyed. But it is their own fault, for learning to think."

"You mean they didn't use to think?"

"Not as we know it. They perceived directly."

"Like animals?"

"More than that, I believe. Each moment to them is different— or you might say each moment is the same. Nothing is like anything else. It is absolutely unique in space and time."

"But I've flown over the temples on the Isles of Fire. That seems to be evidence of thought."

"They were built by the Grungee. Who are controlled by the Coneys. Who in turn are controlled by—"

"By the Eshom."

"By the high priestesses. The distinction is vital. The average Eshom male is pragmatic as an insect. Love, honor, duty—he knows nothing of these things, absolutely the opposite of the Dubha, for example, who are known to die of chagrin because of a personal insult. But for the Eshom each 'thing' is its own individual self. No collectives. They do not hate in groups, which is the reason they were unable to unite against the Jelks. They simply met them individually, and were killed. They do not know how to hate . . . unless their reaction to the Grissig, whose trap is inactive, inorganic, invisible, in fact ungnarshable, is a threat, and they kill them when they can."

"Then I don't see how they have high priestesses. If they are different each time . . ."

"But that's it. The priestesses are *Yival*—that is, always in the same place-time-form. They have a linear dimension in time, they know past and future, which to the common Eshom is completely magical. They are able to plan, and so they are more than priestesses. They are goddesses."

"So what has changed now, that they should be destroyed?"

"They have a new leader. They call him Xoh'ne, the bubble god. He is male, and half Ungul, but he has the female power to kill the Grissig beast. They say he was eaten by a Grissig when young, and killed it from within."

"What does this god do to the Jelks?"

"He has shown the Eshom how to use their gnarshing in battle. Individually the Eshom have always been invincible. But massed formations defeated them; they merely, as individuals, got out of the way. You would have to see them in battle now to appreciate the infinite unity of the scene, but as though a pool of water became sentient, each atom able to act independently, but unified . . ."

"Yes, but what are they doing?"

"Laying waste the entire width and breadth of Queen Maud's Land. They paralyze the Grithy guards with poison from the Grissig beast. They drive the Ungul herds off and train them to fight their former owners. These have no fear of death; they are known to continue fighting with their teeth after both arms have been burned off."

Two days later she watched Yakov land his flier and start up the steps. She called down from the top:

"Koffee, I'm sick of being treated as a child. I want to know what it's all about!"

He stopped and looked up. His face was taut and haggard. "How much do you already know?"

"I know you've got me down as a breeding animal. All right. 'If 'twere done, 'twere better done quickly.' I got that off the ancient tapes."

"I'm afraid you'll get your wish, Abi."

He resumed climbing, and she tried to sound more confident than she felt. "I don't intend to be limited to one, anyway. I plan to have a dozen, each by a different male. This tradition of one woman, one child—it's stupid. Nature designed it so that the strongest individuals should produce the most offspring . . ."

He paused beside her, breathing heavily. "Abi . . . it isn't what . . . you think it is."

"Then I want to know what it is!"

"You're part of a highly secret government experiment." He hefted a small satchel in his hand. "Let's go inside."

It was half a minute before she found the strength to follow him. "You know, that's the one thing I never suspected. Never! I grew up thinking I'm a normal person—*trying* to think of it, anyway, and now one month after my fourteenth birthday, you—" She ran in front of him and blocked his path. "Well, how did it turn out? Am I all right?"

He spoke in a flat, heavy tone: "It isn't finished, Abi."

"Isn't—! Oh this is too much. You mean . . . and that's why all the boys— Oh, you *filth!* You *pig!*" She swung her hand against his face. She heard the sharp spat! and saw the mark of her hand on his cheek, and she had a sudden urge to put her arms around him and climb into his lap . . .

But she managed to rekindle her rage. It was not *his* body being violated . . . not *he* whose very existence was an insult to human dignity. She looked out into the distance and asked coldly:

"What's his name?"

"He . . . it doesn't have a name, that I know of."

"It? What is it, an Ungul?"

"Only half. The other half is Eshom."

She saw in his face that he was telling the truth. Her mind whirled, and she turned away and walked to the wall which overhung the courtyard. In a pen below several laboring Unguls were taking their noonday rest, moving their massive jaws from side to side as they chewed their grain. Out in the center a scarred old bull was mounting a heifer, tearing at her udders, bawling and slobbering while his horny feet kicked up clouds of dust.

She walked back to Yakov. "I want to see him . . . *it.*"

"Why?"

"Because I might decide to commit suicide instead. You can't force me into this, Koffee."

"I can, Abi. I'd rather not."

"You can't! I'll bite through my wrists—"

"If necessary you will be put to sleep, injected, and taken through the entire operation under a Sensi hookup. Your body will be controlled by someone else. So let's not talk of can or can't."

She stared into his face. "Koffee, have you gone insane with power? What could be so important?"

"The survival of the race." He tapped the little satchel. "I have the proof here. If you'd like to hear it. Let's go into your study."

It seemed unreal, almost mystical, to hear the record of that longago council meeting, with its coughs, burps, and wheezes, and to realize they were talking about the creation of . . . herself. *"The strategist Su-shann then asked: Does this imply that the genetic traits are available but have not yet been combined in the manner required?"* And her mother's cool confident voice: *"We do not have genetic tapes on all the parahuman races, such as the Androxi and the Pteroni. But yes, those we have will be used. Including Unguls."* And later the mellow tone of the computer: *"You understand that this will count as the single child permitted to you by law?"* And her mother's calm reply: *"I assumed it."*

After it was over she sat for several minutes without speaking. Then she turned to Yakov. "She really got me into something, eh, Koffee?"

"She really did, Abi." He cleared his throat. "I had hoped to wait until you were sixteen. But the Vim are pressing hard. Megrez is now being evacuated by the fleet. And the Eshom are much worse than I expected. We have not been able to bomb, or to dust the Eshom stronghold, for fear of injuring the young male."

"You mean . . . Xoh'ne, the bubble god?"

"How did you learn his name?"

"From the Pteroni. It is Xoh'ne. How will you get him out?"

"We've done it already. Dusted the entire area with sleep gas, and lifted him out like a harpooned seal."

"You didn't hurt him!"

"Of course not. His health is as important to me as to you."

"Where is he?"

"We have him in a bubble orbiting the earth. He is . . . dangerous; unbelievably ferocious. Remember, he was reared as a god, and has devoted his adult life to killing Jelks. This was the only way we could bring you together without risking your life."

"Does he know about me?"

"I can't say. He does not communicate."

Bride and Groom

Q: What has two legs, two arms and flies?
A: A dead Eshom.

Popular joke of the Eshom war period

He sat with his ankles crossed, the hard soles of his feet turned out. Abi could not see the division of his toes, but the glitter of five obsidian claws was all too apparent. The thick short spur on his ankle looked as if it could disembowel her. A nap of velvet fur lay so close to his skin that it merely smoothed out the corded muscles of his body. A silver fringe hung from his forearms, which were folded across his broad chest. His hands were not clenched, but they looked like fighting weapons, combining the knobbed knuckles of the Unguls and the curving dagger claws of the Eshom. These were retracted now, but she could see the black needle points resting inside pads of flesh.

She continued looking at Xoh'ne through the wall of plastic, but tuned her ears to the voice of the geneticist who was explaining the structure of the space bubble to Yakov Ras.

"It's actually five concentric spheres, each one enclosing a smaller one. All are implanted with copper gridwork charged with electric current, and each sphere revolves in a different direction."

Strange . . . to think they'd put years of research into building this station, all for one *Yaga*. The blunt Grithy word for sex awoke a tremulous excitement in her loins.

"What is the purpose of the spinning motion?" asked Yakov.

"To disorient the prisoner. According to rumor he's capable of teleporting himself, but he can't do it without a directional fix."

It occurred to Abi that any creature who could teleport would not allow himself to be taken by sleep dust. But she said nothing.

The geneticist was a stooped, wizened Jelk who had spent nearly a century in the gene-warping labs and seemed stained by the loathsome evil of his profession. The fact that he'd been chosen for his expendability—and would probably not long survive the experiment—failed to arouse Abi's sympathy. It only made the whole situation more monstrous.

The geneticist continued his lecture in oily sycophantic tones:

"The outer sphere comprises the landing and supply sections. Inside the second sphere are offices, kitchens, sleeping quarters for the Grithies who maintain the bubble. The third sphere, in which we are presently standing, contains my quarters and the controls for the entire complex. Between us and the inner bubble is a vacuum which will instantly fill with deadly gas if the inner sphere should be broken open."

And if I happen to be inside it—too bad. She sensed that the two men were talking merely to avoid silence. *They're waiting for me to say I'm ready—so much easier than strapping me spreadeagled to a tree trunk.*

Forcing a lightness she didn't feel, she said:

"Let's begin, shall we?"

The geneticist cleared his throat. "With your permission, excellency . . . I should point out that although Xoh'ne is a prince among his people, the general rule is that sexual custom supersedes temporal authority. Is that . . . uh, clear, Landess?"

"You are saying that even a queen lies on the bottom occasionally?"

The old man coughed and ducked his head. "Uh . . . exactly. But the Eshom being female-dominant, the sex roles are reversed. Our field observations indicate that the female arouses the male by dactylographic means . . . that is, by touching him in certain ways. He remains passive until the female's skin flaps retract. At this point—"

Abi interrupted. "Does the female Eshom receive instructions before mating?"

"No. They function by instinct."

"Then I'll do the same. Will you make the bubble opaque?"

"But then we can't monitor!"

"Why should you?"

"Your safety, Landess . . ."

"Once I am inside, you can neither help nor hinder. I have no desire to provide entertainment for you and several dozen so-called scientists and technicians. Opaque the bubble or I refuse to enter."

The geneticist looked at Yakov, who nodded. He mumbled into his collar mike, and the inner sphere clouded into a milky whiteness. He turned to Abi and said: "There is a barrier down the center. As soon as you are inside, it will be withdrawn."

She stepped inside. A thin line divided itself in two and faded back into the walls. She stood looking at Xoh'ne's broad back, the spreading wedge of his deltoids, the powerful bulge of shoulder and bicep. She caught the sense of his body: alive, yet unmoving, absolutely poised, yet totally rigid. She knew he'd been born only a few months before her, yet he seemed ageless. A clot of darkness which radiated nothing. She recalled that the Eshom manner of hunting was to sit motionless and summon their prey by mental power. *Am I to be eaten?*

Still she felt no fear as she walked up and pressed her finger against his shoulder. The pelt had a dry slickness, like moth wings. Soft, yet impervious. Resilient, but hard. Kneeling, she pressed her palms to his back and felt the warmth of his body. She moved her hands and felt his skin slide loosely on the flesh. A tingling warmth filled her hands and raced up her arms. It exploded in her chest and filled her breasts until they seemed ready to burst with pleasure. She shuddered and threw back her head to laugh . . .

The milky dome brought her back to sanity. *I am here. In this awful place.*

She lowered her eyes and saw that he had turned his whole body, so swiftly and silently that she had not been aware of movement. Now he sat facing her. In the unbroken blackness of the face appeared two round glowing orbs. She could read nothing there and for a second it terrified her. *He is alien. Graceful and beautiful, but alien still* . . .

What you want?

The words boomed in her inner ear, clean and echoless. But no sound had struck her eardrum.

"You speak Ungul. How?"

Not speaking. Make feeling.

Concentrating, she could feel the ripple of fluid which carried sound waves from the eardrum to the nerve sensors. He was producing the effect of sound by contracting her muscles. She tried to follow the intricate steps of the operation, the countless transfers from mental to physical, multilevels of meaning translated into nerve impulse, and her mind gave up under its weight. It was like looking up at a mountain she could never hope to climb.

A new message exploded in her head: *Think-forms. You. What you want?*

She understood that she was being asked to form a mental image. But then something like little cat feet began padding about on her naked brain, and all she could think of were two Unguls mating face to face.

Something like laughter reached her, and a warmness. Then came a series of flashing erotic images, all ludicrous, involving herself and some android, weirdly inhuman travesty of a male with grotesque robotic movements.

She understood that too. She was being asked why she did not mate with a male of her own kind.

How to convey that they were too weak, too stupid? She formed a picture of a Coney, the hairless white monkey which rode the backs of the Grungee. Then a contemptuous picture of a great woolly Ungul drooling at the mouth . . .

She felt that he understood, though there was no evidence of it. His hand came out and tugged gently at her tunic. He was getting to the meat of the matter. She had to get undressed.

She lifted herself and peeled off her loose trousers. She felt awkward wearing only her short tunic, so she removed that too. She could feel him examining her body with . . . whatever sense he used. But he made no move. She wondered if he found her lack of body hair revolting. She had only the little patch at the crotch and these annoying tufts in her armpits . . .

Then she remembered: The female initiates. What must I do?

Insistent images pushed against her mind: a white hourglass shape which obviously stood for herself, and a square black figure representing Xoh'ne. They were in the jungle. She smelled the perfumed air and felt the soft cushion of vegetation under her feet. He pulled down bunches of tree moss and made a bed of them to lie on.

Then the picture changed. It showed the bubble wheeling, spinning. The black figure put his hands to his head and rocked it from side to side.

"I know," she said aloud. "I would rather be at home too. But I am not in control."

He sat motionless for another minute. Abruptly he moved forward until their bodies were only a foot apart. She felt her legs lifted, pressed down upon his thighs. She had always imagined herself without false modesty—but she could not bring herself to look down and examine his male organ. Instead she looked into his face, which was only a foot from hers. He lifted his inner eyelids, and it was like looking upon the whirling disc of the sun. She felt her mind scooped out, overturned, exposed and trembling like a poached egg on a plate.

Within her body was awareness of alien flesh, probing, searching without regard for her modesty. It touched something so tender that she arched her back and cried out in pain. Then there was a white flash, as though two charged wires had touched, fusing together in a blaze of energy. Blindness came like a hand clamped over her eyes. She would have screamed in panic except . . .

She had no voice.

She could not hear.

She could not see . . .

She had become . . . Xoh'ne.

She understood his world. The jungle was a living mind, a dark organic mirror which reflected what the viewer most feared. For Jelks, a steamy hell. For Xoh'ne, a perfumed paradise. The jungle was his mother and father, it fed him when he was hungry and covered him when he slept and would receive his body when he died.

But the big-eyes had come with fire and death, so the jungle had created Xoh'ne to protect itself. It had ordained his mating with the hairless blue-skinned female who is also a captive of the big-eyes.

That's me! thought Abi. Am I a captive?

I gnarsh that you also serve a higher power. You call it the computer but it is a living mind like the jungle. It also seems to sit doing nothing but always it moves in the form of creatures like yourself . . .

His thoughts hammered at her brain until she felt her mind collapsing. Stop! You are . . . too strong for me . . .

The pressure softened. Better?

Yes, but I would like to see, please . . .

Suddenly she was facing him across two feet of space. His yellow eyes were no longer a blaze of light, but shielded now by the second eyelid, so that they emanated a warm golden glow. Realizing they were still connected sexually she drew away and tried to get her senses back in order. She was aware of her body as something alien, a property she owned rather than a part of her being. She could feel the flesh lying on the bones and the bones strung together with ligaments and all the oils and secretions and hormones that kept his wonderful machine running . . .

Is that your perception, Xoh'ne?

Ours, yes.

I hear you much more clearly now. Before, it was all flat. Now there is something inside me that resonates.

I am inside you.

But I see you outside.

It is nothing but an empty form. In our tradition, the female eats the male as soon as he gives up his seed.

Her stomach wrenched in revulsion. She gasped and said aloud, "I won't do that!"

Have I placed my seed in you only to have it die for lack of nourishment?

She sensed a lilt of irony in his thought. *You are joking about the eating?*

It is a false legend, designed by the females to limit the power of the males, by not allowing them families. This is something no female will ever reveal to a male, of whatever race. But I know it is false, because my father was an Ungul and did not permit himself to be eaten.

He is alive, then?

He was killed by Grissig poison a week before I was born. His life thread could not be lengthened. Neither can mine.

You expect to die soon?

I gnarsh that they will kill me as soon as you leave.

I will help you escape.

If you can shut off the mental shield, I can do the rest.

Does it bother you?

Yes, when I try to extend my mind. Touch, and you will know how it feels.

She bent forward and touched her forehead to his. A chaos of whirling lights pressed in upon her mind. Jolts of current ripped her brain like fire. She cringed, twisted, jerked back gasping . . .

Her teeth grated with the pain. *If the current were cut off, you could escape?*

No matter what we do the thread will run out. But I want to give my body back to the jungle.

She was about to ask another question when he said: *No time now. Those outside grow uneasy.*

The milky opaqueness of the globe disappeared. She saw Yakov Ras and the geneticist peering through the clear plastic. The gleam in the old man's eyes reminded her that she was naked. She snatched up her trousers and pulled them on, then stood up and pulled on her tunic. Xoh'ne had turned his back and folded his arms.

She stepped back and saw the shield rise into place between them. *Goodbye, Xoh'ne.*

We will graze together in the star-meadow. The Unguls say it when one is taken to the slaughterhouse. His chuckle caught her by surprise. *Goodbye, Abi.*

What a strange dark sense of humor, she thought. She walked out through the opening and straight to Yakov Ras. She was slightly taller than he, so she had to look down to meet his eyes.

"The spheres hurt his head. Release him, so that we can carry out the mission on earth."

Yakov blinked. "But I understood that—" He glanced at the geneticist, then at Abi. "You mean nothing happened?"

She stared at the geneticist, noted his crooked smile, and realized that, despite the bubble's opacity, he had somehow observed what took place inside. Her quiet fury gave her words a clipped edge: "It isn't finished. It won't be until you set us down on earth."

"Abi, there are tests we can perform—"

"Now listen, Yakov Ras." She seized his collar. "I've had enough government manipulation of my body. There will be no tests, no dirty scientists poking their instruments into me. You understand? I am a Landess, don't forget that. I have rights."

Yakov closed his hand over her wrist and gently pulled her off to one side. "Abi, you must understand that your safety depends on your silence. If word leaked out that our project had caused the Eshom war—and the rising of the Unguls—the people would demand that you be sterilized. They might even stone you to death. They are half mad with fear."

"*You* created that fear."

"I did not create the Vim. The Unguls. The Grithies. The Eshom. Do you realize we Jelks are outnumbered a million to one?"

"I am not a Jelk, and neither are you."

His face went stiff as dried plaster. "Abi, I intend to carry out the aim of the computer .despite your desires. We must make laboratory tests on you before we . . . release Xoh'ne."

"You intend to kill him, don't you?" He would not meet her eyes, so she reached out and grabbed his chin. "If you do that, there will be no child."

"Abi, don't force me to anesthetize you—"

"It has nothing to do with my wishes. The insemination is not complete. Ask the old man."

Yakov strode to the geneticist and spoke inaudibly. The old man scratched his scalp, then called to an assistant. The Grithy produced a thick notebook and after a quick shuffling of the pages, held it open in front of the old man, who read aloud:

". . . The Eshom female couples as many times as she wishes without conceiving. The purpose in most cases does not seem to be fertilization, but rather a conveying of some vital life force from the male to the female, which invigorates her and permits her to generate the power to detect the Grissig. Thus it is necessary for the males, in order that they may eat and live, to feed her this life force through intercourse. On occasions when the female does conceive, which is about once every four months, she then eats the male and provides nourishment for her child."

"*Eats* him!" Yakov stared at Abi. "Did you know about this?"

"Certainly I knew about it."

"But . . . you were willing to be released with him . . ."

"He would have offered no resistance."

"You really intended to eat him?"

She lifted her chin and spoke in a solemn voice: "For the good of humanity, Yakov Ras, I would have done it."

Yakov tugged at his chin. "I can't believe it isn't just a superstition." He turned to the geneticist. "What if it isn't done?"

"Field workers have documented cases where the child is born dead, or an imbecile. But there can be no certain proof until we are able to observe the entire gestation period. This has been impossible because the Eshom refuse to copulate in public—I mean in captivity."

"But there is nothing that says he must be eaten in the jungle, is there? Why not here?"

Abi gasped: "No!"

The geneticist nodded his head. "There is no reason why it couldn't be done here."

"In that case, let's go into the control chamber. I'm anxious to get this off my hands."

The control chamber was a twenty-foot segment of the third sphere, with dials, gauges, levers, and switches set into a long curved console. A green-coated Grithy tech stood at each end, and a white-smocked Jelk occupied a stool in the center. Abi surveyed the situation with a feeling of dismay. Yakov and the old man made it five against one. But . . . possibly their numerical advantage would work in her favor, since the Grithies were conditioned never to touch a Jelk without permission.

"Yakov, how are you going to do it?"

"The gas, I think. It must be inhaled, so it won't be retained in his body."

She watched him move down the aisle and stretch out his hand toward a red lever set apart from the rest of the controls. She ran forward and seized his wrist: "Koffee, I have to do it myself."

"Come now, that's completely mystical—"

Still holding his wrist, she threw her weight backward and swung him around, throwing him away from the console. With a gape-mouthed expression of shock, Yakov staggered against the old geneticist. Abi seized the nearest Grithy by the seat of the pants and heaved him up, onto the control board. Glass shattered, electricity flashed. The tech shrieked and began thrashing his arms and legs. More dials shattered. Smoke boiled up from the console. She could hear alarms ringing and Yakov shouting: "The net! The net! Throw the net on her, you fools!"

The white-smocked Jelk approached her with a metallic net held between his hands. Abi leaped onto the control board and swung her foot, hitting him in the jaw. She felt the soft bones crack, saw him stagger against the wall and sink down to the floor. She strode down the control board, kicking every switch and lever she saw, grinding the dials beneath her heel. The bubble lurched, the lights flickered and went out.

For a moment there was absolute silence in the control chamber. Then the lights flashed on, and a magnetic net fell over her head. She tried to freeze, but too late; the woven strands had been activated by her movement and began drawing together. A cocoon of metal pinned her arms against her sides, squeezed her chest until she could only breathe in short gasps. She lost her balance and fell to the deck.

A breathless Grithy rushed in. "The inner capsule is gone!"

Yakov spoke into his collar mike: "Commander Torguil! Situation B! Alert the fleet!"

A minute later Abi felt herself jerked roughly to her feet. Yakov pushed her in front of a viewscreen. "There. See what you've done for your lover."

The screen showed the little capsule several miles out in space. It disappeared, and a nuclear flower bloomed in its place.

Yakov shouted into his collar mike: "Good one, Commander—!"

The capsule blinked on the screen, twenty miles farther away.

"Fire again!" shouted Yakov.

A minute later the nuclear sunburst flared—but Abi noticed that the capsule had blinked out a millisecond before. She tried to imagine what Xoh'ne was thinking out there in the cold night alone.

The capsule appeared again. Cursing, Yakov ordered another torpedo fired. It also missed. He ordered firing in groups of three. Each time the capsule danced back onto the screen like a taunting fingertip.

"He can't evade us forever," muttered Yakov. "I've got ten thousand ships deployed around us in three layers." He lifted his mike and barked: "Fleet Commander Torguil! His jumps appear to be limited to twenty miles. Does that give you any ideas?"

"Sir, I don't know—unless we pinpoint his next appearance, then hit him with a planet wrecker."

"That's exactly what you should do, Commander."

"But it would destroy part of the fleet."

"I'm making it an order, Commander."

A minute later a blinding light flared inside the chamber. A shock wave slammed into the sphere and sent it skittering like a soap bubble in a draft. As she bounced off the plastic wall, Abi saw the blazing fury of a miniature sun where the bubble had last appeared. Nearby were a dozen secondary flares, like moths who had flown too close to the flame.

She heard a familiar sound in her ears: *Nothing but an empty form . . .*

Yakov Ras turned up his mike: "That did it, Commander."

"Yes, sir. It also did for twenty cruisers."

"You will report that a Vim raider penetrated our defenses and was destroyed at great cost to our heroic fleet. Pick out fifty men for decorations."

As he turned to her, Abi said: "Another lie, like the one you told me about my parents."

Yakov looked tired and old. "There seems to be no other way . . ." He shook his head as if to clear it. When he looked at her, she saw a pleading look in his eyes: "Abi, it was only a premature truth. Su-shann and Ben Abo are dead now, almost certainly."

"Why do you say that?"

"The Vim have broken through our perimeter and encircled Megrez. There has been no word since then."

Requiem for Mergez

"In the language of the Blue Men, defeat is synonymous with death. They have no word for surrender."

Bak-Ti, on semantic differences
among the EVOs

Bojak the Ungul was a genius of his breed. He had a vocabulary of two hundred words; he knew which levers to pull to send his little fighting ship through the three dimensions of space, and which buttons to push to release the giant warheads. He had a doppler screen, but he didn't know it was called that; only that the red blobs were targets and the violet blobs could be ignored.

This was his life—to cruise beyond the periphery, through a no-man's universe of shattered planets and floating hulks. He had a harem of four. Once he'd had five, but he had killed one of the females when she annoyed him. The others were usually docile; now they were frightened and nervous, for the attack had been gathering intensity, and he had been confined to the control seat for five days of ship time. The ringing of the alarm bell had been almost constant, the other ships of his squadron had one by one flared into nothingness, and now Bojak was alone in this sector of space.

A moment came when no enemies showed on his screen. Bojak said the word that meant food, and the females brought it. Two were with calf; he noticed their swollen bellies and heavy breasts and felt a peevish anger. Soon there would be blood and bawling and probably screams as he carried the little one to the airlock and flushed it out into space. That was the reason he'd killed the fifth female; she'd grown morose and combative after her calf was pushed out into the black void.

One of the pregnant ones had been his favorite; now he pushed her back and motioned another to come forward and take her place. She was the youngest; she had been only a heifer when his ship was launched. He shared his bowl with her, then mounted her while the others watched with bright interest.

When he was finished an enemy ship appeared on his screen, and another behind that, and then a vast swarm trailing back into infinity. He set his controls and homed in on the first, watched it flare in his screen, then aimed himself at the second. He was vaguely aware that something rare and strange was happening; they were breaking through the barrier in a great river of light. Some had already flashed past and gone on toward the unprotected rim of the empire. Those were not his concern; he was a Fighting Ungul, genetically engineered and trained since birth to attack. He had no concept of defense.

The second enemy died, and he scanned the oncoming swarm for a third target. He heard the missiles crashing around him, and the whimpering of the females, but he cuffed the nearest ones and concentrated on driving his ship down the invisible line of the aiming beacon. He heard air whistling, and barked the commands which led to the patching of the holes. Still the air shrieked out, and his vision dimmed, and the death of his third enemy was only a luminous puffball in a world turning dark.

Bojak knew nothing of death or love, and had known happiness only once in his life. Now he remembered a blue-white spark in a lavender sky above rolling fields of purple. The happiness had a name: Megrez. He felt himself leave his body and return there. He ran free across the fields, playing with the others until it grew too dark to see. Tired, he lay down in the warm circle of his mother's arms and slept.

Os-a-nin was a Grithy herdswoman, an overseer of laboring Unguls. The job that day was to unblock field drains. She carried a power whip and a holstered sleep gun in case one of her laborers went berserk. She had males and females mixed; the rebellious ones were manacled at the ankles. The better ones were allowed to leave the group and approach her to beg for tidbits of dried molasses. They were seven feet tall, with biceps as thick as Osa's waist. Their massive jaws, full of thick flat grinding molars for pulverizing their fodder, could have crushed her skull like a cashew.

Osa had tamed the big riding male herself. She sat on a pad strapped to his shoulders, astride his thick forward-sloping neck. Her boots fit into stirrups fastened under his arms; her hands loosely gripped the halter which ran around his forehead and under his chin. He was jumpy and nervous today; one of the females had come into heat after leaving the barn. Had Osa known in time, she would have turned her in to the breeding pen. Now she was a storm center of magnetic energy, twitching her hips as she shoveled purple muck out of the canal. One of the shackled males nipped her shoulder. Osa pressed the button of her electric whip. Blue lightning crackled out and touched the chrome bracelets on the male's wrist. He went rigid, trembling and stiff, and Osa released the button. The male bent over his shovel and the muck flew out in huge spattering gobs.

Time to eat. She rode back to the carrier, dismounted, and dumped the mash into the trough which ran along its side. She called the group, letting her pets eat first and clubbing the greedy ones back until they had finished. Only then did she walk away to a grassy hillock and unpack her own lunch. While she ate, her mount came over and lay down beside her with a deep sigh. She broke off a chunk of canned Ungul beef and put it into his mouth. It was illegal to feed meat to an Ungul, but who would tell? Nobody listened to their grunting. Anyway, it kept his muscles in tone. He chewed listlessly and swallowed with another sigh. She knew he wanted to mount the heifer (who had gone off from the sleeping herd and was pretending to crop the short grass, glancing over her shoulder to see if she'd awakened any interest). But of course the heifer was reserved for the sleek, expensive breeding males and would perhaps give birth to one of the Fighting Unguls which were swallowed up by the thousands each year on the periphery. After she was bred, then the gelded males of the working crew could play their pointless games . . .

She saw another herdswoman, Y-al-son, striding across the field. Her crew napped beneath the bridge they had been repairing across the canal. Al-son brought news of a battle in space and rumors of a Vim breakthrough, but nothing definite. Anyway, there was nothing they could do since they were part of the ground-defense system. Battles in space were not their concern.

Al-son wanted to talk about her male, and the trouble she was having with her den sisters. They would not agree to share him properly, and he was too weak-willed to decide the matter. Even when Al-son managed to win her conjugal rights, the other two remained on the communal mat instead of moving to their single pallets according to custom . . .

Osa grew bored and roused her group from their nap ten minutes early. She had just gotten them into formation when the alarm bleeped on her carrier. She climbed into the open cab, flicked the switch on the communicator, and heard that the Vim had penetrated the barrier and were homing in on Megrez. All members of the planetary guard were ordered to draw weapons and rush to the nearest defense point.

Osa was a noncommissioned officer in the guard. She herded her crew into the carrier and chained them in their places, seating her own mount nearest the gate. As she drove along the paved dike, she saw a herd of Beef Unguls being driven at a run toward the corrals. They were of the imported Hyades breed, and their silver manes rippled in the wind.

Osa felt exuberant, aware of the blood surging hot in her veins. She would fight, now, at last, after the daily combat practice which had been her lot since weaning. She was a warrior first and a herdswoman second, descended from the clan of the great HaM'ho himself. She saw the rocket trails rising into the sky, and her heart went up with her clan sisters who piloted the ships. She saw the bright flare of missiles, watched the guard ships fall like burned little bugs, and she knew the enemy would soon be landing. She felt a tremor of fear—not for herself but for her male.

She pulled into the unloading shed and jabbed her bawling crew down the chute leading to the underground pens. Then she parked her carrier and raced to her cubicle. Her den sisters had seen to the male already; he was underground with the other males, safe but frightened. She petted him and stroked his ears, said goodbye to her children, then went to the armory and drew her weapons and combat harness.

Her squad waited inside the carrier; there had been no time to hose it out, so it was rank with the smell of Ungul dung. She jumped into the cab and swung into the file of carriers leaving the estate. They headed toward the city, twenty miles away in the center of a basin. It was already bleeding from many wounds; red fire mottled the entire west end. Over the industrial flats hovered a sheet of coruscating blue where a magnetic bomb wreaked havoc among all objects of metal. Osa could feel it tugging at the carrier. The vehicle in front of her veered left and spilled over the edge. It tumbled down the dike and came to rest on its top with a great floomp! of dust. There were girls pinned under it, but Osa had no way to stop without suffering the same fate.

A shadow passed over, and Osa saw the dull looming curve of metal. A Vim warship, immeasurably close! Her nerves were electrified. An arc of blue fire speared the head of the column; Osa heard a sound like the gigantic ripping of a rotten Ungulhyde. The lead carrier dissolved into fragments of flesh and twists of metal. An instant later she crashed into the carrier ahead, felt her neck snap back as the following carrier smashed her rear.

Osa grabbed her blaster and leaped out of the carrier, commanding her squad to take cover beside the dike. They came over the sides, carrying a sister who had suffered a crushed foot in the smash-up.

Osa looked across the plain and saw the giant ship settle to the ground about a mile away. It was larger than all the barns of Yendo laid end to end. Black holes opened at its base and hundreds of two-legged, four-armed creatures spilled out. Their numbers darkened the ground as they streamed toward the city, along a route that would take them within a quarter of a mile of the wrecked caravan.

Osa unclamped her distance glasses and brought the figures into close focus. Here was the legendary enemy, the Vim. She had expected something huge, but these were no larger than her own warrior girls. Their features could not be discerned, but they ran on two short clumsy legs. Their most prominent feature was the tail, which curved up behind them as they ran, ending in a knob which they carried as high as their heads.

Osa gave the range, and the girls set the dials on their guns and opened up. The tight energy beams shot out like spears of light, spraying the flanks of the spread-out and running Vim. Fire blossomed at the end of every spear. The Vim fell by the dozens, turned black, and lay still. Osa screamed in triumph and shouted the order to advance. The squad raced forward, discarding their empty charges and reloading from their belts as they ran. They got off three more volleys, and fifty more Vim died. Then Osa heard the crackle of a magnetic grenade over her head. Her rifle was nearly torn from her hands, and two of the girls lost their weapons. Osa felt a rush of anger: why had not the commanders issued them nonferrous weapons, since the magnetic bombs had been known about for years? Then she felt ashamed of her near-sedition. The Jelks knew what they were doing; even HaM'ho had said they were ordained to rule the Grithies, and she had seen it written and heard it in the estate chapel every worship day . . .

One of the girls shouted, and Osa saw a detachment of the Vim leave the main body and come toward them. But . . . what speed! Faster than the best racing Unguls. She saw that they were hopping, their short legs sliding up into their bodies and then shooting out again like pistons, bouncing them forward in leaps of a hundred feet. But they would be vulnerable in the air; Osa directed her troops to switch to needle fire and aim for their stomachs. (She'd heard it from a survivor of one of the fallen planets.) It was like spearing moths; they went rigid in the air and then tumbled to the ground . . . dead.

The survivors went prone and continued their advance with only their tails raised. Some kind of seeing organ in the terminal knob, Osa decided. She told the girl beside her to shorten range and try arching fire. As the girl nodded, a sooty puffball exploded between them. Osa shielded her eyes but the spore missile had done its damage.

Her right eye burned for an instant and then went blank. Through her remaining eye Osa saw the other girl throw down her gun and claw at her eyes, screaming.

They are trying to take us alive, thought Osa. Why? No time to ponder. A Vim rose up in front of her. She dropped to her belly and fired, taking off his head and half his shoulder. She saw him fall and swung her gun to another target—then hesitated. This one was looking at her. She met his eyes—a mistake a soldier makes only once. They were big and perfectly round, with huge black pupils centered by yellow ovals. They seemed to reflect fear and bewilderment, as if he shared her own thought: *What am I doing here?* She saw that his weapon, held in four arms and a whole cluster of spiny tentacles, was pointed away. He wore a harness like her own but no clothing. Probably the number of protuberances made clothing impractical: four arms, the pistonlike legs, and the long tail ending in a ball studded with horny spikes. He was obviously male; she saw his hanging organ and thought: *It would be possible* . . .

But she looked too long. The first one she had shot was getting up. With horror she saw that his head was gone; all that remained was the stump with wet cords hanging from it. She saw the tail bobbing up over his shoulder and realized that the knob must contain some kind of secondary brain. She fired a jagged lightning burst which dissolved his gun and ripped his midsection in two . . .

A searing blast raked her left side. She turned and fired at the second Vim, sweeping her ray like a scythe and slicing off his legs at the hips. She watched him topple, the funny tentacles around his mouth writhing. Then she herself fell, and saw for the first time that the blast had torn away several ribs and a part of her lung . . .

Some time later she raised her head and saw that the Vim troops had gone on toward the city; her own girls lay dead among the bodies of the enemy, and she herself was dying. She struggled to her feet, using her gun as a stave, and turned back toward Yendo. She moved slowly, sliding one foot forward and dragging the other up behind it, holding her hand to her side to suppress the bleeding. To see her male once more, and her children, that was all she wanted . . .

Topping a rise, she saw the gold-roofed castle on the heights. A small white figure stood in the garden; his bald dome reflecting the slanting blue-white rays of the sun. She saw him lift his hand and beckon her, and she altered course. She would not survive to reach the barns, but that could not be helped, for the master summoned.

Qal—Quar'ahan, Landark of Yendo, Jelk of the first rank, sipped wine on his terrace and watched the warrior girl approach. He had watched the fight through his glasses, had seen her and her girls slay dozens of the enemy, and had felt a bitter rage against the custom that Jelks must not engage in physical combat. He lifted his wineglass, looking at the small delicate fingers curved around the stem. That was all they were good for—yet he was sure he could hold a gun. The warrior girls had handled them as if they were part of their bodies.

Something had to be done. The Vim were taking the city, and would soon spread out and overrun the country estates. With all his warriors killed, he and his family would be helpless . . .

He saw that the girl was wounded, with blood and other matter streaming down her hip. Steeling himself against unpleasantness, he drained his wineglass and walked down the marble steps. She had fallen by the time he reached her, but rolled her eyes and tried to rise to her feet. He knelt beside her and put his hand on her forehead, averting his eyes from the ugly wound, and asked in the Grithy dialect: "What is your name, girl?"

"Os-a-nin, my Lord Qal."

"Show me how to use the gun, Osa."

She gasped and groaned as she showed him the dial setting, how to grip the butt and to press the firing button. When Qal said he understood, she lay back with a deep gurgling sigh and did not breathe again. Qal removed the harness from her body, folded her arms across her chest, and walked back to the garden.

After mounting the steps, he paused to catch his breath beside a statue unearthed from the ruins of the First Empire. Muscled like the Grithy warrior girls, yet he had the small ears of an Ungul. Certainly, he was not a Jelk, for he had a navel. Hair covered his groin, chest, jaws, and scalp. Yet he was no Ungul, for he stood like a commander, and the lines around his nose were marks of intelligence. Could it be that Jelks had not always ruled, as he'd been taught? That the First Empire had been the creation of men who resembled Unguls more than they resembled human beings?

He found his household waiting in the central patio, lounging on couches around the fountain. His wife, in her brief diaphanous tunic, stared at the gun he held in his hand. His son, narcotized and heavy-lidded, dozed with his head on the shoulder of his bride. She was a lovely blue girl, native of Megrez, with titles and genealogy going back to the First Empire. The ripe swelling of her stomach showed that their honeymoon had borne fruit, the continuity of the family was assured. The knowledge was ashes in Qal's mouth.

Beside his wife sat Tibi-sal, Stafi poet and tutor of the household children, tall, thin and pale, his eyes invisible behind smoked glasses. Haron, his Milark aide, stood erect behind his wife, wearing his full-dress uniform with medals. No need to ask why he had not been out commanding his troops in battle. Combat was not for Jelks; theirs to review parades and interpret directives of the War Council. There was also his manager, a rotund, snippish Burok whom Qal did not like personally, but who had made Green Yendo the largest-selling narcotic beverage in the empire. Qal suspected that his great-great-great-great-great-grandfather, who had first brewed the famous drink, would have spat it out . . . but then the quality of everything diminished in troubled times.

"My people," he said, "the city has fallen. We have only an hour or so before the Vim arrive."

His wife nodded. "We have been waiting for you, Qal. I have your potion mixed already."

He looked at the glass beside her, felt himself weakening. Death would be easy . . . But then he straightened his shoulders and threw out his chest.

"I have a gun. And I know how to use it." He lifted the heavy blaster and shook it.

"Rather messy, don't you think?" said the poet. "The potion is far more pleasant to taste."

"I'm not going to die, you fool. I'm going to fight!"

His wife gasped. His son looked up at him through heavy lids and groaned. Only his daughter-in-law seemed to sit up straighter and look at him with her yellow eyes alight.

The Milark asked: "How will you avoid being captured and turned into a Vim puppet?"

"I'll go down into the tunnels the blue men used during the time of the deep snows, before we rounded out their orbit. There's a trap door leading down from the dungeon. We'll take food with us, and come out at night to kill the Vim."

His wife sighed. "Qal, that is no life for a Jelk." She lifted the glass. "Make the final toast, and let us all drink together."

Qal felt a heavy futility. "Nobody wants to fight?"

The poet shuddered. "The very thought revolts me."

"And the thought of dying, that does not revolt you?"

"On the contrary, I find it a most natural end to life, in fact the only conceivable end."

"But have you no hatred for the Vim? Those vicious beasts drove the human race out of space once before. Are you going to let them do it again?"

The poet shrugged. "Perhaps it will rise again from the ashes. Who knows?" He lifted his glass and squinted through the pale-green fluid. "Who cares?"

He drained his glass and bent to set it on the edge of the fountain. He kept on pitching forward until he lay across the low wall with his arms in the water and his feet trailing out behind him. His back heaved once and then settled.

"It works quickly, Qal," said his wife. "Come sit with me. We have had a good life. Let us end it in tranquillity, not with blood and fighting."

He felt his energy drain away. He sat down on the low couch and took her hand. He lifted his glass as she did, but only touched his lips to the rim. He watched her swallow, saw her sudden wide-eyed look of terror. The spasmodic clutch of her hand nearly broke his fingers . . .

Gently he pried his hand loose and closed her eyelids. Falling glasses tinkled around the patio. All the others lay dead—all except his daughter-in-law, who stepped away from the body of his son and came to him.

"I will go underground with you, Qal."

He followed her down the stone steps into the dungeon. At the trap door he suddenly remembered: "We didn't bring food."

"Don't worry about it," she said.

He noticed how skillfully she lifted the slab, applying no more force than was needed. "You already made preparations?"

"Yes." She walked ahead of him down the dark steps. "I am a woman of Megrez. We never give up anything without a fight." At the bottom of the steps, she threw open a heavy metal door and called: "Behold! Here is a fighter, the only one from my household."

The arched tunnel stretched in both directions as far as he could see. Opposite the door stood about fifty men and women of mixed racial stock: Grithies, Unguls, blue men, a few amphibians, and a winged Pteroman. A tall blue man detached himself from the group and came forward. His cold yellow eyes and his air of savage strength made Qal feel small, weak, and anemic.

"Qal, this is my brother, Ben Abo."

Qal laid down his gun and raised his hands, pressing his palms to Ben Abo's in the standard Megrez greeting. "We heard that you'd returned. We expected you to stage a revolution."

"No need, as you see." The blue man smiled, showing the red tips of his fangs. "Instead, we spent the last ten years booby-trapping the entire planet. As soon as the Vim settle in we set off our charges. The atmosphere will become radioactive and the soil contaminated to a depth of fifty meters. The Vim will abandon it and pass on to other conquests."

"Leaving you with a contaminated planet. What good is that?"

"It's only for twenty years or so. We'll use the time to increase our numbers. We're only about four thousand."

"Am I the only Jelk?"

"There is one other."

She came out from the group, looking like a child beside the others. A moon Jelk. He had forgotten how delicate they were, how small and fragile the bones, how transparent the skin. He dropped to one knee and took her small hand in his, raising it to his lips as Ben Abo said:

"This is my . . . uh, partner, the landess Su-shann, late of Enderby, Antark, earth—"

A Weapon Is Born

The crushing of the Eshom-Ungul rebellion was bloody butchery. The Isles of Fire were bombed, strafed, and burned; Abi saw the ships fly over and a few days later a vast windrow of burned and blasted bodies washed up on her beach. The free Ungul bands which roamed the Princess Astrid coast were too numerous to fight; the Grithies merely killed their leaders and left the remainder to break up into small groups and starve in the rocky highlands. The sport of wild-Ungul hunting attracted hundreds of Milarks. Even a few Jelks were sold on the idea that it was healthy to hunt in the open air.

Abi took them in and fed them, ignoring the government order that all Unguls who had made contact with the Eshom must be eliminated. When the executioners came to her estate, she and her loyal servants drove them off. They threatened to come back with orders for her arrest, but Abi knew that Yakov Ras would not move against her as long as she carried the child. Not long after this her herd of tainted Unguls was secretly poisoned.

The pogrom became totally racist. Since the Pteroni warned the roving bands of the approach of hunters, they were considered allies of the Eshom. There were public demonstrations against them, and thousands were killed. Those who survived had to flee the continent.

The Isles of Fire were depopulated, the jungles burned off, and the lands parceled out among the Milarks. The Landarks saw their power decreasing. By allowing the military to protect them against the Eshom, they had placed themselves under the power of their protectors.

The war situation deteriorated rapidly after the fall of Megrez. The rich agricultural world of Tarfil was lost, the sphere of defense shrank, and the zone of military control was pushed inward until it became a noose tightening around the home system.

Through all of this Abi forced herself to remain silent, because of the seed which was growing within her. Not until Yakov Ras visited during her fifth month of pregnancy did she give vent to her feelings:

"This stupid caste structure is killing us! We must unite all the people of earth."

"Easy to say for one of mixed ancestry." Yakov slouched in a foam contour chair in her study. Pouches sagged under his eyes. "People don't fight for equality. They fight for privilege. And they'll defend their place in the system rather than risk getting pushed into a lower one."

"*You—!*" She shook her head in disgust. "You are one of the problems, Yakov. You play Milarks against Landarks, Jelks against Grithies, just so you can stay in power."

"Abi, I am only an instrument of the computer. If my actions sustain the caste system, it is because the computer demands it. I assume that the computer knows what is good for humanity."

"The computer is only a thinking machine."

"But it contains all of man's knowledge."

"Is knowledge all there is? What about emotions? Have you lost the capacity to *feel?*"

"Of course I feel—but it distorts and weakens my intellect. Usually I manage to suppress my emotions. You'd be better off if you did the same."

"Koffee"—she had not used her pet name for him since her ordeal in the bubble—"if I operated on intellect, I would not be sitting here now with my belly puffed out like a balloon."

She saw his eyes slide over her body. She had exaggerated slightly; her midriff had thickened to a tubular shape from hips to armpits—except for her breasts, which thrust out in embarrassing prominence against her loose sack garment.

"That brings me to the reason I came, Abi. I've set up a floating medical facility in the Greenland Sea. Tomorrow you can move there and get ready to have your child."

She felt her will set like a block of concrete. "I will have the child here, Yakov. And I require no attendance."

"Abi . . ." He sighed. "Do you realize that the father of your child weighed over three hundred pounds? And the average Eshom weighs thirty pounds at birth? We simply can't risk a miscarriage."

"Can you promise that I will be released as soon as the child is born?"

"I can promise that."

She thought of her mother, Ben Abo . . . and Xoh'ne. Death had been their release. "No, Yakov."

"Don't you believe me?"

"I believe," she said, "that you could make the promise in total sincerity, then break it again without a tingle of guilt under the stress of duty."

He rose heavily, nodding. "Duty is sometimes hard."

"Duty is the excuse government officials use for exercising their sadistic tendencies." She got up and followed him out, feeling awkward and heavy. "Yakov, if you try to take me away from here, I'll drive my fist into my belly and kill the child."

He paused at the top of the steps and looked at her. "You won't do that, Abi."

The following day a fleet of twelve guard ships landed in the open space surrounding the pyramid. Abi climbed the highest wind tower, a series of platforms rising on fluted pillars to a height of eighty feet. When Yakov stepped out of the lead ship, she called down:

"If you try to take me, I'll jump!"

He squinted up at her, then turned and spoke to his Milark aide.

"No sleep-dust either. If I lose consciousness, I'll fall." She wrapped her arms around a pillar and leaned out. The hot wind whipped her garment up to her waist. Yakov looked like a squashed bug far below.

"What do you want?"

"I want you to leave my property!"

"Agreed. But let the doctor make an examination first."

"I'm not coming down until you leave."

An hour later Yakov gave in. Not until the departing fleet's contrails had dispersed in the stratosphere did she climb down from the tower.

In the following weeks she spent a lot of time in the birthing barn. She saw no reason why the herdswomen who assisted the Unguls could not also assist her. Ungul babies were indistinguishable from Jelk babies, except in size. It amazed her that the Grithy girls could cuddle the little creatures and even let them nuzzle playfully at their breasts— and when they attained the age of tender veal, could slaughter and eat them with great appetite. She would have liked to get out of the whole monstrous business of raising Unguls, but there was no way. If she sold them, they would be butchered. If she freed them, the patrols would kill them, or another rancher would capture them and send her a feeding bill . . .

In the seventh month she walked spread-legged, shoulders thrown back to offset the weight of her womb. Her swollen breasts swayed like the udders of a Dairy Ungul. She rubbed oil on them every night, and massaged the spreading worm tracks in her hips. Every day she walked five times around the pyramid. Often she broke into a giggle when nothing was funny. One night she woke up screaming with pain. She knew that pregnant mothers sensed the moods of their babies, but this was too much. The embryonic mind submerged her own . . .

She began to feel panic, as if a monster had crawled inside and was devouring her alive. Soon she would be only a thin membrane surrounding this creature who had usurped her body . . .

One afternoon in her eighth month she awoke with a feeling of nausea. She started toward the birthing barn and had just reached the top of the steps when the first contraction seized her. She set her teeth and waited until it passed. The steps would be too risky. She turned and went back into the central courtyard. At that point the bottom dropped out of everything. Warm water splashed over her feet. She sat down on the mosaic tile and pushed at the swollen lump of her stomach. It heaved and writhed under her hands. She sensed the child's rage at being disturbed. She closed her eyes and saw a long roseate tunnel with a chink of light at the far end. *Cold out there. Don't want to go but I must . . .*

Pain tore at her mind. Part of a scream slipped out and she bit her lip. Darkness came with a taste of blood.

Blue sky overhead. The thing was done. She raised herself on her elbows and saw a pair of flat almond eyes studying her. The pupils were black, with a pointed oval slit in the center. Yellow like his father's. *His?* She glanced between his chubby legs and confirmed it. A boy, with crimson skin . . . *Oh, no, that's blood.* She got to her hands and knees. Slipping on the wet tiles, she hauled him to a patch of turf. She pulled off her garment, ripped away the sodden hem, and cleaned his body. His skin came out creamy white, glowing with health. His hair was black, long and glossy. She propped him up on the grass like a doll. Pride lumped in her throat.

"Hello, I'm your mother."

It sounded inane, yet he seemed to consider her words with a thoughtful expression, as if wondering what he should say in return. He began to look around him, at first in puzzlement, then in agitation. He worked his mouth as if he were trying to cry. She thought he might be cold. She wrapped the remainder of her gown around him and carried him toward the bedroom. A uniformed guard bulked on the wall above her. She opened her mouth to order him away, then saw the gun in his hand. Instinctively she arched her back and wrapped the baby in her arms. She felt the sharp sting of the dart between her shoulders. Cold enveloped her like a bath of ice.

She awoke in her own bedroom. Someone had put a clean nightgown on her. Sunlight streaked through the colored arches of her windows. *Morning* sunlight. It had been afternoon when she'd had the baby.

She ran to the door, her breasts aching and full. It was locked. She pounded and screamed, and a peephole opened. She looked into the bristly face of a D'Yabelt guardsman.

"Get my baby, you stinking pig!"

Yakov Ras brought him, wrapped in a soft blanket of Ungul wool. He held out the bundle and said solemnly: "The will of the computer be done."

Abi laughed at his pretentiousness. She sobered when she saw the guardsmen standing behind Yakov with their blasters angled toward the floor. She was a prisoner—but at least she had the baby.

She took the bundle and carried it to her bed. Peeling aside the fold, she looked into his face. His mouth opened, and she saw tiny fangs peeping out of his gums. She motioned Yakov to close the door, and slipped out her breast. She felt a sensuous thrill when he started nursing . . . blissful relief as the pressure drained away. She settled herself and slipped the woolen blanket off his head.

His black hair had been shaved off. A pink net of scar tissue covered his scalp.

"Imbecile!" she hissed at Yakov. "You've tampered with his brain."

"We only implanted a grid of copper under his scalp. It doesn't harm him. The threads are tiny, invisible to the naked eye, powered from a transmitter on the moon." His eyes pleaded. "Abi, we couldn't risk having his talents released on earth."

She said bitterly: "You don't even know what his talents are."

"I know this: so far the combination of genes has produced an expansion of power on all levels, physical, intellectual, and paranormal. Su-shann's power of deductive reasoning and her—willfulness, to use a mild term—were passed on to you in double measure. You've also got Ben Abo's inventiveness, as well as his rebellious spirit. You're four times as strong, four times as smart, as the average Jelk. As a child you tied up whole regiments of guardsmen, platoons of spies, and laboratories full of specialists.

"And Xoh'ne . . . descended from a killer Ungul and a mother with unknown telepathic powers. Who knows what his child has inherited? As an infant, he'll be greedy and self-centered and immoral. All babies are. Suppose he has the Eshom talent for mirroring emotions and intensifying them? Imagine it doubled, quadrupled. He might cause us to tear our throats out because his dinner is late. Or he might cause an entire division of soldiers to walk off a cliff, just for amusement."

The reasons were logical—in the context of Yakov's paranoia. She couldn't resist saying sarcastically: "You imagine he will instruct the Vim to commit suicide?"

Ras shook his head. "I don't know. The computer has so far offered no understandable predictions on what form his power will take. I suspect it might be something I would not even recognize as power."

Abi decided to walk in the garden. She got up and started toward the door, but Yakov shook his head.

"*What?* Am I a prisoner in my own house?"

"It is security—"

"For the child. I knew you'd say that. Can't I feed him in privacy?"

"All right. When he is done, knock on the door and the baby will be taken. He will be brought back for nursing every four hours, as the computer has instructed."

So the computer condoned her imprisonment. *Yaga* the computer. She tried the other door, found it unlocked, and stepped out onto her tiny private patio. She surveyed the eight-foot walls, saw the bores of laser cannon peeping from patches of new cement, and decided not to scale them. No doubt there were spy eyes everywhere, plus audio pick-ups to record her slightest gut rumble. She would bide her time, and plan her escape carefully. Meanwhile the child would get stronger.

She pushed her forefinger into his clenched fist, then yelped as the fingers squeezed. She twisted free and sucked her throbbing digit. At least the copper grid had not weakened him. Or had it? There was no way of knowing . . .

One night she heard the soft flutter of wings on her patio. A soft melodious whistle sounded. Abi translated mentally from the Pteronian:

"It is Untas. May I enter?"

She unlocked the door and slid it back. "How did you get past the lasers?"

"A momentary power failure, due to a copper bar being dropped across two wires." He hunkered down under his folded wings. "The Eshom say the child is born."

"Two weeks ago. How did they know?"

He lifted his pinions in the Pteroni equivalent of a shrug. "They know. They call him X'ra X'rakhim. It means 'Fire of God.' "

"Kim? Kim. Yes, I like it."

"I am living with them now, in Patagone. They are much reduced in numbers, but ready to fight to obtain the child. They can come whenever you say, at night, in numbers sufficient to overwhelm all resistance."

Her heart leaped at the thought of freedom. But she said:

"Too dangerous to take him out during a battle. He might be killed by accident. Let's wait until he's stronger."

"I will tell them. Now I must go."

She let him out onto the patio. He leaped to the top of the wall and gave himself a kicking boost into the air. Seconds later a searchlight tunneled through the night. Guns chattered. Tracers stitched the darkness. She saw Untas fold his wings and plummet, then spread out and glide beneath the beam. None of the bullets came close. She closed the door and went back to bed.

Yakov returned to the moon in the third week. Kim crawled on the same day. A week later he was tottering on his feet, and within two days he was walking easily. Sometimes she caught him looking at her with a speculative frown, as though he wanted to ask her a question but didn't have the words.

She found evidence that he was being studied like a bug under glass: Pinpricks on his heel where blood samples had been taken . . . rashes on his scalp where electrodes had been clamped . . . allergy patches on his skin. She realized then that Yakov Ras had no understanding of the computer's instructions. In his ignorance he might ruin everything. Well . . . she had the gem, the weapon which would destroy the Vim. She had only to get him away from Yakov and his thumb-fingered scientists, get the grid off his skull, and let nature do the rest.

Grithy nurses brought him and carried him away, but the armed guards always stood in the door. The D'Yabelt were widely reputed to shun the company of women, and from the cool looks they gave her she knew it was true. They were immune to sexual distraction. She felt sure Yakov had planned it that way. Bribes were useless, for these were elite troops on special duty, selected for loyalty and lack of imagination. To Abi both words had the same meaning.

One day she asked the guard what would happen if she seized the baby by the ankles and hit him over the head with it.

"We will be executed if any harm comes to the child," he said.

"What about me?"

"We are permitted to kill you to save the child, or to prevent you from carrying him off."

And there it was. To Yakov she was a throwaway—a container that had served its purpose. A second-stage booster rocket. Each day brought her nearer to the time when Kim could be taken off the breast, and she would come to the end of her immunity. On that day, she was certain, she would be silenced in the only manner that Yakov trusted.

She thought of asking the Pteroni for help, but they'd dispersed around the world. Now they were involved in a struggle for existence on a thousand mountaintops, fighting against giant mutated bats; against insects, web spinners, and the intelligent mites of Madagascar; against the shaggy three-toed beasts who claimed the high caves.

The Androxi had been left alone during the pogrom because they'd stayed out of sight. But the screen she'd put across their bay no longer functioned. With Antark under military travel restrictions, nobody came to buy their artifacts, so they lacked the gold to pay for power. Seal herds had begun to breed on the beach across the mountains, and the Androxi were too busy fighting them off to worry about anything else.

Bad times all around. Even after the wild Unguls had been killed and the Eshom driven north, the killing machine went on. The Eshom returned in the night as raiders, to steal the Ungul herds and kill the Milarks. Rumors arose that certain Grithies were guiding the raiders. (For this she blamed Yakov. It would be his answer to population pressure, and a poor one in her opinion.) First there was a trial and execution of Grithies who had joined the Ungul uprising. Then the fear-crazed Grithies began to lynch those of their own number who had taught their Unguls to read, and to speak in the tongue of the rulers. The lynchings spread to those who had merely treated them kindly. There were witch-hunts throughout the army, and the factories, and in the guild of domestics. There was treason within mating groups— almost unheard of before—where one wife denounced another wife. In the villages one grew accustomed to seeing a neighbor stoned to death . . .

The old happy times were going fast under the pressure of the Jelk collapse; they were like insects in a horde, irritating each other to a killing frenzy. Abi wondered if that was part of the computer's plan . . .

Her inquiries were reported to Yakov, who came flying down. He looked harassed; his hands shook and he kept pacing the floor. The Milarks were getting out of hand; they wanted to dissolve the War Council and replace it with a general staff under their control.

"If I should lose power, the entire program will be scrapped. You and the child will be killed. You know that, don't you?"

"The methods you use force others to use the same methods. We are all trapped in a spiral of increasing brutality."

Wearily he passed his hand over his face. "I have no time to discuss philosophy. If you agree not to escape, I will give you freedom to raise the child as you see fit. Do you agree?"

"If I have no choice, there can be no agreement. Only acceptance of the inevitable."

He shook his head. "The argument is too abstruse for me to follow."

"Just this: any freedom that you grant can also be taken away. Therefore it is not really freedom. Therefore you may go *yaga* yourself."

He gave her a narrow look, then nodded as if to himself. "That means you are still planning escape. So the situation remains unchanged. Do not try to involve the guards. You will only cause their deaths."

Next day her guard was doubled. A squadron of skimmers was stationed on a nearby mountain. The patrols followed a random pattern, so she had no idea when a flier would hover over her patio, churning the air to a froth while the pilot gazed down at her through his belly-port.

She examined her room carefully. Magnetic door seals, controlled from elsewhere. She thought it could be jammed, but did not experiment. Within her bedroom was a damping field in which not even a phosphorus match would light. No good grabbing a guard's rifle. It wouldn't work inside the room, and she couldn't get out without it.

The only way out was straight up. Therefore she had to capture a skimmer. Only the child had access to the outside world. Therefore he must be the instrument of her escape.

When Kim was in physical contact with her, she was aware of an expanded mental power. Intermittent, diffuse, unpredictable, it brushed her at odd times like a summer breeze. When it did she could pick up the thoughts of the guards. Most of them were mere cogs in the military machine, their brains crippled from birth by Jelk conditioning. Their minds were armored; she could touch them, but she could not penetrate.

There was one exception. One of the patrol pilots had done duty on the shores of the arctic sea. She caught his guilt-ridden thoughts of the Dubha—wistful because their nonviolent culture was being destroyed by brutal and tenacious Grithies, guilty because he had burned their friendly villages and killed their women and children . . .

She increased her rapport with him each time Kim nursed. His name was Hut-Mo. D'Yabelt descent . . . but a pervert among his own kind. He liked to visit the Grithy village at the head of the bay and copulate with the prostitutes. She planted the idea of escape.

But they will simply shoot me down.

Not if you have the woman and the baby with you.

Where do these thoughts come from? I'm going crazy.

You must cut off the power. Drop a bomb on the booster station.

I can't do it. I'm afraid.

She aroused suspicion in his commander's mind. Hut-Mo was watched, and his efficiency dropped off. He was due to be relieved of pilot duty and sent to a reindoctrination camp.

They will turn you into a mindless robot. You must escape.

I don't dare.

Escape! Tonight! Run! Flee!

I'll do it.

At twenty-one hours. The woman and child will be waiting.

At twenty hours Kim was brought for nursing. He had a mouthful of teeth now, and his fangs were sharp as a kitten's. She never nursed him without a tingle of apprehension. As he drew on her nipples, it felt as though some chemical fixative had entered her brain and crystallized her thoughts.

We will go to the northern hemisphere, she decided. Not to the Dubha, for they are defenseless, and would only die trying to hide us. If I could reach those caves where they worship the ancient bomb, Yakov wouldn't dare touch us.

They will kill us both rather than let me go.

The words rang in her mind like a gong. She looked down into the yellow eyes and had no doubt of the source.

Why didn't you speak before?

You were doing fine.

And now . . . not so good?

The grid is a tracer. The thin man with the long nose will always know where I am.

We'll get it off.

If it is tampered with, I die.

The diabolical bastard!

He serves his purpose, though he does not understand it.

She heard the rumble of a distant explosion. The lights blinked out. She felt a sinking despair. What can I do?

Go. They do not believe you will leave me. Their attention will be focused on the grid.

But you will be left in the hands of Yakov Ras.

I shall be a troublesome dependent. I feel no apprehension about the future. Our lives are long worms crawling through the apple of time. I perceive no end.

You perceive time?

Only when I am linked with you. When we are separate, I am quite an ordinary child.

If you think of yourself as an ordinary child, at the age of three months . . . then you are not an ordinary child.

Possibly. Go now. The pilot is coming.

She set him on the bed and jammed the door with a floor tile. In the dim light from the patio, she saw that he had put his thumb in his mouth and assumed an expression of absolute blankness. She bent and kissed his forehead, and his thought reached her:

I'll be all right, Mother.

As she slid back the door, she saw the skimmer hovering over the courtyard. It descended with a deafening roar of exhaust. At that moment the lasers spat tongues of fire, impaling the skimmer like a bun on a spit. Chips of stone whined off the walls and buzzed around her head. The skimmer crunched down on her marble fountain. While lasers crackled overhead, she tore open the door and threw herself inside. The pilot sprawled beside the control chair, his jaw gaping. She found a neatly cauterized hole going in under his left shoulder and coming out the right side of his chest.

Good try, Hut-Mo. She slid into the control seat and threw the turbines on full power. The skimmer shot straight up. Through the belly-port, she saw lights flaring around the palace. Guns winked brightly from the walls. She jammed the ship into full forward speed and felt herself thrown back in the seat. She aimed between the twin peaks of the Sleeping Virgin, flying so low that brush raked the bottom of her ship. She corkscrewed through the mountains, then veered left above the phosphorescent wiggle-worm of the surf. After an hour she saw lights winking on the rocks at the southern end of the Isles of Fire.

She decided to skirt them, since they would already be on military alert against the Eshom. She swung out over the open sea, flattening wave tops with her exhaust.

Hours of this. She had time to think of the baby she'd left. For the first time she understood how her mother had felt when she was forced to abandon her.

To her right, the River Plate Burn. Energy forms rippled and dived like dolphins, leaving corkscrew loops in the radiation glow. Ships had been known to disintegrate in the vortices, and most pilots took the stratospheric route to avoid them. But that would simply get her shot down by the Guardian Fleet.

Dawn found her skimming the jungle of Patagone. She followed a glowing track of phosphorescent matter for a couple of hundred miles before she came to the end. A giant worm, perhaps a half mile long, was eating his way through the jungle, laying down an ooze of slime which stretched behind him in a shimmering highway.

For the next few hours she dodged through the high peaks of the Andes. Once she was caught in a shimmering web stretched between two cliffs. She gunned her engine and broke through, trailing thick sticky strands.

The land became bleak, gray, and lifeless. Yawning cracks revealed the blood-red heart of the planet. This was the magma flow of Central America, heaving and falling like a viscid sea. Two volcanoes, thirty thousand feet high and a hundred miles apart, had ruptured the earth and vomited huge rivers of boiling lava. She tried to pass between them, but the whirling convection currents flung her ship upward and back. She veered off to the right, where the magma met the sea. Cloud banks of steam rose to a height of several miles. Unable to gain altitude, she flew blindly into the cloud. She steered by her compass and watched her radar screen. Something spattered on the front of her bubble and left a long smear of blood. Some kind of bird? A minute later the steam cleared, and she saw flying reptiles diving in the superheated air, spearing fish which had been killed by the boiling water. She wondered if they'd evolved for just that purpose.

Hot in the cabin. She saw steam leaping through the laser holes. It drifted through cracks where plates had sprung. The smell of burning sulphur choked her . . .

. . . Beyond the volcanoes now. She crossed over several hundred miles of stagnant water, clotted by floating islands of sickly-yellow vegetation. She buzzed a fleet of floating purple bladders and watched their skins ripple in the underblast.

Swamp now. Endless green tidelands. Dead insects formed a greasy sludge on her bow screen, and she had to keep blowing them off with an air blast.

Getting low on fuel. The mountain of the science-priests was said to be at the northern edge of the great talc desert. She must be getting close; the vegetation had thinned out to low thorny scrub. Fifty miles further it disappeared altogether. Dust began to sift into the cabin. She pulled on a respirator, but still it got incredibly stuffy. Her ground-speed indicator showed three hundred miles per hour. She'd been cruising at two hundred. That meant a hundred-mile-per-hour tail wind.

Barrier up ahead. Thousand-foot cliff. She tried to gain altitude, but the skimmer lurched and twisted like a berserk Ungul. It was like shooting rapids in an air mattress. Only a gap in the cliff could create this wind-tunnel effect. She searched and found it. Two vast slabs of rock had pulled apart, then tilted together at the top, leaving a triangular hole several hundred feet wide. She set her teeth and maneuvered her ship into the jetstream.

Ground speed, 600 m.p.h.

She was sucked through the needle's eye and spat out like a melon seed, flipping end over end. She got a scissors hold on the steering column, hugged the wheel, and tried to keep from getting smeared on the bulkhead. The body of Hut-Mo slammed into her back and knocked the air out of her lungs. She saw the black fingers wiggling behind her eyes and programed herself to hold on . . .

Silence fell, like sudden deafness. The wind had stopped. So had her engine. Ground speed 200 . . . 150 . . . 100 . . .

The ship lurched. There was a long screech, like sand sliding down a chute, then a billowing bumpety-bumpety-bump-bump . . . *bump*. She stopped, almost gently, then started sinking. She saw the white powder coming up to her ports. This was the great talc desert . . .

She tried to start the engine, but it only sucked her deeper into the fluffy white powder. She wondered how deep it was. Estimates ranged from twenty feet to a mile. The stuff flowed like quicksilver, but the sunlight should have fused a crust on top which could support her weight.

The stuff poured in through the cracks and flowed across the deck. When it touched her skin she gasped. *Hot.* Thermometer read 140 . . . and that was in the shade. Could she survive in the sun?

She delayed a half minute to strip the shirt from the dead pilot. It stank, but it would protect her from the sun. She pushed up the hatch and climbed out. A minute later would have been too long. Now it was a level jump to the jagged edge of the crust. She gathered her strength and leaped, sailed through the air, and caught her toe on the edge. She sprawled full-length, heard a muffled crack, and scrambled away from the hole.

Her palms burned where she'd touched the packed surface. She stood up and held the shirt over her head. Which way to go? Did it matter? It was like being inside an oven. Each time she breathed she felt the hot air frying the cells in her lungs. It was like standing on a sheet of frosted glass. Her feet burned inside her shoes. Impossible to look down, her eyes would fry. In the middle distance, the horizon was blue-white. To the south she saw the dim red fire of the volcanoes, to the east billowed fluffy cloud castles of talc dust. She looked north and saw the heaped-up spires of a mountain range. They looked cool and blue in the distance.

She started walking, but knew it was hopeless. Water rushed out of her pores and dried at once. She touched her skin and watched it slide off her arms. She wrapped the shirt around her head and pushed her arms inside her gown.

In the sky she saw a hovering speck, circling in lazy overlapping sweeps, wheeling and turning in the Pteroni pattern of search. What could he find here? Animals living in the talc? Never mind, he might help her. She tried to give the Pteroni distress whistle, but found it impossible to shape her cracked lips. She wished for something black. Her hair was red. Thank the computer she wasn't bald like her mother. Then she thought: *That isn't enough. Movement will attract him.* She started walking in a zig-zag most likely to capture his eyes. Her nose puffed out in a huge blister, her eyesight faded . . .

* * *

She had fallen . . . how long ago? She gasped for air, her cheek against the blistering sand. Each breath seared her lungs. She was dying. Without water her blood oozed like thick honey. Already her hands and feet were numb. Brain cells drying up, her outer skin shrinking, wrinkling, turning black like a dried apple . . .

She was being mummified.

Something thump-thumped on her back. Her cells awakened, swelled out. Her flesh firmed up. Sensation began to return. Her eyesight came back, and she saw vapor curling up from the sand. Vapor meant moisture. She lifted her head and felt cool water splash onto her face.

A man was standing there. She tried to see his face, but the sun dazzled her. He was naked, not woolly like an Ungul, but with hair on his groin, chest and face.

"The Pteroman is coming. He'll help you to his cave."

The voice was one she had heard long ago: *In the desert lives the water-giver, who appears to thirsty lost ones, and water flows from his hand.*

"Who . . . ?" The word came out in a dry croak.

"You knew me when I was very young and you were . . . not much younger than now. I told you I'd be all right."

"Kim?" For the moment it was possible to believe it. "You mean you can travel . . . in time?"

She got no answer. She looked up, saw only the hovering shadow of the Pteroman. The sand around her was dry. Had it ever been wet, or was it all an hallucination from the sun?

The Enemy . . . Within?

> "Oh, the Jelkies may eat us
> But they'll never beat us
> For we are the Khoom-na
> We're seven feet tall . . ."
>
> Ballad, translated from
> the Hyades dialect

Now Yakov Ras, grown more secure in his power, indulged in second thoughts, a luxury confined to the winner of any given struggle. Had there been a way to save Abi? He missed her bright vivacious eyes, the vigor of her mind. Knowing that he'd been secretly afraid of that vigor, overwhelmed sometimes, he wondered if his subconscious had played tricks upon him, if he had somehow arranged her death without knowing exactly what he was doing.

Metal detectors had found the little skimmer at a depth of two hundred feet. There were no bodies, but the talc worms had the ability to scent water-bearing tissue from afar, and would not have taken long to find her. She was most certainly dead, and from the point of view of the government and the computer, she had been expendable, having served her purpose as the launching cradle for this superweapon of the Jelks.

The weapon itself made Yakov terribly uncomfortable. Even as he toddled about and played with the toys Yakov brought, he had a feeling the boy was mocking him. He moved him to an island off the coast of Enderby, one of the "new" islands, with a volcanic cone leaking streams of magma like wax melting down a candle.

Yakov had two reasons for choosing the island. It was separated from the Eshom by the entire Antarctic continent, and it was a place of maximum security, having been a penitentiary for miscreant

Grithies before the vast prison complex was built in the Greenland Sea. It was ringed with submarine monitoring stations and pocked with surveillance chambers buried beneath the ground. Boiling currents from the Tasman Burn lashed the island's eastern shore, and packs of sabre-toothed seals prevented escape toward Afrik. With the beach of Enderby garrisoned by loyal D'Yabelt troops, and a trusted staff on the island, Yakov felt it safe it let the boy run free as the computer had instructed.

At the age of five he was as big as the average Jelk adolescent. He climbed trees like a Coney and swam in hot springs whose temperature was near the boiling point. There was no pretext of a formal education: Stafi specialists were periodically flown to the island and then taken away again—knowing only that they'd been highly paid for sitting around and answering the questions of a bright lad of undetermined race and ancestry. Those who broke their oath of silence were said to be suffering mental fatigue, and were granted long rest cures in the free government clinic on the asteroid of Pallas.

Yakov himself undertook to teach the boy topographical chess. On the third game he was startled when Raki—a name Yakov preferred to the one Abi had called him—shifted from an awkward defense to a skillful attack. After several defeats, Yakov realized that the boy could improvise with lightning speed, making all the calculations necessary to change a plan in a split second.

Yakov found himself stimulated, somewhat awed, each time he visited the island. He marveled at the way the computer's design was taking shape, and worried that it might get out of control. Raki could not be led, or commanded. Yakov's only hope was the sleep conditioning which had taken place nightly since his birth: *You must destroy the Vim computer,* a command planted so deeply that the experts promised it would function without his knowledge.

It was Yakov's nature not to trust even his own experts, so he ordered the installation of a secret spy eye, expertly camouflaged as a wisp of vapor, maintained at an altitude of one hundred feet by 1-t-a gas, designed always to be focused on Raki through magnetic attraction the grid in his skull. Nobody on the island would know of its existence, and it would project only to Yakov's private chamber on the eighth level of the moon. With this safeguard, Yakov felt he could relax.

In Raki's tenth year the spy eye began to function.

* * *

The boy was climbing down the rocks on the eastern side of the island. Long Eshom muscles rippled beneath his sleek creamy skin. Drops of moisture condensed in the tight, silver-tipped mat which capped his head. They dried immediately in the hot brassy sunlight. Dry cindery dust filled the air, and the red-scaled bushes quivered in the wind.

Raki paused at the edge of a low cliff and looked down onto the steaming, rust-scummy beach. A horde of insectile sea life tried to reach him. Some looked like giant scorpions, with long segmented tails and bulbous scimitar-shaped stingers arched over their backs. Their mandibles were composed of a substance so hard it scarred the rock. Centipedes, twelve feet long and resembling huge red sewer pipes, tried to scale the steep cliff. They kept falling on their backs while their hundred legs, each the size of man's arm, rippled in sinuous motion.

Yakov held his breath as the lad jumped onto the back of a centipede, raced down its length, then leaped onto another, landing just behind his head. Yakov saw the hairs rising where his feet had trod, and knew they gave off an electric shock which killed smaller animals. Raki seemed to have no fear, and Yakov knew he'd done it many times before.

He switched on his console, tapped out the sending code, and saw the bristly, mustard-skinned face of his guard commander fade in on the screen.

"Do you know where the boy is?" growled Yakov.

The commander stiffened to quivering attention. "He is out walking with his jester, excellency."

"What is the temperature on the surface of the island, Commander?"

The guardsman's eyes flicked to a dial, then widened. "One hundred forty degrees! The wind must have shifted—"

"And the jester is holed up in a cave somewhere. Find him."

He clicked off the screen and turned back to the spy-eye receiver. At first he did not see Raki in the surf. The waves were twenty feet high. They did not crash and foam like cooler water, but rolled in like hot oil, curled into spiraling tunnels, then smoothed out with a muffled crumping sound. Steam blurted from trapped air pockets, and the backwash formed scummy bubbles which looked like rust.

The redness came from billions of button-sized rotifers, and these had attracted a giant jellyfish which floated offshore, sustained by an air sac the size of a space cruiser. Thousands of tentacles floated to the beach on bulbous air bladders. One touched a giant centipede. It writhed, stood on its tail, then collapsed on its back, dead.

Raki was playing among the tendrils, sidestepping and leaping from one patch of bare sand to another.

The communicator buzzed, and Yakov turned on the face of the commander.

"I have the jester, excellency. He was sleeping."

Xip-tah stood in loose baggy smock and shorts which flared around his knobby knees. A former minstrel, he'd arrived three years before to entertain Raki with songs and music and had stayed to teach him the arcane secrets of Bola-bol and other Grithy vices. He made a slovenly contrast to the starched commander. His posture was more slouch than stance, and he spoke in the aggrieved tones of one unjustly accused:

"Your strategic highness, sir. Raki has gone to the beach because the hot winds blow. He has done it many times, and I have never been able to follow beyond the line of storms. What can I do? I wait, but the heat makes me drowsy. Always before he has returned and awakened me, and no harm has been done."

"What does he do?"

"He says he goes fishing, that is all I know."

The commander said: "I will go and fetch him."

"Wait," said Yakov. He looked through the spy eye. Raki was still dancing among the tentacles. Yakov saw that there were three kinds: one a thin red whip which lashed about, another a deep, ugly coruscating blue, which touched the creatures and made them dead. Only then did the third tentacle appear, a white slimy mucosity which flowed over the corpse and smothered it in sucker discs. Extruded stomachs, thought Yakov. The reds were the finders and the blues the killers.

And Raki was trapped by a red one. Ah, no . . . Yakov let out his breath. Raki seized the tentacle and wrestled it toward a blue one. There was a blinding flash, and the sudden dead cessation of motion on the beach revealed to Yakov how much of the roiling life had been the creature itself. The tentacles were limp. Raki tied them into a double bow and got between them like a draft Ungul. The muscles bulged in his thighs—and the monster started gathering speed like a ship under sail. It bobbed on the rising swells, then tumbled into the breakers and rolled up onto the beach. The giant bladder shriveled visibly as the hot wind sucked moisture from its tissues . . .

Raki tipped back his head and smiled directly at the spy eye, white fangs gleaming against the bright pinkness of his mouth:

"Why don't you come down and go fishing, Yakov?"

* * *

Two years passed. The Vega system was lost, only twenty-seven light-years away. Vast numbers of people awakened to the knowledge that five hundred years of attrition had become a rout. Three hundred thousand sleep-frozen refugees would reach Juno in the same year as the sixty thousand who had escaped from Megrez. A law was passed in council that none could be thawed until land was ready for them. Stilt homes of the new Grithies covered the swampy inland sea, plagues carried off thousands, and infant mortality was one in three—but still the new Grithies increased at twice the speed of other races.

Yakov, in one of his periodic examinations of key personnel, called in the chief of the educational task force he'd assigned to Raki.

"What sort of questions does he ask?"

"He has asked none—for at least two years."

"Does he talk to you?"

"Rarely. I'm afraid we bore him. Frankly, he mocks us. He proposes no new theories, but shows the fault in ours. Two of our people have requested transfer back to Ganymede. Another has committed suicide. It is impossible to love him, or resist him. We have our knowledge in little boxes. He breaks open the boxes and scatters our knowledge until we are reduced to idiots laughing at our own pretension."

"Is he serious about nothing?"

"I would say . . . he is not even serious about nothing."

Yakov hesitated, then asked: "Insane?"

The Stafi shrugged. "What is sanity?"

It seemed to be one of those philosophical cloudlands to which Stafis were addicted. Yakov surprised himself by asking:

"Do you know anyone named Novii?"

The man nodded once. "I know him. He has gone to join the navel-contemplators on Jupiter."

Yakov's mind drifted to the memory of Abi and the young man dancing in their captured ship. Her hair had been a blazing torch and her eyes had flashed like bits of gold caught in the sunlight . . .

Pain lay heavy in his stomach. He dismissed the Stafi and tuned the circuit to the island. (On the old maps it was Amry's Isle, but the boy's personality dominated, and in his mind Yakov called it Raki's Island.) The guard commander was new, fresh from the Dunkirking operation on Vega. His troops were so happy to be alive that they offered no problems in discipline.

"I want to speak to Raki. Where is he?"

The commander wore a harried expression. "Your excellency. Eight hours ago he went swimming. The fleet has been alerted, submarines are patrolling the continental shelf, and skimmers are hovering over the water. So far he has not surfaced."

Yakov studied the commander. His skin had an amphibious green tint which made him think of his grandmother, but it wasn't that which caught his eye.

"You seem remarkably calm. Has he done it before?"

"Many times. He swims with the young Androxi. They like to tease the killer seals, which they say are stupid and clumsy."

Yakov left the console and went into his private chamber. He looked at the holy-g map which was connected to the copper grid in Raki's head. A red dot glowed in the Androxi undersea city. Yakov went back to his console and told the commander: "Prepare a submarine. I'll be down within the hour."

The Androxi city was composed of metal spheres which glowed dully in the dark water outside the submarine's searchlight beam. Yakov saw half a hundred swimming figures spread out in front of them. It was obvious that they meant to use their bodies to prevent the sub from penetrating farther into their city.

The pilot asked: "Shall I plow through them?"

"No. Get me a pressure suit."

Yakov went out through the airlock and approached the group. The Androxi were blue-skinned on the back, off white on the underside. An extra layer of fat under the skin protected them from extremes of temperature and gave them a streamlined look. They had gill slits above their collarbones and expelling vents under their arms.

Sharp, clear sounds beat against his ears, seeming to come from the water around him: *"Welcome to our city, Yakov Ras."*

None of the individuals had moved his mouth, so it was impossible to tell which one had spoken. Three males were swimming toward him, moving their webbed feet up and down in a flutter-kick motion. It was this swimming technique, Yakov assumed, which caused their bodies to develop most widely at the hips, with two huge bulges in the gluteus maximus region. He felt no fear, though the harness on their bodies held guns and concussion grenades.

"I am Oongu-anga," said the voice. *"We will take you to our meeting house, where we can talk."*

They swam upward into a region where the sunlight came down in pale streamers. They led him through an opening and emerged in a transparent dome with a platform built around its edge. Yakov stood up and found that his head and shoulders protruded into the air pocket trapped beneath the dome. Samples of artifacts hung around the wall, and he realized that this was their trading center.

"You may speak Jelk," said the spokesman. He had a small rounded head and ears which were nearly invisible in surrounding pads of flesh. Coarse hair stood out on his scalp and pointed in Yakov's direction when he spoke:

"The boy from the island comes here often," said Yakov.

"The son of Abi is always welcome," said Oongu-anga.

"Where is he now?"

The Androxi ducked his head beneath the water. Yakov recalled that the high-pitched sounds of the Androxi had great penetrating power, making it possible for them to converse at a distance of more than a mile.

"He is coming," said Oongu-anga.

The Androxi projected a tranquillity, an equilibrium of nature which came through to Yakov and calmed him, like a gentle wave. He asked questions about their culture, and they were proud to answer. The Androxi were the least changed of all human types, and some could trace their ancestry back before the first solar expansion period, when the earth had been so overcrowded that many people had to live under the sea. Many of these were later employed by interstellar traders to deal with suboceanic races on other worlds. From one such nucleus had grown the present Androxi. Now their civilization was spreading, thanks to the impetus given them by Abi. Colonies had been established off Patagone and Afrik. Explorations had been carried out in the northern hemisphere, and suitable lands had been found on the continental shelf off Baffin. Thousands of young Androxi were ready to emigrate, but they needed submarines to protect them from the seal herds during the trip.

"That can be arranged," said Yakov.

At that point Raki's head popped out of the water, surrounded by a half dozen young Androxi. One who stayed close to him was female, with glints of gold running lengthwise down her body. She had long conical breasts which looked human except that they were composed mostly of muscle tissue. Yakov recalled that the female Androxi squirted nutrients into the mouths of their young by muscular contractions, since oceanic pressures did not permit sucking. He noticed that her hair stood out like spines when she spoke to Raki.

Raki accepted Yakov's offer of a ride back to the island. As the sub churned through the dark sea, Yakov asked:

"How long can you stay under water?"

"Oh, for half an hour, without air. But many species of animals carry oxygen down into the depths. You find them and steal their air, and you can stay under for hours . . . days. Actually there's no limit."

Yakov asked why the young female's hair had stood out.

"It happens when they feel emotionally drawn to someone. She wants to have little ones."

"Ah? With your cooperation?"

Raki shrugged. "We have fun together."

For the next few weeks Yakov was haunted by the fear that Raki would disappear with his bride in the dark oceans of earth. Instead, Raki appeared one day in his private cavern on the eighth level of the moon. With him was the Androxi leader, Oongu-anga, clad in something which resembled a Jelk atmosphere suit, except that it contained water instead of air.

"With these," said Raki, "they can walk on the surface of the earth, ride in spaceships, and go wherever the rest of us go. They are ready to take their place with the rest of humanity. They desire representation on the council."

"Impossible," said Yakov.

"Wouldn't it be helpful to have one more member hostile to the racist policy of the Milarks?"

Yakov was surprised that Raki knew of his political bind. In those terms, the idea had merit . . .

Six months later, after a series of deals and manipulations, Oonguanga became the first Androxi to sit on the council. Hov Torka grumbled: "Fish on the council, then what? Shall we install a perch, and invite the Pteroni?"

Yakov smiled. "All in good time, my dear."

* * *

A year passed. The guard commander called in a state of gibbering panic to report that Raki was poised on the edge of a thousand-foot cliff, about to jump into the boiling pool of Yaqwer with a pair of plastic wings strapped to his back.

"Let him jump," said Yakov. "I don't believe he's suicidal."

Curiosity impelled him to cancel a meeting and fly immediately to earth. He found Raki soaring in the updraft from the boiling lake, accompanied by a covey of adolescent Pteroni. The boy glided down, spread his gauzy wings, and braked himself with a jet of gas released from a tank on his back. Alighting gently beside Yakov, he called to the covey in the shrill whistling warble of the Pteroni. A figure detached itself from the group and circled down to land beside him.

"This is Paq-linn. Isn't she beautiful?"

She was, thought Yakov, if you liked them seven feet tall and thin as a flagstaff. Skin flaps ran from below her ears to the tips of her shoulders. Membranes under her arms were attached to her ankles by a thick tendon. She had a high domed skull and unblinking violet eyes set in deep sockets. Small pink breasts peeked from the downy white fur which covered the front of her body.

Yakov noticed that she seemed nervous, flapping her wings and rising a few feet off the ground.

"This is her mating flight," said Raki. "She has selected her group and is anxious to be off to her nesting place on Menzies Peak."

"You really feel an urge for her?"

"It is communal," said Raki. "One cannot help it."

With a jump and a hiss of escaping gas, he flew into the air. Yakov watched them wistfully until they were mere wheeling specks in the sky.

When Raki returned a week later he would say only that the flight had been successful. Paq-linn had become pregnant and was now in-

volved in nest building with her four surviving males, an enterprise
which bored him.

On Raki's third disappearance, Yakov was not disturbed until his
absence stretched into the fourth week. Then he consulted his tracer
and found the red spot in Gafronkil, the Grithy slum built on stilts
over a marsh. An informant told him that Raki was touring the bor-
dellos, supporting his sexual researches by playing Bola-bol, a gambling
game in which five ivory marbles are thrown onto a board containing
five numbered holes. Each player tries to calculate the combination of
the numbers on the balls multiplied by the numbers on the holes.

As a lightning calculator, Raki soon ran out of opponents. He got
bored and started a walking tour of the continent.

At this time Raki was taller than the average Grithy, roughly six
feet, but broader and heavier. His ears were small, almost Ungul size.
Tight-curled hair covered his chest, his groin, chin, jaws and upper
lip. His yellow-green eyes glowed with friendliness, but Yakov perceived a white-hot flame of violence lurking behind them.

Raki wound up his tour on the family estate of Enderby, and informed Yakov that he intended to live there. Yakov did not object,
but was shocked to learn that Raki often went down to the Ungul pens
when the females were in heat. He liked to prowl the range, weapon-
less, and take his choice of the young heifers on their first mating. The
neighboring Landarks were stunned with horror. To placate them, Yakov
flew down and asked Raki if he would like to have a few Grithy courtesans come and live on the estate.

"Too tame," he said. "Their actions are not spontaneous like the
Unguls. Although even among these there are great differences. The
common Beef Ungul is least appealing. Hyades heifers are best, though
they have a strong taboo against mating outside their race. They call
themselves the Khoom-na, which means human. They keep the history
of their race alive through ballads."

"Doesn't this taboo include you?"

"Oh, no." Raki smiled, showing his fangs. "I am a descendant of
Silvertip, who in their language is called Yoquin. They have a legend
that I'll free them from bondage to the Grithies."

Strange, thought Yakov, to see the computer's design working.

"Why do you suppose they're different from other Unguls?"

"An accident of history," said Raki. "In the home world their Hossips died of disease, and the Grithies lost control, and the Unguls ran
wild for three centuries. They had the beginnings of culture, religion.
They built a gigantic stone monument on the site of their first city.
I've seen films, though today nobody credits the Unguls with having
built the thing. Of course, when the Grithies retook the planet—
under Jelk officers—they destroyed the culture and kept the Unguls in

a state of barbarism, capturing a few now and then for the combat arena. Someday I think I'll visit the home world. For the present, I have no trouble identifying with them. The females love me . . . which is quite enjoyable."

Yakov flew back to the moon and went into private communion with the computer. "Is it possible that the boy can reproduce at fourteen?"

"It is possible."

"Is it good that he should spread his seed among the races?"

"It is not opposed to his purpose."

"Should I permit this . . . dalliance?"

"Permit what you cannot prevent, Yakov."

Yakov left feeling dissatisfied, as usual. He wished the computer would issue clear instructions; this way, it left all the thinking to him.

Still, when Raki said that he was flying to the Pteronian *weeya* in Patagone, a breeding orgy generally accompanied by much drinking of tikula, Yakov forbade him to go.

"An accident might happen. Those are Eshom lands."

"I don't fear the Eshom. Their blood is partly mine."

"Yes. That is why I forbid it."

For the first time Yakov saw the blazing yellow fire beneath the invisible membrane of Raki's eyes. "You can't stop me from doing what I want, Yakov Ras. You can only make it difficult for both of us."

He was gone three weeks and came back to inform Yakov that the Androxi, the Pteroni, and the Eshom were talking about forming a single nation. "Their representation on the council is a sop, the geno-cide continues, the Eshom desire an end to Jelk forming, which destroys their hunting land and makes it fit only for Unguls."

They were sitting in Abi's old study, and in Raki's face Yakov saw the same belligerent defiance that Abi had so often displayed.

"You didn't spend all your time wenching and drinking, then."

Raki gave a boyish grin and ducked his head.

"I have three minds. One is seeking fun, all the time. I want to learn all there is to know, make love to all the females. And then on another level, I can see the power that is being wasted in these people. The Androxi, with their deep wavelike patience. They make their plans in terms of hundreds of years. The Pteroni . . . so carefree, but absolutely merciless toward their enemies. Their system functions without rules, entirely on intuition. And the Eshom, weird, silent, deadly. With all their special powers. Do you think if they ever united under a single person, that your unhappy regimented Grithies could stand against them?"

"You see yourself as that person?"

"It tempts me, Yakov. With the Androxi and the Pteroni I inherit the reputation of Abi. They see her as a goddess. I could command the

Unguls in the name of Silvertip. The Eshom call me 'Fire of God' and believe I will do something superhuman. Maybe I will, someday." He raised his head and fixed Yakov with a piercing look. "But first I want to know what the government has planned for me."

"You know about the grid?"

Raki winced. "Every filament runs through my cells. How could I help but know?"

"It was put on when you were young. We had no idea how you would turn out."

"Now you know I'm not a mad killer. So you can take it off."

"I'm afraid not, Raki."

The boy looked at Yakov in a calculating manner. "If I held you by the heels above the pool of Yaqwer, you would order it taken off."

Yakov shook his head. "It was predicted that you would be able to influence those around you. So the cut-off switch was sent twenty-five years into the future. It's a tiny thing, but it took a year's reserve of power to send it. There is no way to bring it back."

"So I'm a prisoner in this cage for eleven more years, eh?"

"Only if you stay in the Jelk sphere. Once you go outside the periphery, you will be in full possession of your powers."

Raki laughed. "That puts me in Vim territory."

Yakov nodded. "That's the plan."

"I see. And I'm expected to do something unpleasant to the Vim?"

"Yes. Defeat them."

Raki scratched his chin with a short, rounded claw. "So ends the children's games. Get me into the Horlick Academy. I want to learn military science."

* * *

Three months after Raki entered the Horlick Mountain Military Academy, the commander came to Yakov with a request that he be removed. He was destroying the academy's hallowed traditions.

Raki was contemptuous. "It's a losing tradition. Why should it be perpetuated?"

He gave Yakov a list of changes to be made in the training program, then flew off to the Space Academy on Ceres. His classmates knew him as Requal, a descendant of proto-human forebears from the Mizar sector. He left after eight months, having completed the normal five-year training course.

"We spent our time working out tactical problems in textbook situations," he told Yakov. "Based on the defeats of last year and the year before. So what I came out with was a perfect strategy of defeat."

"What would you suggest?"

"For one thing, abandon the tradition that a Jelk is not supposed to pilot his own ship. He sits and directs the Grithies, and the Grithies run the ship. The whole thing could be automated, you could eliminate all these time-wasting steps in the chain of command."

"Yes," said Yakov. "And you could also eliminate the careers of about a hundred thousand middle-ranking Milark officers . . . but before you got it done, you'd have an officer's revolt."

Raki sniffed. "You overrate their fighting spirit. Better risk it, anyway. You'll need an offensive strategy to push the Vim out of human space, even if I manage to knock out their central computer. Which reminds me, I'm ready to study *our* computer. I want to learn how it's put together."

Yakov felt a prickly discomfort. "Nobody knows *that.*"

"Well . . . what's its basic premise? There must be an ethical system which governs it."

"Nobody knows," said Yakov. "There is a job for everyone who serves the computer, but there is no overall direction. The computer actually fixes its own purpose."

Raki was determined, so Yakov went against the united power of the Progs to have him assigned as an EVO trainee in the sector of strategic planning. His stomach felt queasy for an entire month, then Raki appeared one day in his private chamber dressed in the smock of a programing tech.

"Something's missing from the computer."

Yakov stiffened. "What do you mean?"

"It's like a puzzle where all the pieces fit together, but there's this big blank space. Circuits bypass it. Energy comes out but nothing goes in. Suppose it's been infiltrated. Maybe this is why we're losing the war, because our computer is directing us to lose it."

Such talk made Yakov sick. One had to take something on faith— and he had built his life on the premise that the computer was basically beneficent toward man. To consider an alternative was to stare backward into a wasted life.

"I'll . . . ask the computer that you be permitted to examine that area."

"I already asked."

"And . . . ?"

"Permission denied. So I tried to break in. Don't look so horrified. I didn't succeed. The sector is out of phase, somehow. Either the node of the computer is actually a time machine, or . . ."

"Or what?"

Raki shook his head. "The concept is too abstract to describe. Anyway I can't penetrate wih the powers available to me now. I want to capture a Vim ship with its crew—alive."

"Impossible. The Vim ships invariably self-destruct."

"They wouldn't if they were clamped in a stasis field."

"But there's none large enough to seize a whole ship."

"There was once . . . on Hidalgo."

"How do you know?"

"There are records in the computer . . . taken from people who were captured by pirates. Ben Abo used a stasis field on cruisers."

"Ben Abo is dead. And Hidalgo's a blasted cinder."

"There may be enough left to put a machine together. Anyway, I'll go see."

He declined Yakov's offer of a cruiser escort, saying he wanted to get used to working alone. Three months after he blasted off in his one-man shuttle, the guardian station on Callisto received a message from the cruiser *Mira*, patrolling the asteroid belt with a complement of five Jelk officers and three hundred Grithy crewmen:

UNIDENTIFIED SHUTTLE CLOSING FAST. AM PREPARING T

The message ended. The solar fleet went on red alert. Planetary guard squadrons scrambled. Space satellites bristled with atomic cannon. All leaves were canceled. All pleasure ships and passenger vessels streaked for the nearest base.

And Raki's face materialized on the screen in Yakov's private chamber. His fangs showed in a broad grin. Beside him sat an officer of the *Mira* with his hand frozen to a communicator key, his fixated eyes staring into space.

"No need to tell you I found enough parts. Clear me with Callisto and I'll bring in this boatload of stiffs. I'd rather not be aboard when they come out of stasis."

* * *

One month later the stasis field went into production. Five ships were equipped with one unit each, and the fleet spun out toward Arcturus on f-t-1 drive, with orders to seize a Vim ship and bring it back with crew alive.

Raki slept for a week in Yakov's private cavern, then got up and said he wanted to get in touch with the Jovian Entities.

"But Jupiter supports no life measurable by instruments," said Yakov.

"Which may indicate a fault of the instruments, rather than absence of life. When the fleet returns, I'll be on Amalthea."

Amalthea, only 113,000 miles from Jupiter, had once housed a scientific station. Now it was the site of the Temple of Jovian Truth, a religion invented by Stafi hucksters, who made a fortune hauling believers out from earth and giving them a spin around the awesome planet.

"Why can't you work with the group on Ganymede?" asked Yakov.

"It's structured for people who have a hundred and fifty years to sit around, and I haven't."

Time, the black bird of expediency, perched on his shoulder. But quiescent now. Somehow Raki, after two years of frenzied activity, fell into a complete trance.

Reports from Amalthea indicated that he'd reduced his food intake to zero. They showed his countenance on the screen: hollow jaws, sunken empty eyes. Yakov ordered him awakened, and after several hours, Raki opened his mouth and growled: "Have they got the Vim ship?"

"No. They haven't had time to reach the periphery—"

"Don't bother me until they come back."

Then he shut himself off. His vital signs dropped to the minimum required to sustain life, and remained their for seven months.

A message came in on the subspace relay. A Vim cruiser had been seized. One officer had blown himself to molecular paste as the stasis field took hold, but the other two were frozen intact. So was the troop contingent of three hundred Vim.

Yakov flew to Callisto to watch the fleet come into normal space. It was an eerie sight, to see the ghost images of hyperspace, each ship magnified forty times, the whole fleet spread out in flickering haze from the belt to Neptune's orbit. With each flicker the ships grew smaller and sharper, until at last they were normal size. The Vim ship looked like a strung-out mechanical toy. Three flexible whips grew out of a central sphere and terminated in lozenge-shaped control pods. A long solid shaft ran from the troop section to the drive unit a half mile to the rear.

Yakov decided not to awaken either Raki or the Vim until he'd taken adequate security measures. First he imposed a total news blackout. Most people believed the Vim had superhuman powers of hypnotic control, and would have gone into paranoid convulsions if they learned that over three hundred live Vim were within the system.

Mars, an almost waterless and airless world already gutted by mining interests, was chosen as the prison site. The Vim ship was brought down on the equator and a copper-sheathed plastic dome built around it. Atmosphere was created to duplicate that inside the ship. Jelk dieticians reproduced their food supply without much trouble, mainly by substituting carbohydrates for the proteins in their own gruel. A surveillance station was built on the satellite Phobos, 5800 miles from the center of the planet. It was a tiny moon, only ten miles in diameter, with a sidereal period of seven hours, thirty-nine minutes.

Yakov ordered the Vim removed and laid out in rows under the dome. Many had to be taken out through holes cut in the hull. It would have been easier to thaw them first, but Yakov couldn't risk having them take control of the ship. With their many appendages frozen in working position, it was like moving trees with limbs and roots intact.

Yakov had the empty ship transported to Callisto for study. Then he flew to Amalthea and awakened Raki. The boy was a frightening skeleton, but after a few hours' intake of food concentrates, he regained his usual vigor. During the flight to Mars, Yakov asked if he'd made contact with the Jovian Entities.

Raki shook his head. "They don't seem to function on this level."

"What did you do for ten months?"

"That long? Seemed like hours. I traveled into the past."

"But you didn't move."

"No, of course not. One bisects the circle of time, but one cannot enter the stream physically. What I did was project a thought form, which then functioned according to the will of those present in that time. I myself had little control . . ." He shook his head. "It's a metaphysical problem. I can't explain it."

On Phobos, Raki wanted to thaw out the Vim immediately and go down and mingle with them.

"Too risky," said Yakov.

"I can't learn anything at this distance."

"They might kill you and eat you."

"They're vegetarians."

"In that case they might mistake you for a vegetable."

Raki finally agreed to Yakov's security precautions. He flew his little shuttle into the dome and stayed inside it while the Vim were brought out of stasis. For ten hours he observed them through his viewport, describing what he saw to Yakov:

"Head is covered by a bony plate, like a helmet. Through this, on each side of the central ridge, grow four tentacles. These have no grasping function, but point in the direction of food. Neck is composed of resilient discs, probably containing nerve trunk and blood lines. Clusters at joints are roller bearings, allowing completely free motion at shoulder and elbow. Cohesion must come from a magnetic field, which is probably controlled by the brain. If caught, the Vim could merely detach that appendage and flee. The Vim are probably capable of regrowing body parts, including the head. Four powerful tentacles grow from the back. These are prehensile, but seem to have no function that I can see. The tail is an extension of the spinal cord, culminating in a secondary brain equipped with sensors.

"In the legs, the area between joints is composed of resilient discs which provide spring when hopping. They seem to underestimate their range quite frequently, hitting their heads against the top of the dome. This would indicate evolution on a planet with about two-point-five earth gravity. Knee joints lock, permitting the Vim to sleep standing up. Eyes are lidless, fixated during sleep. There are four barbels around the mouth which seem to have no relation to eating or speaking. Possibly a sex function, but this cannot be determined until females are examined. All these are males. The male organ has a structure similar to humans. Physical connection would be theoretically possible with a Vim female, if any such exist. Signing off now, will go out and attempt to learn their language."

After two days of silence, he came back on the audio:

"They seem to accept me as a fellow prisoner, though I am obviously not a Vim. Apparently they are used to seeing other races among their fighting forces, which leads to the conclusion that the Vim are not alone in their fight. One may postulate an interstellar federation of many races, expanding in many directions at once. Their culture is single-sex, despite the presence of reproductive organs. Possibly they are segregated at an early age and trained entirely for combat. Their vocabulary is small, their songs simple working chants.

"So far they have not permitted close contact. When I eat, they move away and leave me the entire trough. Wherever I go, they step aside. It's too bad the Vim were taken out of the ship before I arrived, since I have no way of knowing who were the pilots and which are the troops. They wear no insignia of rank, which may indicate a military structure different from ours. Possibly the orders are given on a sensory level I can't pick up. In any case I can find no leaders."

And two days later:

"Today I found the leaders. There were two who sat and had their food brought to them by others. I thought perhaps they were injured, or this was merely a gesture of friendship. But it isn't. When I tried to talk to one of them today, he hopped away from me. It's hard to corner a person in this round dome, but I got him backed against a wall and planned to coax him into the shuttle for a private talk. The minute I grabbed his tentacles he died. Now they're all bunched around the body. They've grown hostile, so I think it's time to go. I'll take the dead one along, because I want to dissect the brain."

Two hours later Raki's shuttle eased into its cradle on Phobos. He came through the airlock and dropped two dead Vim like two bags of coconuts. Gashes streaked his shoulders, and a purpling lump oozed blood from his forehead.

"They got between me and the ship. Damned hard to knock out, with their double brains. The only fatal spot is the solar plexis." He held out his hands. "I'll clean up and then we'll slice into those brains. One is a pilot and one is a trooper, and I suspect we'll find a difference."

The difference was that the pilot's brain contained an encysted area the size of an apple, but porous like a sponge. They found nothing inside it but a white flaky substance. The microscope revealed it as dried organic cells.

"The leaders were infected by a parasite," said Yakov.

"Occupied by a control organism," said Raki, "which is slightly dif-

ferent. The parasite gave them power over the ones who didn't have it."
He scratched his chin. "Were the brains of the yellow-eyes ever examined?"

Yakov shook his head. "None were ever captured. We had no stasis
field in those days."

Raki wiped his hands. "I've got a feeling the Vim aren't the real
enemy. But the only way to check it out is to infiltrate. Let's get to work
on that Vim warship."

Three control cabins . . . three pilots. It seemed pointless, until
Raki discovered that each of the pods controlled a different kind of
drive. One functioned in normal space, one in hyperspace, and the
third . . .

"It might relate to a different order of physics," said Raki. "Anyway
I don't want to test it until I have my full powers. Let's weld the three
pods together so I can move from one to the other. I'll fly out beyond
the periphery and kick it on."

"Too dangerous."

"Yakov, there's no waiting time left. This is a new thing. I don't
know how the third pod worked, but it got the ship through our defense screen. With a few thousand ships like this, they could wipe us
out in five years."

When the ship was ready, they hauled it in a cruiser to the orbit of
Pluto. Yakov hated sentimental farewells, but he needn't have worried. As soon as Raki was strapped into the control seat, he said:

"Something I didn't mention before. I saw Abi while I was time-
traveling."

Yakov felt his pulse leap. "Where?"

Raki showed his fangs in a grin. "Maybe I'll tell you . . . after the
grid comes off my head."

Yakov stared. "Is this blackmail?"

"Insurance of a safe homecoming. I listened to the record of the first
council meeting, you know."

Yakov nodded slowly, remembering. Nothing had changed; that was
the saddest part.

Raki's Log

I kicked off the hyperdrive as soon as I left Jelk space.

There's really only one thing you can say about the Interdicted Zone. It's empty. Five light-years of nothingness, home of a thousand dead worlds and ten million fused hulks, populated by myself and about thirteen million guard Unguls with their ships and their harem crews. I felt a warm kinship with them. I almost wanted to seek one out and share a cup of tikula with him while we talked about home . . .

But I didn't have time. A violet flare on my doppler screen showed a heat-seeker missile homing in on my drive. I hit the button which would side-slip me into an oscillative speed pattern. The Vim control panel was much more compact than ours, with buttons no larger than pinheads . . . logical for beings who used tentacles, but awkward for a fingered man. I compromised by using the tip of my claw.

But the missile came on. Two more were coming up behind it. I ran into the next hull and hit the hy-dee. The universe became a bouquet of colored vortices pinwheeling in endless slow motion. A prickly rotifer of energy swam toward me. I identified it as a ship-finder, one of those mysterious Vim missiles which destroys ships in hyperdrive. I launched an interceptor and watched the pair collide in a silent orgasm of yellows and blues. That seemed to draw more rotifers. My screen looked like the inside of a blizzard. I leaped back into the normal-drive pod and dropped out of hy-dee.

The transition from one form of space to another is like being run through a meat grinder, and you come out of it with body senses all mixed up. Synesthesia, the psychs call it. You try to see with your big toe and smell with your ears. Ordinary people need an hour or so to recover normal perception, but my Eshom heritage gave me the ability to make the switch in no time.

No sooner had I dropped into normal than the heat-seekers got on my tail again. So it was back to hy-dee. I could see how the Vim beat their way through our screen. One pilot ran the hy-dee and the other ran the normal, and they just kept batting it back and forth. Of course, I had to make the switch again right away, because the damn rotifers were waiting for me . . .

A couple of ship-days passed in this manner. Then I had a long breathing spell when I didn't run into any missiles. I used the time to set my course for Rigel, which showed in my viewport as a brilliant ruby. It was 540 light-years away, and I could see the warp of space as a curving black line between my eyes and the star.

When I finished plotting the curve, I sensed a trickle of energy from the voice speaker. It was activating itself, about to release a recorded message. I projected a mental current which bypassed the speaker and brought the message directly into my mind, something the Eshom do when communicating with Jelk types. It came in, blip! in one big clobber of word concepts. In order to transcribe it I had to arrange them in time sequence. It was from Yakov and it went:

"Since you are hearing this message, it means that you have gone beyond our periphery. You have also gone beyond range of the transmitter which powers the ESP-baffle buried in your skull. You understand this precaution, I'm sure. By now you perhaps know the nature of your latent power. If not, you should begin experimenting in order to develop your faculties before you encounter the Vim. . . ."

I'd been so busy I'd given no thought to the copper grid in my head. I sat still for a minute and let it happen. It started as a cellular swelling in my skull, as if the bone were becoming porous and letting in streamers of light. They were dim at first, like sunlight shining down through a murky sea, but soon a pearly radiance suffused my entire brain and a lifting warmth spread through my body. I looked down and saw that my feet were six inches off the deck. I checked the gravitometer and saw that it registered .70 EG, so I knew I was levitating. The radiance inside my head leaked out into the surrounding air. I moved through a glowing murk. My passage stirred little sparkles and eddies of color. I could sense the binding force of every atom, I understood how matter was created, and I could even, maybe, create some myself . . .

So I tried. Out of the atoms before me I created a little round Bola-bol bearing the number 13. Then I created the rest of the balls and a table too, and I thought: why not create a partner? She was tall and fair, with breasts like delicious melons. I asked if she could play and she said, "I am here to do whatever you want me to do." I said, "Do something original." She said, "That would be totally impossible, since I am a creature of your will." That's when I said, "Dissolve," and she did.

How could Yakov have failed to realize that once I possessed my full powers I would be lord of my own universe and would need none of his petty victories and rewards? And what had I to fear in death when the very idea was laughable, because I was immortal and indestructible?

Then I glanced at the viewscreen and saw a missile homing in, and I decided that my immortality was still an open question. I depressed the interceptor switch with an arrow of thought—then just to make sure I tapped it with my finger. Then came another missile and another, and I began to look back upon that first outburst of *hubris* as a flirtation with madness . . .

I had a month to spend in the hy-dee. That's outside time. Within the hyperdrive field itself the old equation was being balanced according to the speed-of-light constant. Since my speed was forty times that of light, I had forty months in the can. I tried out all my powers, but I kept running into the need for an outside observer. Did I actually tele-port from one control pod to the other? (It's simple if you know how. You just think yourself into another place.) Or did I just block out the memory of walking over there? Did I really deflect the rotifer missiles by mental energy, or was I just deflecting phantoms of the mind?

I never quite abandoned the possibility that I'd gone insane.

But I was an eighteen-year-old, with a superabundance of hormones, so I created a succession of houris that would have shamed a Landark. I copulated with Unguls and Grithies and Eshom and Pteroni and Dubha . . . I even created the haughty Jelk wife of the Horlick Acad-emy commandant, with her gown and jewels and her air of supercilious contempt. I degrade her; I created a gigantic Ungul who ravished her from the rear while she kissed my feet and begged forgiveness . . .

I had to drop that line of endeavor.

It was none too soon, either.

The rotifers were getting so thick I seemed to be headed toward a solid barrier of swirling energy. I flipped into normal drive, and found the heat-finders thick as spines on a digger's back. I went back into hy-dee, but the rotifers were packed so tightly there was hardly a ship's width between them. Any one of them could have hooked my ship and spun it off into unknown dimensions.

This was the Vim barrier, and it was obvious I couldn't make it either on hy-dee or normal drive. That left only the third pod, whatever it was . . .

The controls looked about the same, except for fewer buttons. And no acceleration lever. It was either on . . . or off.

I pushed the switch on.

Nothing happened.

I let it spring back to off then pushed it again.

Nothing. Or at least I felt nothing. But when I looked in the view-screen the rotifers were gone. I was still in normal space . . . that is, the stars shone in their usual variegated hues of green, purple, red, white, and yellow. Rigel was still dead on my nose—but much brighter now. And the constellation of Orion had spread out slightly. I looked in the rear viewscreen and saw the familiar stars of what we call the home constellation: Procyon, Fomalhaut, Sirius, Altair, Sol, and the Alpha Centauri Twins, Abe and Bayka. I took a quick triangulation and discovered that in one great leap—or was it two?—I had gone twenty light-years past the Vim periphery.

Incredible. As far as I could tell I hadn't come out of normal drive. I pushed the switch again, and this time I assessed my sensations. There was nothing, except a sense of *wrongness* which seemed to loom up behind everything, a swelling feeling that the universe was about to burst like a soap bubble and leave nothing but a great blinding light.

But nothing happened—except that I jumped ten light-years closer to Rigel.

That figure clicked an association in my brain. After three more jumps, I realized that the Vim . . . or someone, had invented a quantum drive. Somehow they'd managed to hook into the fluctuating force of the electromagnetic field. Instead of riding the humps and hollows of the sidereal universe, I was stitching through it like a needle through folded fabric.

For a minute I forgot my mission. This would put Sirius on our doorstep and move the Magellanic clusters into our back yard. One could eat breakfast on earth and have dinner on Procyon, ten light-years away. But how could he get to Centauri, only four light-years away? I looked for a calibrating mechanism which would reduce the length of the jumps, but found none. The drive was tied to the wavelength of the magnetic field.

That explained the three hulls. The quantum drive moved between constellations, and the hy-dee moved between the stars. Once you got into a planetary system, you dropped into normal drive and sort of walked the rest of the way.

I mentally congratulated the Vim. Their engineering was a pleasure to behold . . . But a little frightening when I remembered that they were the Enemy.

And that line of thought brought me back to my mission. The quantum drive would be useless to mankind if he got himself annihilated.

Time to start looking for Vim. I knew they'd come from the direction of the galactic hub. Their home world had to be at least three hundred light-years from earth, because that's how far we'd explored when we met them. Even though I'd come sixty light-years beyond the periphery, I was still in space formerly controlled by man.

I thought of visiting Megrez, but it was on the other side of the Jelk sphere.

Logically, it seemed that the farther I went from the Vim frontier, the more likely I would be to find an unguarded world.

I took another five stitches before I began my hunt.

I learned that if I held the switch on for five seconds, it made another jump automatically. That gave me time to scout the surrounding area for stars between F2 and K1—the only ones which could have habitable planets. I was taking a beeline toward the Hub, and I had no time for side trips.

During the first hundred light-years I scouted thirty habitable planets. Several had once been occupied by humans, but were now abandoned even by the Vim. I ached with temptation to survey these ancient ruins—so many people I knew had left ancestors buried on these faraway worlds—but I hadn't the time. I found other worlds veiled in smoke and laced with the sickly fire of radiation, where war had ended the possibility of life forever.

And I found a world which looked so earthlike, so lovely with green and brown continents swimming in a blue sea, that I momentarily forgot that I was in enemy territory. Under full magnification I could see waving fields of purple, and a few scattered domes . . .

That warned me that it was a civilized world. I was reaching for the hy-dee switch when the universe flared white. The atomic missile missed by about six miles, but it was close enough. My time sense jumped into an accelerated state. I could see the shock wave approaching like a compression of lines. I doubted that the hull would hold, even though it was made of compacted matter, by an atomic wedging technique which Jelk science had not yet mastered.

I must have teleported automatically. I found myself in the third pod holding down the button on the quantum drive, watching the viewplate and wondering if the drive would kick on before the shock wave hit . . .

Then everything jumped sideways.

Later I figured out that both things had happened at once. When I came out of shock my finger was still holding the quantum drive button. I heard it click twice more before I realized my time sense had slowed back to normal. I released the switch and looked out the port. The Hub was farther away, and off to one side. Apparently I'd been slewed sideways when the quantum drive came on. If I'd been out for ten minutes that would mean three hundred jumps. Three thousand light-years.

I decided that figure was as good as any. Looking out the viewport, I could recognize nothing. I felt suddenly lonely. My desire to touch dirt was an ache in my fingers.

There were no planet-bearing stars in the vicinity. I hit the quantum drive button and waited for the star shift which told me I'd made a jump.

Nothing happened.

Of course, everything had its limit. Whatever had fueled the quantum drive, it was now gone, expended in that last sidewinding burst.

The nearest star was fourteen light-years distant. It didn't look like much, but I threw the ship in hy-dee and started toward it. The closer I got, the better it looked. The sun was GO, maybe a bit hotter than Sol. It had a similar planetary system. It would naturally be governed by Bode's Law—but there was only one supergiant doing the balancing job that Jupiter and Saturn did in our system. Instead of an asteroid belt there was a planet about twice earth size which looked like it might catch enough heat to sustain life. I went into a planetary orbit which crossed the poles. The equatorial region was desert, but the temperate zones contained vegetation reaching all the way to the polar snowcaps. No cities. I saw clumps of stones which might have been ruins but I wasn't sure.

I picked the sea as the best hiding place for the ship. I made a skip-landing just off the point of a long fingerlike peninsula. I started sinking the moment I lost forward momentum; not even the air in my hull was enough to keep the superdense metal afloat. I came to rest on the bottom, two hundred feet down. I filled my belt with food concentrates and started to strap on a gun. Then I thought: *Man, you don't need it. You've got all these special powers.*

I threw the holster aside and snatched off the belt of food concentrates. In a burst of exhilaration, I took off everything and went out through the airlock naked. It seemed an appropriate way to appear on a new world.

Waheera of the Golden Crest

Raki's Log II:

I surfaced just off a sandy point of land where some Vim were grazing. They fed squatting, stretching out their long arms and plucking
the flowers with boneless prehensile fingers. I had no problem defining
male and female. Those lacking back tentacles had belly pouches, some
nearly flat, others distended by the presence of young. Mothers with
large burdens rested their pouches on the ground while feeding.

I stayed mostly submerged and moved in closer, trying out my new
mental power. There was a yammering of surface thoughts: *There's a
nice bloom, yummy . . . if I move over there my feet won't get wet . . .
when the new blooms appear there will be a new mating, and I will
choose Okban of the blue crest . . .*

I found no evidence of a ruling entity—but there'd been none among
the prisoners on Mars either. Deciding to take the risk, I walked ashore
and gave the collective greeting: "*Ig-awa-sarumli,*" accompanied by the
placing of both hands over my mouth. (Meaning: I come in peace
and have no desire to steal your crop.) They stared, then babbled
among themselves. Out of the isolated thoughts of terror and awe, I
picked up one quiet reflection: *He speaks the ancient tongue. How can
this be?* Source of the thought was an ancient gray-skinned individual
with a mottled purple crest running the length of his skull. He was also
the only one seated. I walked over to where he sat and, indicating that
I would stay, sat down about five feet away from him. There was a
hushed silence, then the entire tribe, with the exception of the old individual, turned their backs and curled their tails above their heads.
This gesture, which I had already seen on Mars, had a variety of
meanings: military capitulation, respect for authority, obeisance to a
god. Of course, its original meaning was sexual submission, but it was

unrealistic to suppose that I could be sexually interested in all the hundred-odd members of the tribe.

Having completed the gesture, they returned to their grazing. The old chief didn't move. I recalled that the Vim name for chief was *Omnar-bundu*, He-who-sits. Obviously I was a challenge to his authority, but he did not seem to mind. He glanced at me a couple of times, then a blankness came into his eyes, and he seemed to go into a trance.

I watched the others graze. They drank no water; it wasn't needed, since there were beads of moisture on each petal. They didn't chew, but rolled the petals with their tongues against the roofs of their mouths and flipped them back into their throats. I picked a handful of petals and stuck them into my mouth; the bitterness set my teeth on edge, and I spat them out. The Vim stared at me—their wide round eyes always seemed to express surprise—then looked away as if I had committed some breach of good manners. Now what? Would they assume a god did not eat? When the blue-white sun reached its zenith and beat down upon my head like bullets, the herd left the field and walked to the over-hang of a cliff where deep cool shade awaited. There issued an uproar of burpings and gut rumblings, followed by contented cud chewing. Female breasts appeared for the first time. Normally hidden by a tough flexible skin covering, they were long at the base and terminated in a soft round sac equipped with a nipple. They had four, two on each side of their chests, which seemed to correspond to the average number of offspring. These crawled from their pouches and sucked noisily.

Only the old chief and I had not gathered blooms. I watched three females walk up to him, offer their lifted tails in a sort of homage, then turn and vomit about a quart of whitish-yellow slime into his bowl. It was the flower petals, already chewed and dissolved in digestive fluid. I was so engrossed in watching the old chief lift the noxious brew and slurp it into his mouth that I did not notice one of the females detach herself from the group and come toward me. She held out a small bowl filled with the same substance. Though I hadn't seen the stuff issue from her mouth, I knew where it came from. I made the sign of negation and she looked shocked—but then the Vim always look hurt and bewildered by Jelk standards, which will someday wreak a curious psychological effect upon the conquerors—assuming that's ourselves. She turned to the old chief, who made some sort of sign, then she set her bowl down and turned her back on me, planted her legs wide, and lifted her tail to display . . .

I'd examined the sexual attributes of many humanoid and proto-human females, from the Androxi maidens, who accept the male member by means of a retractable tube which they draw into their bodies and manipulate with great skill until it surrenders its burden, to the Grithy girls of Gafronkil, who tattoo their labia with intricate designs

to attract and entertain the male . . . but here I was surprised to see
nothing, not even an aperture for the elimination of waste. Only a fluff
of soft fur . . . no, not fur, as I realized when I looked closer, but a
growth of downy white feathers. I didn't touch it, having learned
caution from the prisoners on Mars, but merely mouthed the phrase
the old chief had used on the other three: *"We-zuk-h'na . . ."* which
means something like "Go in peace." She didn't go, but turned back
around, burped up her cud, and stood there chewing and regarding me
with an expression of utter tranquillity.

I gazed at my image reflected in the green vertical slits of her pupils.
I probed further, using my new powers, and found myself looking at
the world through her eyes. It was a flat image but with infinite detail
carried to the most distant objects. I found, like a trap door, the channel leading to her subconscious. Her thoughts were of me, and I
learned that I was neither god nor chief, only a strange creature who
had offered the polite greeting and therefore, under their moral code,
was permitted to graze with the tribe. Going deeper, I found areas of
sadness . . . a thought of little ones . . . *My pouch is empty, can he
fill me?* She was called Waheera of the Golden Crest, and she had
taken many mates, without issue. Soon she would be committed to the
status of a barren female, assigned to pulling the carts or casting spells
and other witchcraft.

Unless . . .

I seemed to be her last chance, but there was no urgency in her
mind, only an idle speculation. The cud chewing went on for two or
three hours, and the tribe drifted almost imperceptibly into sleep. I left
them and strolled across the flatland of waving grass and purple blooms.
I saw a distant mesa of some red mineral which had formed itself
into odd crystalline blocks. As I strolled closer I saw that it was an
artificial structure. There were no openings at ground level, but beginning eight feet up I found slits large enough to provide handholds
while I climbed to the top. I found myself on a circular wall which
surrounded nothing but a heap of rubble, overgrown by fleshy red-
leafed foliage. Impossible to imagine what species had inhabited the
planet before the Vim took over. Some race dead and lost even to memory . . . and there might someday go the race of man, if I should fail
my mission.

I saw Waheera coming across the field, hopping a few times, then
pausing to look and listen. I climbed down and joined her on the
ground.

"We returned to the field and I did not see you," she said.

I thought, *Alone at last,* and I put my hand on the fluff beneath her
tail. She looked more puzzled than usual, and I asked if she would like
me to fill her pouch with little ones.

"Of course, but it cannot be done until the time of the new flowers."

She treated it as a self-evident fact, and I did not pursue it. We rejoined the herd and they munched and crunched until darkness. Then I lay down to sleep, staring out at the forest of legs, with knee joints locked, their five-clawed feet spread out to maximum width, asleep with their startled eyes fixated on space, moving their small pointed chins from side to side as they ruminated their cuds.

A few days later I learned that the brilliant yellow tentacles which grew four to a side along their narrow skulls were sense organs which told them that a field of kusa plants had made their arbitrary decision to bloom. One moment they were squatting amid the plants, their long ropy arms swiveling out and the finger tentacles stripping off the petals. The next moment all heads came up, the tentacles quivered and circled, then stiffened out in one direction. The males started off in great springing leaps, each bound carrying them higher and farther until they disappeared over the horizon in jumps which encompassed one hundred yards. The young ones climbed on the tails of the nearest females and they too were traveling, a little slower than the males, but still faster than I had ever run.

Waheera hung back, obviously distressed. "The new flowers, it is the time of the new flowers!"

I picked the rest of it out of her mind: There would be no pollen for her, and therefore no filling of her pouch with little ones. I couldn't teleport without a point of fixation, so when we topped a low hill I saw our group headed toward a field of bright waxy flowers. But another tribe approached from the opposite direction, already closer and moving just as fast. I picked up Waheera's thought: *Gyuli's tribe will be first, and we will get no blooms.*

I understood, on a deeper level, why speed was so important to the Vim. The first tribe to reach a field claimed all the blooms. Without new flowers there could be no little ones, and no perpetuation of the tribe.

I concentrated on a spot in the center of the field. I created the smell, the feel of the wind, the appearance of the land around me. I cast my mind free of the spot on which I was standing and . . . Lo, I stood in the center of the new field. I made motions of stripping the petals, and when the other tribe came up they halted quickly, then turned and lifted their tails and ran. A minute later my own tribe bounced to a sudden halt at the edge of the field. The males remained there but the females came in and started plucking out the central stamens of the flowers. They had one clawed tentacle I hadn't noticed before. They were popping the stamens into their mouths, rolling them around, and then spitting them out. I was puzzled, then I realized they were collecting pollen. Waheera joined the group without a word to me.

I walked out to join the other males. There was much joking and what passed for laughter—clattering the bony plates inside their mouths—but they did not seem in awe of me. They talked about how the tribe would grow much larger now, with a fleet-footed member such as I. They gave me a new name, *Ra-kusan,* which meant bloom-finder. It was better than my old name, He-who-hops-on-one-leg, a mildly derisive sobriquet like Stinky, or Melon-head.

As the women gorged, I could feel a growing excitement among the men. It seemed to affect the women too. Now and then one of them lifted her head and released a high-pitched gurgling squeal which I took to be a sign of pleasure. When the first one came out of the field I noticed that the barbels around her mouth were distended. The males stood waiting, jiggling on their springy legs. The female seemed to hesitate, then walked up to one of the males and pushed her face into his. I didn't see what happened exactly, but the pair bounced straight up and then hopped away across the field. They stopped at last in a little cirque in a stony cliff. I tried to see what they were doing, in order to know what would be expected of me, but all I could see was two tails waving and jerking in violent motion.

One by one the women left the field, chose males, and took them into the tall grass. Even the females with young in their pouches went off to wallow in lust. Waheera was the last to leave the field, having been the last to arrive. She brought her face close, her fixed green eyes looking into mine. A kiss? I tried that, but she seemed puzzled. The barbels around her mouth were trying to push themselves between my lips. They felt warm, pulsating . . . not too unpleasant. I took a pull and spat out the bitter bilious fluid.

Waheera drew back. "You refuse my nectar?"

Since she put it that way . . . I took a tentacle into my mouth and sucked. Bitterness was only a first sensation. Next came a prickly astringent chill which drew my taste buds into knots. I swallowed, and felt an explosion of warmth in my stomach. The colored plates on Waheera's head began to shimmer and glow with indescribable beauty. I felt a softness in my legs and a hardness elsewhere. She was extending another barbel. I emptied that and she gave me another, full and distended. The operation grew difficult when she began jiggling and making gargling sounds in her throat. I felt her tentacles enwrap my male member, gently, though they had enough strength to pinch me off at the root. I was ready, and yet . . . puzzled. I found a horizontal opening in the front of her stomach, but my attempt to penetrate there only evoked a look of consternation. Below it was the opening of her belly pouch, fine for the children but hardly suited to my purpose . . .

The problem was solved when she turned and lifted her tail. The flesh under her muff had grown hot—at least 105 degrees F. An opening appeared where none had been before. Apparently the pollen caused the retraction of a covering membrane.

I enjoyed her immensely, far more than the idealized houris I'd created in my ship. I explored her strange body with fascination, thrusting my hand inside the warm belly pouch, exploring the aperture—in exactly the same location as a human navel—from which her young would emerge. I parted the tough ropy shield on her chest and tongued her hot pink nipples . . .

My virility was limitless, as long as the nectar flowed from her barbels. But these, which regenerated full in four hours, eventually were exhausted. So together, man and wife, we rejoined the group. Waheera displayed her nectar sacs, empty, while the females looked upon her with . . . was it envy, or did my ego imagine it? Later there were many fights which resembled drunken brawls, with the males grappling back to back, clutching each other with their tentacles, and trying to brain each other with their knobbed tails. But fights occurred only when two males went for the same female at the same time. Otherwise it was a complete saturnalia. I saw Waheera coupled with a male with a spotted purple crest, and then a few minutes later with another in a green crest.

The effect of the nectar lasted thirty hours, and during that time I copulated with at least twelve tribeswomen. I also suffered a bloody nose and a bruised rib from various combats, before they discovered that my two fists were more than equal to one knobbed tail. After the orgy, everybody went back to monogamy. Waheera was mine again. She had little tricks of possession, nuzzling, slipping her tail around my waist. A familiar lover's trick, to entwine tails. She didn't seem to mind that I had no tail to entwine. I had other things . . . most important being an organ that would rise without the stimulus of pollen. This evoked mutterings from the other adults of the tribe, and I gathered that it was sinful to copulate between times of the new flowers. So I quit, and when I checked ten days later, Waheera's membrane had regrown.

The other females began to swell, but not Waheera. She fell into a despondent state. I told her not to worry, she would have little ones. I recalled the Jelk practice of nurturing their young in the wombs of Grithy nurses. One night I teleported four fetuses into her womb, one from each of four females. She awoke and told me she'd had a dream; a god of the Old Ones had visited her, and told her she would bear little ones . . .

I was not to see these. The nights grew chilly, and we wandered southward. I was puzzled at the lack of warlike spirit in these Vim, who were obviously members of the same race that was devastating the Jelk empire. Even the old chief, whom I suspected might harbor one of the controlling parasites, seemed more interested in sleeping than in governing his tribe. He had three young wives who pulled him everywhere in a two-wheeled cart. He managed to avoid touching me, and I didn't seek it, since I had no desire to cause his death. I found that I could influence the entire tribe when their attention was focused on the storytellers, or in dancing. But the old chief's mind had been opaque since that first instant of seeing me, as though something inside had pulled down a curtain.

The vegetation thinned out to scattered clumps. The carts were filled with dried dust paste, and the skins with water. We began our summer migration across the great equatorial desert, toward the blooming lands of the southern hemisphere.

I had no problem, since the heat rarely rose above 130 degrees F. Each night I teleported back to the last waterhole and took a swim. I brought water to Waheera, but usually she wasn't thirsty. Their hard leathery bodies required little moisture. A heavy dew kept them refreshed all day.

One day the old chief sat down, called his tribe together, and said farewell. He told them to depart across the burning sand, all but his successor, the next *Omnarbundu*, He-who-sits. Then he motioned me to sit down in front of him. I remembered Waheera telling me that when the old chief died, he would pass his soul on to the next chief. I had teased her. *"What does this soul look like?"* She said, *"Like the souls of the little ones you gave me."* And I had thought, *Sperm?*

Now the old chief said: "This body is old, it is finished, there is no need to keep it any longer. Let us mingle tentacles, and you will be the new chief."

He held out his arms, but I drew back. The old eyes went dim, and he toppled onto his side. Little white worms, no larger than hairs, came out through his pores and waved in the air, seeking, questing, finally gathering in a little puddle on the sand. It sank in and disappeared. Overcoming my revulsion, I started digging in the spot. While I squatted, I felt an itch in the soles of my feet. I lifted my foot and saw that it was stuck in some stringy, whitish-transparent gluey substance. It crawled into my pores. I forced myself to stand still, and felt it creep up inside my leg. It followed the veins, avoiding arteries, careful not to impede the flow of blood. It spread through my pancreas, oozed through the interstices of my guts, flowed into my pleural cavity. It sent an exploring tendril into my lungs, then drew back. It seemed hesitant, unsure of itself. I felt it wriggle into my spine and climb the nerve ganglia toward my brain. *So this is how it feels to be inhabited,* I thought.

I projected a question: *Who are you?*

It recoiled in horror and shock. I gathered an impression of fear . . . then resignation. After a minute the thought croaked into my brain.

Wroqna.

Why are you afraid?

I recognize you as one of the ancient enemy, the human scourge which must be eliminated before the Wroqna can live in peace.

That's exactly what we say about the Vim.

They are our creatures. They have always been ours. How did you get in there?

I sensed an ancient withered being in a fit of shrill panic. *This is not a Vim body. This is my own.*

A stunned silence, then:

I thought it seemed strange. The old chief was deaf and nearly blind. I should have transferred fifty seasons ago.

You're still in trouble. This body is taken.

A fiery needle stabbed at the base of my brain. I'd been expecting it, and I clamped down on the nerve nexus at the top of my spine. It recoiled, hissing with rage.

I fired a conciliatory thought: *Why not give mankind a small part of the universe, and keep what you have?*

Wroqna must grow.

Why?

No reason. It was a muttered snarl.

I wanted to keep the creature engaged in conversation. *How many Wroqna are on this planet?*

Ten mating units. We landed three hundred.

What's a mating unit?

Three individuals. This is tedious. Let us make direct contact, and you will know what I know.

I felt a gentle, thrusting tendril. *No tricks.*

They would be useless. I am doomed. You will see.

I decided to take a chance, and let the tendril enter. In objective time the transfer of information took place instantaneously. Subjectively, I lived through all the ancient creature's life, since the time it landed on this world fifteen hundred years ago. I understood how the Wroqna controlled the Vim, and why the Wroqna could never share the universe with humans . . .

16

Festival of the Fallen Gods

The Wroqna, of course, were man's own ancient enemy, whose long-ago explorations had seeded our legends of demonic possession and beings who lived in the ground and dead men who rose up and walked . . .

I had no time to reflect on my new knowledge.

The Wroqna, devious, deadly devilish creature, had taken advantage of my distraction to block the valves of my heart. I nearly blacked out before I took conscious control of my autonomic system and accelerated my heartbeat to the point where he had to withdraw. There was no way to kill him: he attenuated himself and slipped between my cells, taking up residence in another part of my body. He stayed away from nerve fibers so that I couldn't tell where he was—until I felt a lash of pain in my thalamus. I blocked him with all my concentration, only to discover it had been a feint. He flowed into my lungs and began to smother me. I began deep diaphragm breathing, pumping my lungs like a bellows until he had to pull back or be blown out onto the sand. He chose retreat. The creature was learning all the time. Next he blocked my kidneys, and I nearly died of uremic poisoning before I flushed him out.

But each effort weakened the Wroqna. He tried to draw energy from me as he did from the Vim—by tapping the nerve bulb under my brain. But the secretions of human adrenals were poisonous to Wroqna. The harder he fought, the more of my energy he used, and the more he hastened his death.

He lasted three days, and during that time I could not spare the energy even to twitch a finger. When he was finished I lay in the sand and sweated his dead tissue out through my pores. It left a scummy whiteness like a snail track. I immediately fell asleep.

When I woke up the whole tribe had gathered around me. They expected a new chief to spend several days on his back, and be fed from the mouths of all members of the tribe. I knew this had been the Wroqna's way of building his strength and reestablishing control over his tribe. Since I had no need of it, I decreed that we push on across the desert.

We began to encounter a few scrawny thorn bushes, then clumps of grass, and at last a few fields of withered flowers. On the day the first new flowers were found, I sat out the ensuing revels and marveled that the Vim could be so carefree.

Had it not been for them, the Wroqna might still be living beneath the subsoil of their home continent, as they had been doing for countless millennia before the Vim found them. In those days the Wroqna had several appendages, one a flexible sac which slid over a yamlike tuber which grew underground. A shearing mechanism severed the tuber from the root, and the sac filled with acids which then seeped down into the body of the Wroqna. They had another called the *gremsh* organ, which located and killed the subterranean rodents which shared the Wroqna appetite for the kusa yam. A poison was squirted from the tentacle which dissolved the cells of the rodents, reducing them to a jellylike slime palatable to the Wroqna.

The Vim also enjoyed the kusa yam, but their appetite was confined to the blooms. Since the blooming season ranged from the lower to the high latitudes, the Vim formed small tribes with high mobility. As population increased, they began to develop a mechanical culture which emphasized speed of movement, culminating in airships. Landing on the home island of the Wroqna, the Vim used heat rays against the giant worms which ravaged their crops, failing to recognize them as part of a large animal which lived underground. (The Wroqna's brain and digestive organs floated inside a gelatinous mass which filled their rock cavities. The surface exuded a chemical which slowly dissolved the rock and allowed the Wroqna to grow.) The Wroqna retaliated by destroying the Vim's metallic shields with a chemical which acted like gray tin, breaking down the molecular structure of metal, rock, and everything else the Vim might bring in contact with it. Since the Vim bred slowly, and the Wroqna could double their population each breeding period, the Vim decided to abandon the planet. They built spaceships and established colonies on hundreds of virgin planets. Within three generations the Wroqna were firmly entrenched beneath the surface. The Vim assumed at first that the Wroqna were stowing away on their ships, but then they learned that the Wroqna had managed to implant their young inside the bodies of the Vim.

(A peculiarity of the Wroqna is that they were hermaphroditic. Each had identical sexual apparatus. During the mating season, the tentacles which carried these organs became extremely long and hard, winnowing their way through cracks and cavities until they met the opposite sexual organ of another Wroqna. The cilia of the two intermingled and a small sac appeared, which gradually filled with the body fluids of the parents. When the offspring began to grow its own tentacles, the parent organs withdrew and remained dormant until the next breeding season. The minimum number required for breeding was three, since one organ would not function until the other was hooked up to a third member of the species. The usual breeding complex consisted of twelve to three hundred Wroqna, who were incapable of any other activity as long as the breeding hookup was maintained.)

The Vim-Wroqna war entered a new phase. The Vim could find no way of killing the Wroqna young without killing themselves. Even worse, the Wroqna learned to inject their communicator tentacle into the host brain of the Vim and override their thoughts. Usually the Vim died under the impact of alien mind patterns. But some were only reduced to morons. Within a generation 90 per cent of the Vim died in slobbering idiocy, and the rest became Wroqna puppets. In time the Wroqna learned to control Vim minds without destroying their efficiency, and the mechanical science of the Vim was put into service of the Wroqna. A civilization of symbiotes—one eating the roots, the other the blooms, of the same plant—began an expansion which spread over half the galaxy.

The usual practice was to land several hundred Vim on a new world, along with a few dozen riders. (The Wroqna occupied only one Vim in a hundred, but these were endowed with weaponry and superior brains, and so stood at the top of the power pyramid. None of the Wroqna enjoyed rider duty, since they were never comfortable inside an alien body, but all had to serve their turn when young.) The Vim would clear the ground and plant the kusa yam, while the Wroqna went underground to await the harvest. Then they could begin the orgy of eating and breeding which would overpopulate the planet within a century.

Their cataclysmic encounter with the First Solar Empire might have been delayed for centuries, had not one of the Vim barbecued by the Sha'al explorers been a carrier of Wroqna, who managed to survive the cooking process and travel from the brain of the Vim to the stomach of the Arab. There ensued a period of confusion for one and indigestion for the other, as the Wroqna found its way through unfamiliar passages to the brain of the Arab. Since the man happened to be an astrogator, the Wroqna knew immediately the source world of the invasion, and the precise direction and dimensions of its flow. The race of man was biting into the Wroqna galaxy like an apple. This could either be a disaster for the Wroqna, or an opportunity. Expansion through the Vim was slow, due to their haphazard method of breeding. If these hairless, tailless, pocketless bipeds could serve the same function, so much the better.

The Wroqna lost no time—the moment his host sat on the ground—

in making contact with his fellows underground. These knew only that some disaster had occurred involving the food supply. The moment their communicator tentacles were meshed, the awareness became universal to all, and the solution began to be applied. Three Wroqna joined in a breeding unit and created three young. These three, each no larger than a man's thumb, were hand-carried by the astrogator to the tent of his wives. He had three, as befitted his rank as a senior officer. One of these went into convulsions and died the moment the Wroqna was introduced into her body during sexual foreplay. The other two immediately became puppets of the Wroqna. (The only visual change was a subtle shading of the eyes, caused by chemical change when the Wroqna overlaid the sclerotic layer with its own visual sensing apparatus. The change took place gradually, beginning as a yellowish tinge and darkening within a week to a glowing saffron.) Meanwhile, all three Wroqna-humans held hands, intermingled their sexual organs, and produced three more Wroqna young. These three were carried to neighboring tents, so that by morning the entire colony was Wroqna in all but appearance. It was a crude take-over, done in haste, and the process destroyed the identity of all the colonists. Since the Wroqna could not detect the slight color change of the eyeball, and did not have access to any part of the human mind except their memories, they assumed that their presence inside the humans were invisible. Flying the Arab spaceship to a neighboring world, they hooked themselves into the vast communications network of the Wroqna empire. The threat of mankind was quickly assessed, as well as the potential. It was decided that the Wroqna-humans would attack immediately, proceeding to the center of the human-dominated sphere and seeding on the way.

The ship landed on the planet Hwu Hsi, pretending to be in distress, dropped three Wroqna-humans, and proceeded to the planet Yakovitch, where the same procedure was followed. They had penetrated no more than one hundredth of a galactic diameter when a customs agent on the Spanish-speaking planet Rinconcito put the ship in a quarantine orbit and would allow nobody to disembark until it was determined what had caused their eyeballs to turn yellow. The Wroqna realized that their chance to assimilate mankind was shattered; a new order was transmitted instantaneously throughout the Wroqna empire: Annihilate mankind. Attack with all ships, at all points.

More than a billion spaceships, which only yesterday had been hauling yam tubers to the settled worlds of the Hub, converged on the bubble of man's infant empire. There was no waste, no duplication of effort. Each ship had its own planetary target, its own crew of humanoid marsupials controlled by Wroqna riders.

But conquest was not like colonization, which sustained itself as it went. Conquest was a running sore on the body politic, drawing strength from the interior and burning it off in space. The advance guard had just reached the home system of the earthmen when a message went out from the Hub. Wroqna were starving on the inner worlds. There were no yam ships to haul tubers: the fleet was needed at home. It was an orderly retreat at first; all human worlds were scorched, burned, vitrified to bedrock. But then the need for haste became apparent: Wroqna were dying in the holds of the ships. Those who had inhabited humans were the first to go; next came those who had bred with, or even touched the communicator tentacles of the man-riders. So the Wroqna learned that the human race was a viper in its bosom. Panic ensued. The outer husk of the empire was quarantined. All ships trying to enter were destroyed. But still the disease spread inward. Before it ran its course, nine tenths of the Wroqna had died, and only the riddled core remained of their far-flung empire.

The Wroqna I'd killed had been part of the crew of a huge battle cruiser, manned by a hundred Wroqna and ten thousand Vim. Losing its way during the chaotic retreat, it had crashed on this planet, which they called Illyanola. The survivors had crawled from the wreckage, planted the tubers they'd managed to save, and settled down to wait for rescue.

But help never arrived.

Not only that, the soil lacked a mineral which the Wroqna needed for reproduction. For fifteen hundred years there were no young. Accident and disease decimated the Wroqna until now there were only about thirty ancients left, their vitality low and their spirits resigned to death. The Vim, less sensitive to nuances of chemistry, had increased until they now numbered a hundred thousand.

I had an idea how I would infiltrate the inner worlds of the Wroqna. As soon as the tribe finished their orgy of the new blooms, I motioned forward the tallest and strongest of them, called Okban of the Purple Crest. I touched his tentacle, saying: "I am too weak to lead the tribe now. You will take us to the Shrine of the Fallen Gods." At the same moment I sent my mind into his, playing on his pleasure centers while I projected the thought: *I will be with you always and you will obey me gladly. Do whatever I ask, and I will give you the strength to succeed.*

The cart was bumpy, but I gradually slowed my metabolism until the physical processes nearly stopped. I was to all appearances a corpse, and though Waheera was sad, the others seemed unconcerned. It wasn't uncommon for new chiefs to lie in a coma for several days. Often they died.

Through Okban's eyes I watched the scattered fields grow thicker as we ranged southward. On either side I saw other tribes converging. I could sense the awe that Okban and the others felt toward this ship from another world. It was as though earthmen of prespace times had made a yearly pilgrimage to the actual Ark which had carried Noah to his mountain.

My plan hinged on whether the ship had an atomic drive like those the Vim had used in their first invasion. The moment I saw it I was tempted to scrap the plan. It looked as if half a mountain had caved in on the bow of the cruiser. The seams had split open, and dirt had drifted inside. Giant bladder trees grew up through the cracks, and vines covered its surface until only its general form could be seen.

None of the Vim would approach closer than ten miles. To do so, they said, would cause their bodies to break out in running sores. Ultimately they would die. They were describing radiation sickness, and I knew then that my plan would work.

A few Vim kept walking toward the mountain. These were carriers of the Wroqna. There were only eighteen, and two had to be carried. Only five were as young and healthy as Okban.

I knew the routine. The natives were to be impressed—not deliberately perhaps, but the true meaning of the ceremony had grown hazy even in the minds of the superannuated Wroqna. The ship still contained distress flares, and it was the custom of the rulers to set off one each year, in the hope that another Wroqna ship might be passing through the stellar neighborhood.

By now the Vim filled the valley of the river which curved around the foot of the mountain. They stood munching their cuds and staring toward the mountain. New flowers filled the valley, but these would not be touched until the fireworks ended. That would signal the beginning of bacchanalia, which would last until all the flowers were gone and the vines trampled into dust.

At dusk I sat up in the cart and called my tribe together:

"I make this prophecy: Tonight the fallen gods will return to their ancestors. They will depart in a burst of light brighter than the sun. Those who gaze on this light will find their eyes melted from their sockets. Be warned, and spread the word among the others. From tonight on there will be no more festival of the fallen gods. You will choose your own chiefs now. Be sure to choose only the smartest and the strongest."

I figured that was harmless advice, since it would work out that way in any event. I resisted the temptation to lay down a set of moral commandments. Their only effect would have been to add a burden of guilt to the carefree natures of the Vim, without improving their character in the slightest degree. I had no doubt that my tribe would henceforth regard itself as the Chosen Ones, and would probably end up making life miserable for themselves and others. But I saw no way to avoid it.

I asked Okban if he were willing to accompany me to the land of the gods.

"I have no wives or little ones to keep me here. I will go."

"Even though you might never return?"

He lifted his tail and let it fall, the Vim equivalent of a shrug. "I have eaten the flowers of this world. I am ready to taste new blooms."

At midnight the signal flare went up. A blue streak hissed and sputtered until it reached the height of a mile, then bloomed into a huge flower of green, red, and yellow. Tracers streaked out in all directions, filling the sky with colored lines. The flare died, leaving the after-image etched in black on a purple sky.

The Vim stared, and clattered their bony plates. A few of the younger females edged away from the crowd and moved into the fields of new flowers. This signaled the beginning of the stampede, as all the females rushed in to fill their barbels with pollen. The males began to scamper and prance on the outskirts, working themselves into a frenzy at the prospect of sweet nectar. Even Okban started to jitter, and I had to assume direct control of his mind in order to keep him from joining the masses.

I had him pull my cart to the foot of the mountain. Then I left him in a trance behind a boulder, and walked up to the hulk. I found a trodden path leading to a rent in the hull. I entered and found myself in the dark interior of a troop compartment. I stood still until my Eshom eyesight turned the darkness into day, then I walked to the front of the compartment, crawled down a rubble-strewn passageway, and stopped at the entrance to what had once been the officer's mess. Ranked along one side were still-shiny vats used for mixing gruel. In the center sat the Vim, their tentacles joined in a circle. They were totally engrossed in their own version of the sex orgy taking place in the valley. I had no urge to warn them of their imminent destruction. Fifteen hundred years of life lay behind them already. I felt they'd had more than their share.

I left them and walked toward the stern of the ship. The door to the drive chamber was sealed, and warnings were written on it in Vim microscript. There were also coded instructions for getting inside, which could be understood only by the Wroqna—or by one who possessed the knowledge of a Wroqna.

The moment I entered, a prickling on my skin told me the atomic pile was leaking radiation. But I had visited the Eshom in areas where bombardment was much stronger. It was a simple task to pull the cadmium damping rods. I wondered why the Wroqna had never thought of doing it; possibly their old brains were simply worn out.

Perhaps it would not have worked during the first few centuries of their exile. But now, I was certain, the Wroqna had instruments as sensitive as our own, which could detect atomic explosions at a distance of fifty light-years.

I left the ship and visualized the rock where I had left Okban with my cart. Within a second I was there. Minutes later the ship's pile reached critical mass.

The shock wave ripped away the topsoil on either side and nudged the huge boulder six inches downhill. I was glad to see that the valley where the Vim reveled lay in the shadow of the peak. They would escape flash burns, though there might be several thousand cases of radiation sickness. I crouched down with Okban as the debris whined and fluttered past. In the intense white light I saw the Vim scattered along the river's edge, lying on the ground, perched on boulders, some knee-deep in water. Most were still coupled with their mates, but all were staring at the mushroom of dust, fire, and smoke which rose from behind the mountain.

I had nothing to do now but wait.

17

The Supergiant

Raki's Log V:

The triple-hulled ship came down from the sky phasing in and out in a defense pattern which lit up the land with a flickering purple glow. The Vim ceased their revels and gazed up in awe; when the ship flipped to stand on its tail beside the mountain, they all turned their backs and raised their tails.

Whoever had come to investigate the explosion knew his business. A ramp dropped down from the cargo pod, and a tracked vehicle rolled out and circled the pool of molten rock where the ship had been. It crawled back inside, and out marched a hundred Vim in military formation. I put my body into suspended animation and moved my consciousness into the brain of Okban.

Relax, I told him, and I'll take charge.

He was trembling inside, and only too willing to let it happen. I maneuvered his body between the shafts of my cart and started him up the mountain toward the marching soldiers.

They halted when they saw us. The ranks parted, and through them strode a lordly Vim, a head taller than any of his men. (The Wroqna always chose carriers who were outstanding physical specimens.) He walked up to Okban and extended his tentacles. Had I left the matter to Okban he would have collapsed into jelly, but I caused him to stretch out his own hand. I felt a tickling sensation, and I knew the Wroqna within was trying to insert his communicator tentacle. He wanted to learn whether Okban was also inhabited by a Wroqna. I decided not to try faking it, since I might be hooked into a breeding circuit.

Making no contact, the officer stepped back and spoke in the clipped Vim military dialect:

"Who are you?"

I projected the words into Okban's brain, and he repeated them in a tremulous tone: "I am Okban. The Lords commanded me to await you."

"Who set off the blast?"

"I know nothing about the blast. I was told to say only: 'This is the world of Illyanola. We have waited many centuries, and we are tired. The enemy came and killed many of us before we learned how to deactivate him. Now the rest of us are dying because of some mysterious disease the human possessed. We are setting off the pile in hope that it will draw attention to our world. We have instructed Okban, our loyal servant, to care for the body of our enemy, so that he may be studied.'"

The officer walked back and gazed into the cart at my body. He stretched out his tentacles and Okban said:

"Lord, the others who touched him died."

The officer jerked back his arm. "Are you able to touch him safely?"

"Yes, Lord. The common folk are not affected by the disease."

The officer pointed his head tentacles toward the ship. "Take him aboard and stay with him."

We were led through the troop compartment and shut inside a six-by-six metal compartment. Okban started gasping and rolling his eyes, and I had to put him to sleep. He had never even been under a roof before, much less inside a steel box.

After an hour I felt safe in teleporting back to the rock. I popped into the midst of three Vim officers seated in a circle with tentacles intermingled. I popped out again immediately, and reentered behind a bush ten yards away. The Vim had not noticed, since they were in the quiet throes of breeding.

After a time the troops marched up from the valley herding about fifty prisoners taken from the local populace. Noting their outstanding physical stature, I knew these were destined to become Wroqna carriers. The first was brought forward, writhing in the clutch of two soldiers. His mouth was wedged open with a plastic block. One of the Wroqna-Vim walked over to him and crammed a white gelatin blob into his mouth. The Vim jerked and trembled and fell to the ground. I knew the death struggle which was taking place inside him, and I felt a terrible urge to kill the three Wroqna. But that would have gained only one world and lost thousands, so I forced myself to stand still and watch.

More than fifty Vim were injected with the Wroqna offspring of the three officers. By the time it ended the first new "chiefs" had gone down among the people and started rounding up their tribes. The world I had freed was enslaved again—and 99 per cent of the slaves would never know the difference.

I teleported back to the ship just before it took off.

It was smaller than the ship which had carried me into the realms of the Wroqna, but its design was the same: three control pods, three pilots. I knew now that the flexible shafts connecting the pods contained the communicator tentacles of the Wroqna, enabling them to coordinate their jumps without mechanical aids.

I counted six quantum stitches before the ship jumped back into hydee. Then we traveled for a month in hyperspace. During that time I gave Okban control of his own body, but kept a tight clamp on his adrenals so he wouldn't get ship fever. I sat up in his mind and eavesdropped during his growing friendship with the Vim who served his gruel through a sliding panel in the door. Their conversations confirmed what I'd learned by other means. He knew nothing of the Wroqna. He'd been born on the world of Brel-sik in the Mul system, and has been selected for military service when a child. One never saw one's tribe after that, but there were compensations. The world to which we were going, Uxvaleen, was headquarters for elite strike troops, and so got the best food, and the best females to serve in their clubs. He'd nearly persuaded Okban to join up when he mentioned that those who went off to fight the humans hardly ever returned. No, Friesl didn't know what the war was about. Barbarians were always pillaging the civilized worlds, raping Vim mothers and murdering their little ones. Humans were the worst, and would probably not desist until they were wiped out by the heroic Vim.

How depressingly repetitious, I thought, was military propaganda in any race.

One day I felt the rending cellular twist which signaled our return to normal space. The Vim in the troop compartment crowded their viewscreen, and I managed to tie into their vision . . .

Uxvaleen was a pocked and pitted cinder, a dead lump from pole to pole, victim of some ancient war of conquest. As more of the planet tilted into view, I saw a splotch of green which grew into rivers and trees and patches of purple flowers. It was probably fifty miles across. On its outer edge a solid line of machines chewed up the fused rock and laid down strips of new soil. Near the center was a flat space about five miles across, covered by a substance which glittered like frosted glass. A line of cargo pods, twice the size of our troop compartment, moved on a belt toward a featureless black ball in the center. On the edge of the field clustered vertical structures which could have been office buildings, merging into a belt of factories interspersed with shanty settlements, then spreading out into stately homes where little Vim children played among the purple fields.

It was obviously a class structure based on unequal distribution of resources, much like the Jelk system, designed to yield the greatest output for the least input. Nearest the landing pad stood a group of young Vim females with ribbons tied around their food-finding tentacles. The troops began shouting and jiggling . . .

Landing. I decided not to reactivate my physiological processes but just to lie there and use my Eshom senses to gnarsh the world outside. My mind was drawn toward the black sphere. It was nothing but a gigantic blot in my field of awareness, an impenetrable blankness which radiated zero. Yet I felt something sentient inside.

I felt a jerk, and realized that our ship was moving toward the black ball. I didn't like the idea of going in blind, so I decided to teleport outside the ship. Since my human body would cause panic, I moved Okban.

I could feel the black sphere pulling me off balance as I made the jump. Instead of being transferred just outside the ship, I found myself in the slum area I'd seen before landing. I tried to move Okban again, but my control had grown tenuous with distance. His will overrode mine, and he had no desire ever to return to the metal box. It was as if I were sitting up inside his mind, in a little room filled with controls which I pushed and pulled without effect.

Okban wandered around, jumping each time a little wheeled car buzzed past, gawking at the young females who waggled their erotic barbels at him in a suggestive manner. The place was surprisingly like the brothel slum of Gafronkil. Sidewalk stands dispensed a beverage which looked like the nectar of the Vim girls, in return for pierced discs of plastic which the soldiers carried on loops attached to their belts. I managed a mental transfer of one of the loops to Okban, and he proceeded to buy a bulb of the synthetic stuff. It had a tit at one end which one broke off and sucked. It tasted brassy and metallic to me, but Okban gulped down three quick ones and started jiggling. A Vim girl with painted skin came up and peeled back the ropy shield on her chest, displaying four ripe mammaries. She lifted her tail and offered to retract her membrane in exchange for a pair of plastic discs. Like a stoned puppy, Okban followed her into a curtained booth. During the action I felt a wistful longing for Waheera, who had loved me despite my alien body. Commercial sex was a pale substitute for love, but Okban was more than happy with his new friend, and let her lead him to a gambling game designed to further separate soldiers from their plastic discs . . .

It was played with small rectangles inscribed in patterns of dots. The object was to match up the dots, and the first to play all his rectangles won. I learned how to beat it—a simple process of transferring rectangles from Okban to the other players. My idea was to give him a plentiful supply of discs so that he'd knock himself out on nectar and let me take control.

While his pile grew I heard someone behind me talking about ". . . a huge hairy beast, twice as tall as myself and ten times as broad. Haggers grow from his tentacles, which are stiff and jointed. His mouth is full of tiny sharp knives. He hops on one leg, and cannot move fast, but once he catches you in his huge arms you never see the homeworld again."

He was describing a Fighting Ungul. I managed to turn Okban's head. It was a Vim soldier, with metal rings around his neck inscribed in microscript, listing his acts of valor. I didn't know the Vim symbols for our stars, but I wanted to learn what part of the human frontier we were near. Though I intended to go on to the Hub, it would be useful to have an escape route already planned.

I tried a mental jump—and failed. Not only that, I lost touch with Okban.

Oblivion. For a moment it frightened me. I tried to pull back into my own body and found the way blocked off. Panic was useless. The situation called for a cool head.

Cogito, ergo sum.

I floated above the crowd, a disembodied entity composed of nothing but a concept of being. But the "I-ness" perceived, and remembered, and this nostalgia for my three-dimensional form lifted me up above the crowds and pulled me across the city to . . .

The black sphere.

My body was inside it.

It took a moment for me to realize I could not penetrate the sphere. As I approached it a jangled tangle of magnetic lines compressed and pulled at my identity so that I had to pull back to at least ten yards away. I went around the sphere and across the top. It was completely closed. Even the cargo pods entered through a close-fitting sphincter, which allowed not even a molecule's width between the sphere and the surface of the ship.

But only the surface. I had no trouble getting inside the ship. It was nothing but a huge tank filled with the pulped tubers of the kusa yam, sole diet of the Wroqna. I had a pretty good idea what was inside the sphere.

I don't know exactly when the ship went through the sphincter. A whirlpool developed in that vat of slime, and I let myself spiral downward through a hole in the bottom. Then I shunted myself aside, while the rest of the cargo spilled down a deep striated well which heaved and pulsed like living flesh.

It was flesh. Wroqna flesh. Here was the creature's esophagus, and somewhere a hundred feet below the surface lay its stomach. It must have occupied at least a square-mile cavity, judging from the number of yam-ships it took to feed it.

Then the black sphere must represent . . . what? The head? No point in straining the analogy. I had to find my body, and the smothering mental presence of the creature made it impossible to use my mental powers.

I penetrated the nearest wall and found myself in a circular chamber. Metallic tentacles came from the walls, and these were fitted with drills, calipers, saws, torches and other devices. The creature had created tools which it could use directly, without the need for Vim intermediaries. I could visualize a time when the Wroqna would eliminate their faithful servants, having no more need of them.

I penetrated another wall. This appeared to be surgical laboratory— a giant stasis chamber where all organic processes were frozen. Creatures lay on a long row of slabs in various stages of dissection. I saw one being no larger than a man's hand, with huge eyes and pads equipped with sucker discs. On another slab lay a humanoid female not more than two feet long, with blue-white skin and flesh so transparent I could see her bone structure. She looked human except for transparent wings half crushed beneath her back. I wished that I could have had a chance to know her, but that was impossible now, for the top of her skull had been sliced off and her brains spread out on a tray.

I roved on down the row of slabs, past appendages with scalpels cutting, slicing . . . to the last body in the row.

It was mine.

The creature already had me cut open from collarbone to pelvis. A long flexible arm came down on my skull, and a little circular saw began spinning . . .

18.

Heart of Empire

No!

I leaped, instinctively, impelling myself with all the power of my consciousness. I had meant to leap back into my own body and transfer out of there, but instead I leaped into the brain of the giant Wroqna.

And I learned a curious thing. At each level of the Wroqna culture the knowledge is total, all members share the knowledge of all other members . . . *on their own level.* My contact with the Wroqna inhabiting the old chief had given me the history of the race . . . but only on its own level. The Wroqna which inhabited the Vim actually believed they were the ultimate, the absolute, the true rulers of the universe. They were totally unaware of the creature within the black sphere.

And I understood why the soil of Illyanola had been sterile. A chemical substance had to be injected into these foreign worlds, and the only source of this was the Hub, the center of the Wroqna empire. Each ship which returned from the Hub carried a small quantity of this "life germ." Without it the entire empire would wither and die.

But it was unbelievable the number of functions this creature controlled: construction of new shelters on other planets for more of the giant Wroqna, a program of coalescence which would unite several thousand smaller Wroqna into one of planetary size, a scheme to convert more dead planets into plantations for the tubers, in order to build the strength to conquer more planets to grow more tubers. The question of why did not enter. Wroqna nature was to grow, and it had no philosophy, no more than a river derives a philosophy to explain its inexorable flow toward the sea. No doubt to a river the concept of "gravity" would be a religious principle.

Mere numbers give only an inkling of the resources this supergiant controlled. There were more than a thousand star systems, totaling something like five thousand producing planets. From each of these planets came an average of a hundred yam-ships a day. Only a small percentage landed on this world, the rest were shunted toward the Hub from a station in space. And this giant creature was only one of thousands spread throughout the galaxy . . .

My mind reeled from the effort to comprehend. For the moment I could not encompass it. I felt an urge to shrink, to become a mere atom inside this huge thinking organism. It would allow the sacred "I" to survive at least for a while. But then I felt the link to my puny corporeal body lying on the slab, and I knew that if that link were severed the "I" would dwindle away like a page of wet newsprint drying in the sun. And that moment was drawing near, for my viscera and all internal organs had been removed. The scalpel worked with blinding speed. I could see the inside of my spine, the nerves branching out and the rib cage curving around my empty chest cavity.

I was not yet dead. My cells were locked in stasis, but the element which locked them lay in my thalamus and would soon come under the knife. The locking mechanism would be destroyed and the precious tissue would fall prey to the forces of decay . . .

I found the nerves which controlled the dissecting arm. I felt the force of the creature's nerve energy beating against me, trying to dislodge me from my position at the crossroads. It was like holding to a twig in a high wind. I could not let go without being dissipated throughout that vast brain. It was almost like my combat with the other Wroqna, except that this time I was the invader.

The Wroqna decided to sever the dissecting tentacle, to give it up and substitute other elements. I allowed it to happen, but just before the appendage fell I followed the nerve impulse along the channel to the directing mechanism. Conflict . . . struggle . . . and finally . . .

I am.

I had found the giant Wroqna's squirming ego, a concept of "I-ness" so complete that it had no roots. And I asked:

What are you?

I am . . . me.

Who told you?

Nobody. I am.

Are you . . . really?

A questing spread out. The creature consulted its sensors, seeking reassurance. I confused them, I caused them to send back conflicting reports. Hot became cold and light became dark and everything became something else . . .

The creature groped blindly. The digging machines turned and began chewing back through the suburbs, destroying the stately homes and killing the tubers already planted. Ships began colliding out in space, piles went critical and exploded. Even the vast intestinal sack buried in bedrock began regurgitating its slime, spewing it from the esophagus like a volcano which burst the sphincter and spread out over the field. The cutting torches turned back and began cutting through the walls to the creature's brain. It was trying to destroy me and in doing so was destroying itself . . .

I left the creature's brain and took control of the surgical chamber. I picked up my intestines, liver, lungs, bladder, kidneys, heart, and all the rest and put them back in my body cavity. I cut off the stasis field and reactivated my heart, then I sutured the seam and sprayed it with healing mist. If it had been possible, I would have restored that elfin beauty with the gauzy wings, but it was too late for her, the sense of identity had already dissolved.

I returned to my body and felt the agonizing pain of a thousand cuts. But the healing mist took effect, the cells knit together, and I rose from my slab feeling only a stiffness in my joints.

My perspective had been suddenly narrowed. The tiny chamber was filled with stifling odors of decay. I teleported outside. The black ball had cracked like a giant egg, and white stuff oozed out through the broken seams. The belt had broken, and cargo pods littered the field like cast-off toys. Smoke billowed up from the outskirts of the city, where the digging machines had ruptured power lines.

I teleported to a three-hulled ship which was parked at the edge of the field waiting to be hooked to a cargo pod. The drive was fueled, the pilots had not yet taken their places. I entered the normal-drive pod and lifted off.

More than a thousand quantum stitches later I reached the hub of the Wroqna galactic empire, the very squirming center of the enemy ego. And what did I see? Not a vast communications network, no fairy cities with spidery walkways. Just a huge planet, perhaps the size of our own Saturn, ringed with a similar belt of matter. As I went closer I saw that the belt was composed of millions of ships, some joining the ring and others peeling off. I saw holes opening in the cargo pods, and the cargoes of pulped yam tubers falling down upon the planet in a gentle rain.

I saw a crack open in the planet, and I watched the chasm fill with gray-white slime. Then it filmed over and hardened. I knew that the planet was growing, constantly, endlessly. Why? To no purpose at all. This was the Ultimate Empire, a gigantic mindless self-perpetuating blob which lived to eat and ate to live and knew nothing of art or poetry or death or love . . .

But not senseless, no. As I maneuvered my ship past the ring of cargo pods, a giant pseudo pod rose from the surface of the planet. It

shot to an altitude of a hundred miles in the flick of an eyelash, seized
my ship, and pulled it down with a force that slammed my body against
the top of the control pod. I had only a second to jump, from the ship
to the surface of the giant planet. My feet broke through the crust,
the thirty-g gravity sucked me down.

I was blind, but I gnarshed that I was still in the stomach, in the
outer ring of the Wroqna organism, licked and assailed by digestive
juices which seared my skin. My environment was yam pulp, nothing
else . . . no air, no light. I knew how to stop my breath and live off the
oxygen stored in my cells. I teleported downward, to my maximum
range of five miles. I was still in the stomach. I jumped again, and
again. I lost track of the number of jumps. The creature was all
stomach. Ah, now, here was something, a discrete solidity injected
into the soup, now compressed by gravity to a thick plastic paste. It was
a nerve tendril, perhaps a mile in diameter. I gnarshed the gaps between the long cells and slid inside . . . and found myself in contact
with the creature's brain.

It was not aware of me, no more than the human body is aware of
a single germ, though the leukocytes and the white corpuscles mount
armies to combat the invaders. I followed the nerve through a hundred
branchings, each channel larger than the last, leading ever inward
until I tapped the consciousness of the creature itself.

It was old, incredibly ancient. It held a memory of a time when
the Wroqna had been a small burrowing creature. For this Wroqna
the Vim-human war was a skirmish, a stumblingblock in its inevitable
expansion throughout the known universe. Humans were not merely
carriers of a disease; they were the disease itself, an organic form of
life which killed Wroqna just as the plague virus had once killed humans.

But humans were not the only race fighting the Wroqna. Mindless
expansion had set them at odds all around the galaxy. The Jelk
empire was a flyspeck on a giant balloon; there were hundreds of
races similar to ours, many more humanoid than the Vim. There
were thousands of species of civilized insects, spores, and energy
creatures, and some beings which I sincerely hoped the human race
would never have to fight . . .

There were planetary balloon sacs from another galaxy, which
dusted planets with a substance that caused them to bubble like
yeast, and then devoured them. Creatures from another dimension
raided and disappeared. Cancerous blots appeared suddenly in space,
like black holes in burning paper. They grew as matter collapsed into
them, while around the edges the structure of space-time-matter was
strung out, attenuated.

And I thought to myself: The unity of thought must survive. Man-

and-Wroqna must unite to save the galaxy, *life* must bury its enmity and link arms to destroy . . .

The others.

For a second I considered it seriously, then I realized that the thoughts were not mine but those of the Wroqna.

You great towering majestic intelligence, you supermind, I feel you looking down upon me as though I were a worm vaguely amusing . . .

Who are you?

I am . . . the precision of the Jelks, the courage of the Pteroni, the strength of the Hyades Ungul, the patience of the Androxi, the lethal savagery of the Blue Men, the devious deadliness of the Eshom. I am the Unity of Man, oh destroyer of diversity, assassin of races, malignant beast who eats beauty . . .

What is beauty?

It is the feeling of beyond-yourself, when the universe flows through you like a gentle wind through a lattice.

I am the universe. There is nothing which is not me. I am.

So am I.

What kind of Wroqna are you?

I am Raki. I am not a Wroqna.

Everything which is, is Wroqna. You have not realized your true nature. When you do, you will be Wroqna. It is the ultimate form.

No! With a furious leap I transported myself away from that ego-destroying concept. In another part of the brain I created a blot of unstable atoms. I leaped to another spot and created another blot . . . and on and on, spiraling out of the creature until I found myself in the cold of space. I transported inside the hull of an ancient atomic vessel and caused its pilot to decide upon suicide. He tipped his ship and drove it at full power down onto the skin of the Wroqna. The atomic blast created a mere pimple, but there were other ships, other pilots who found in themselves an irresistible urge to dash themselves down and go out in a burst of glory. Slaves never lose the urge to kill their masters; in the minds of thousands of Vim pilots the impulse lay just beneath the surface.

I played upon these as I did my psychic dance around the ring of ships. They fell like moths, and a thousand fires began to sputter on the surface. Giant cracks began to open up, and the burning fires reached deeper, meeting and joining the atomic reactions I had started in the center. Dark blotches mottled its skin. Pistules burst open, shooting out long streamers of fire which caught other ships and pulled them down.

I transported myself into a three-hulled vessel and pulled away from the dying planet. It would take years to collapse. But the yam boats would arrive and find no way to dump their cargoes. They would mill about and collide in space like the mindless machines they were. Millions would come but none would depart, and in a hundred years this would be a gigantic sargasso of wrecked vessels. In time it might coalesce into a new planet . . .

The giant Wroqna would eventually die, lacking their regular dosage of the life germ which enabled them to breed. They would live for many centuries, but there would be no new ones. I had succeeded; the war was won, though the fighting might go on for another hundred years.

I turned the ship and started for home.

APPENDIX I

Use of Remote-control Sensory Intersex among Jelks

Known as the "Sensi" in popular usage, the Sensory Intersex allows Jelky men and women to enjoy the sensual stimuli of sexual intercourse merely by plugging themselves into a transmitter and dialing the desired partner. If the other party acquiesces in the connection, he plugs in his own connection and the sexual act begins. The apparatus itself consists of microcircuits implanted in the sexual organs of Jelkies at puberty—an operation which some anthropological experts equate with circumcision rites among the ancient tribes of earth.

Like most Jelk customs, its origin goes back to the early days in the Ganymede caverns, when air and heat were at a premium, and several generations of Jelks spent their lives inside heated, atmospheric suits. The need to reproduce the species was recognized, of course—but flesh contact for mere sensual gratification was discouraged as being too wasteful of air and heat.

By the time the science of the Jelks succeeded in supplying unlimited heat and air to the caverns, the custom had become frozen. Progs on the moon still use it extensively, conducting a multitude of "Sensi" affairs without leaving their private caverns. Since multiple hookups are possible, troilism is popular, and connections involving up to seven persons are not infrequent. (Without realizing it, the Jelks have imitated the sexual practices of the Wroqna by electronic means: not only that, but their practice of living in separate caverns on the moon duplicates the life-style of the Wroqna.)

Among the Jelks, body contact is made by females only once per lifetime, and that is to procreate. Males are unlimited in number of body contacts, since the females bear the onus of population control. Consequently, women place a high value on their child, and seek to acquire the best possible genetic ingredients. In practice several females tend to mate with the same male, with the short-term effect of heightening desirable characteristics, but in the long term decreasing the genetic pool. (Thus the computer's solution to the Wroqna problem was ostensibly concerned with knocking out the Wroqna computer, but more fundamentally pointed toward the creation of a new homogeneous race patterned after Raki.)

APPENDIX II

A Psychograph of the Jelk Subspecies

Jelks: Descendants of the scientific colony which survived underground on the moons of Jupiter. Survival characteristics: precision of mind, self-discipline, cleanliness of mind-body, authoritarianism, a certain kind of brilliance. Physically hairless, small, eyes lacking in cones and color sensitivity. Generally color-blind, since recognition of color was not a survival factor in the underground. Eyes sensitive to UV and sunlight. The Jelks preferred to avoid Earth, or to ride around in air-conditioned, sun-shielded bubble cars—looking out so that nobody could look in. (Not like Landarks, who made adaptation to earth through selective breeding and genetic engineering. Which is the reason their star is on the rise.) Special muscular adaptation to low gravity, agoraphobia, which in some amounts to a psychosis, bred in the bone. Sexual customs almost totally sublimated to intellectual level. The Sensi provides mind-contact between males and females which has little to do with sexual attributes on the outside, but rather matches dominants. Thus a physical male whose personality is female-dominant would be matched with a physical female whose male personality is dominant. Also there is a masturbatory element in that the male-female principles in each body can be united to produce mental orgasm within self—but this is frowned upon since it produces withdrawal of person from social pool, which is antithetical to Jelk philosophy.

Childbearing has become increasingly unpopular since the discovery that Grithy women do not reject Jelk fetuses. Thus Grithy *mamus* are employed to gestate the children and nourish them after birth. In view of the rigorous scientific background necessary for maintenance of Jelks on the moon, longevity became a premium since it reduced down-time for training. The cutoff point was found to be the age of two hundred years, at which age efficiency showed a sharp falling off due to boredom and insanity. The only cure was destruction of memory and retraining, and it was found to be more efficient to replace the worn-out unit with a new one. Thus at two hundred the unit was "euthed" and the products recycled into the organic food supply. This was an absolute necessity in the beginning, and continued up to the present time. None of the other developed races practiced it. It was, in effect, a practice of eating the dead which had been practiced ceremoniously in certain ancient cultures—but with the Jelks there was no ceremony, no religious significance—unless the doctrine of no-waste could be termed a religion.